P9-DWZ-651

# MURDER IN CANTON

Strangers in Canton, Judge Dee and his faithful lieutenants Chiao Tai and Tao Gan find themselves entangled
in a baffling web of high political intrigue and vicious
murder. What is the secret of the voluptuous belly-dancer
Zumurrud, who so fascinates Chiao Tai? Is the Arab
merchant Mansur plotting to burn down the city? And
who is the strange, blind girl, whom Tao Gan rescues
from rape?

Judge Dee seeks the answers in the dark alleys and
soaring temples of the great South China port.

LEARNING RESOURCES CENTER
SANTA FE COMMUNITY COLLEGE

# MURDER IN CANTON

*A Judge Dee Mystery*

*by*

## ROBERT VAN GULIK

*With twelve illustrations*
*drawn by the author in Chinese style*

*The University of Chicago Press*

SFCC LIBRARY
6401 RICHARDS AVE.
SANTA FE, NM 87507

The University of Chicago Press, Chicago 60637

Copyright © 1966 Robert  van Gulik

All rights reserved. Originally published 1966
University of Chicago Press Edition 1993
Printed in the United States of America
01 00 99 98 97 96 95 94 93   6 5 4 3 2 1

ISBN 0-226-84874-4 (pbk.)

**Library of Congress Cataloging-in-Publication Data**

Gulik, Robert Hans van, 1910–1967.
    Murder in Canton / by Robert van Gulik ; with
twelve illustrations drawn by the author in Chinese
style. — University of Chicago Press ed.
      p.   cm. — (Judge Dee mystery)
    1. Dee Jen-Djieh (Fictitious character)—Fiction.
2. Judges—China—Fiction.  I. Title.  II. Series:
Gulik, Robert Hans van, 1910–1967.  Judge Dee
mystery.
PR9130.G8M87   1993
823'.914—dc20
                                      93-2456
                                         CIP

∞ The paper used in this publication meets the
minimum requirements of the American National
Standard for Information Sciences—Permanence of Paper
for Printed Library Materials, ANSI Z39.48-1984.

This book is printed on acid-free paper.

# DRAMATIS PERSONAE

It should be noted that in China the surname
—here printed in capitals—precedes the personal name

*Main characters*

| | |
|---|---|
| DEE Jen-djieh | President of the Metropolitan Court, in this novel visiting Canton in the summer of 680 A.D. |
| CHIAO Tai | a colonel of the Imperial Guard ⎫ his |
| TAO Gan | Chief Secretary of the Court ⎭ assistants |

*Persons connected with the Case of the Imperial Censor*

| | |
|---|---|
| WENG Kien | Governor of Canton and the Southern Region |
| PAO Kwan | Prefect of Canton |
| LEW Tao-ming | Imperial Censor |
| Dr SOO | his adviser |

*Persons connected with the Case of the Smaragdine Dancer*

| | |
|---|---|
| Zumurrud | an Arab dancing girl |
| Mansur | leader of the Arab community in Canton |
| LIANG Foo | a famous financier |
| YAU Tai-kai | a wealthy merchant |

*Persons connected with the Case of the Secret Lovers*

| | |
|---|---|
| Lan-lee | a blind girl |
| NEE | a sea captain |
| Dunyazad | ⎫ his slave-girls |
| Dananir | ⎭ |

## SKETCHMAP OF CANTON

1. Governor's Palace, and offices of the Provincial Administration
2. Tribunal, and offices of the City Administration
3. Garrison Headquarters
4. Examination Hall
5. Market
6. Temple of the War God
7. Temple of Confucius
8. Great South Gate
9. Custom-house
10. Kwang-siao Temple
11. Temple of the Flowery Pagoda
12. Muhammedan Mosque
13. Temple of the Five Immortals
14. Kuei-te Gate
15. Wine-house on quay
16. Inn of the Five Immortals
17. Inn where Tao Gan stayed
18. Arab sailors' hostel
19. Liang Foo's residence
20. Captain Nee's residence
21. Yau Tai-kai's residence
22. Prefect Pao's residence
23. Tomb of the Arab Saint
24. Pearl River

In this novel the scene is laid for the first time in an actual Chinese city. Though the exact features of seventh-century Canton are not reliably known, it seems to have comprised roughly what is at present called the 'Old City'. The location of the city gates and the historic sites, marked on this map with Chinese characters, is partly guess-work. In subsequent centuries the city spread mainly towards the east and south-west—where modern Shameen is located—and over to the south bank of the Pearl River.

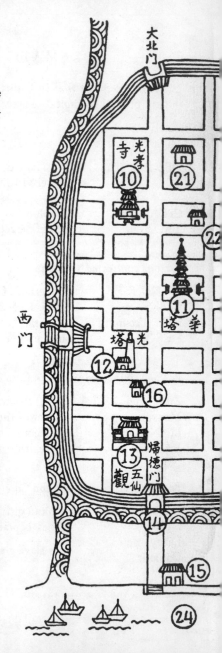

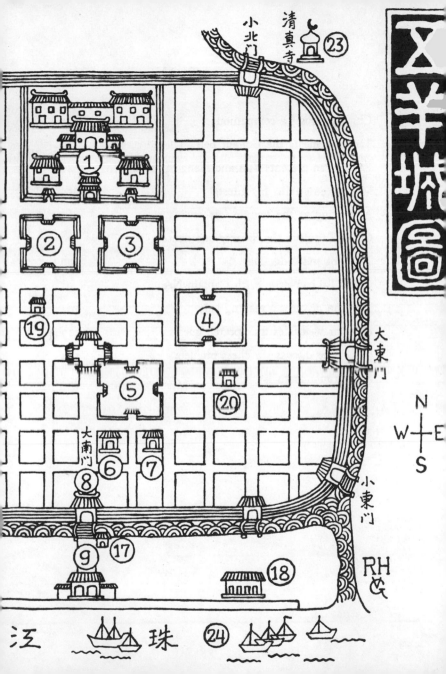

羊城圖

清真寺 ②③

小北門

大東門

小東門

RH

大南門

① ② ③ ④ ⑤ ⑥ ⑦ ⑧ ⑨ ⑰ ⑱ ⑲ ⑳

N
W—E
S

汃 珠 ②④

# ILLUSTRATIONS

# I

The two men standing at the corner of the custom-house silently watched the long, dreary waterfront. The elder's thin, angular frame was wrapped from head to feet in an old goatskin caftan. The other, a burly, handsome man in his late forties, was clad in a patched brown gown and jacket. While they were standing there, the hot, clammy mist changed into a warm drizzle that wetted the worn velvet of their black caps. The still air was very close, for although it was late in the afternoon already, there was no sign yet of a cooling evening breeze.

A dozen bare-backed coolies were unloading the foreign ship moored a little further on alongside the river quay, opposite the arched gate of the custom-house. Bent under heavy bales, they trudged down the gangway to the measure of a mournful catch-song. The four guards at the gate had pushed their spiked helmets back from their perspiring brows. Leaning heavily on their long halberds, they followed the work with bored eyes.

'Look! There goes the ship we came down the river on this morning!' the elderly man exclaimed. He pointed to the dark mass that came looming up out of the mist, beyond the masts of the other craft moored next to the foreign ship. The black war junk was being rowed with great speed to the estuary of the Pearl River, its brass gongs clanging to warn off the small boats of the river hawkers.

'Weather permitting, they'll be in Annam soon!' his broad-shouldered companion said gruffly. 'There's bound to be a lot of good fighting down there. But you and I have to stay behind in this god-forsaken city, with orders to assess the situation! Hell, there's another drop running down my neck. As if this blasted humid heat isn't making me sweat enough already!'

He pulled the collar of his jacket closer round his thick boxer's neck, at the same time taking good care to conceal the coat of mail he was wearing underneath, with the golden badge of a colonel of the Imperial Guard, a round plaque consisting of two intertwined dragons. Then he asked testily, 'Do you know what it's all about, brother Tao?'

The lean man sadly shook his grey head. Tugging at the three long hairs that sprouted from the wart on his cheek, he replied slowly:

'Our boss didn't tell me a thing, brother Chiao. Must be important, though. Else he wouldn't have left the capital so suddenly, and rushed down here with us, first on horseback, then on that fast war junk. There must be trouble brewing here in Canton. Ever since our arrival this morning, I have ...'

He was interrupted by a loud splash. Two coolies had let a bale drop into the muddy strip of water between the ship and the quay. A white-turbaned figure jumped down from the deck and began to kick the coolies, shouting at them in a foreign tongue. The bored custom-guards suddenly came to life. One stepped forward and with a quick swing of his halberd let its flat side thud down on the shoulders of the cursing Arab.

'Keep off our men, you son of a dog!' the guard shouted. 'You are in China here, remember!'

The Arab gripped the hilt of the dagger in his red belt. A dozen white-gowned men jumped from the ship, and drew their long curved swords. As the coolies let their bales drop and scurried away, the four guards levelled their halberds at the cursing sailors. Suddenly iron boots resounded on the cobblestones. Twenty soldiers came marching through the gate of the custom-house. With the ease of long practice they surrounded the angry Arabs and herded them at spearpoint back towards the edge of the quay. A tall thin Arab with a beaked nose leaned over the railing of the ship, and began to harangue the sailors in a strident voice. They sheathed their swords and climbed on board again. The coolies resumed their work as if nothing had happened.

'About how many of those insolent bastards would there be in this city?' the colonel asked.

'Well, we counted four ships in port, didn't we? And two more are lying in the estuary, outward bound. Add the Arabs who've settled down ashore, and you get a couple of thousand, I'd say. And that wretched inn of yours is smack in the middle of the Moslem quarter! A fine place for getting a knife in your back at night! My hostel is nothing to crow about either, but being right outside the south gate, the guards are at least within calling distance.'

'What room have you got there?'

'The one on the corner of the second floor, which gives me a good view of the quay and the wharves, as per orders. Well, don't you think we've been hanging about here long enough? The drizzle is getting worse. Let's go and sample the stuff over there.'

He pointed to the end of the quay where a shadowy figure was lighting the red lantern of a wine-house.

'I certainly could use some!' Chiao Tai muttered. 'Never saw such a dismal place! And I can't speak the language either.'

Hurrying over the slippery cobblestones, they did not notice a shabbily dressed, bearded man, who now left the shelter of the godown further along the quay and followed them.

Arriving at the end of the quay, Chiao Tai saw that the bridge across the moat by the Kuei-te city gate was crowded with people. Clad in straw raincoats, they bustled along, each intent on his own business.

'Nobody takes time off for a bit of loitering here,' he grumbled.

'That's why they could make Canton the wealthiest port city of the south!' Tao Gan remarked. 'Here we are!'

He pulled the patched door-curtain aside and they entered a dim, cavernous taproom. They were met by the smell of stale garlic and salted fish. The smoking oil lamps dangling from the low rafters threw their uncertain light on a few score guests, huddling in groups of four or five round small tables. They were busily talking in undertones. No one seemed to pay the slightest attention to the two newcomers.

When the two men were seating themselves at an empty table near the window, the bearded man who had been following them came in. He went straight to the rear, to a worn wooden counter where the innkeeper was heating pewter winejugs in a basin of boiling water.

Tao Gan told the waiter in good Cantonese to bring them two large jugs. While they were waiting, Chiao Tai put his elbows on the greasy table top and glumly surveyed the guests.

'What a crowd!' he muttered after a while. 'See that awful dwarf over there? Can't understand how I missed that ugly mug when I came in!'

Tao Gan looked at the small squat man sitting all alone at the table near the door. He had a flat, swarthy face with a low, deeply furrowed brow and a broad nose. Small, deep-set eyes lowered from under ragged eyebrows. His large, hairy hands were clasped round his empty beaker.

'The only fellow of decent appearance is our neighbour!' Tao Gan whispered. 'Has the looks of a professional boxer.' He pointed with his chin at the wide-shouldered man sitting alone at the next table. He wore a neat, dark-blue gown, its black sash wound tightly round his slender waist. His heavy-lidded eyes gave his handsome, deeply tanned face a sleepy expression. He was staring into space, seemingly oblivious of his surroundings.

The slovenly waiter put two large jugs before them. Then he went back to the counter. He pointedly ignored the dwarf who was waving his empty beaker at him.

Chiao Tai took a sip, looking rather sceptical.

'Not bad at all!' he exclaimed, agreeably surprised. He emptied his beaker and added, 'Quite good, in fact!' He drank his second beaker in one long draught. Tao Gan followed his example with a happy grin.

The bearded man at the counter had been watching them all the time. He counted the beakers they drank. When he saw the two friends begin yet another round, their sixth, he started to leave the counter. Then his eye fell on the dwarf, and he checked

4

himself. The boxer at the next table, who had been watching from the corners of his hooded eyes both the bearded man and the dwarf, now sat up straight. He pensively stroked his short, neatly trimmed ring-beard.

Chiao Tai set down his empty beaker. He clapped his heavy hand on his friend's bony shoulder and said with a broad grin:

'I don't like the city. I don't like the damned hot weather, and I don't like this smelly taproom. But by heaven the wine's all right, and anyway it's good to be out on a job again. What about you, eh, brother Tao?'

'I got fed up with the capital too,' the other replied. 'Be careful, your badge is showing.'

Chiao Tai pulled the lapels of his jacket close. But the bearded man at the counter had got a glimpse of the golden badge, and his lips curved in a satisfied smile. Then his face fell again as he saw a blue-turbaned Arab with a cast in his left eye come in and join the dwarf. The bearded man turned to the counter and gave the innkeeper a sign to fill his beaker.

'Heaven knows I am not cut out for the part of a parade colonel!' Chiao Tai exclaimed, as he refilled their beakers. 'Had four years of it now, mind you! You should see the bed I'm supposed to sleep in! Silk pillows, silk coverlets, and brocade curtains! Makes me feel like a blooming whore! Know what I do, every blasted night? Take out the reed mat I keep hidden behind the bed, roll it out on the floor, and lay me down there for a good night's rest! Only bother is that every morning I have to rumple the bedding a bit, to keep up appearances for my orderlies, you see!'

He guffawed. Tao Gan joined him. In their happy mood they did not notice that their laughter sounded very loud. Conversation had come to a standstill; the guests stared in sullen silence at the door. The dwarf was talking angrily to the waiter who stood with folded arms in front of his table. The boxer watched them too, then again turned his gaze towards the man by the counter.

'As for me,' Tao Gan said with his sly grin, 'tonight I can go to sleep in peace in my attic. I won't have to first shoo away those young maidservants my house-steward keeps trotting out. The scoundrel still hopes to sell me one as a concubine some day!'

'Why don't you tell the rascal to stop that nonsense? Here, have another drink!'

'It saves money, my friend! Those wenches come to work for free, hoping to catch this wealthy old bachelor, you see!' Tao Gan emptied his beaker, then resumed, 'Fortunately you and I are not the marrying kind, brother Chiao! Unlike our friend and colleague Ma Joong!'

'Don't mention the low wretch!' Chiao Tai shouted. 'To think that after he married those twin-sisters four years ago, he has sired six boys and two girls! That's debasing into hard labour what ought to be a gentleman's pleasure! And he's afraid to come home drunk nowadays. Did you...'

He broke off and looked astonished at the commotion by the door. The ugly dwarf and the Arab had risen. Their faces flushed and angry, they had begun to curse the waiter who was trying to shout them down. The other guests were watching the scene with impassive faces. Suddenly the Arab groped for his dagger. The dwarf quickly took his arm, and pulled him outside. The waiter grabbed the dwarf's wine-beaker and threw it after him. It smashed to pieces on the cobblestones. An approving murmur rose from the crowd.

'They don't like Arabs here,' Chiao Tai remarked.

The man at the next table turned his head.

'No, it wasn't the Arab, exactly,' he told them in good northern Chinese. 'But you are right, we don't like Arabs here either. Why should they come? They don't drink our wine, anyway. Aren't allowed to, by their creed.'

'Those black bastards miss the best things of life!' Chiao Tai said with a grin. 'Join us in a round!' As the stranger smiled and pulled his chair up to their table, Chiao Tai asked him, 'Are you from up north?'

'No, I was born and bred here in Canton. But I have travelled about a lot, and a traveller has to learn languages. I am a sea captain, you see. My name is Nee, by the way. What brought you people down here?'

'We are just passing through,' Tao Gan explained. 'We are clerks belonging to the suite of an official who is now touring the province.'

The captain gave Chiao Tai a judicious look.

'I'd have thought that you were army.'

'I used to do a bit of boxing and fencing, as a hobby,' Chiao Tai said casually. 'You interested in that too?'

'Fencing, mainly. Especially with Arab blades. Had to learn that, for I used to be on the regular run over to the Persian Gulf. There are plenty of pirates about in those waters, you know.'

'It beats me how they manage those curved blades,' Chiao Tai remarked.

'You'd be surprised,' Captain Nee said. Soon he and Chiao Tai were in animated conversation about different kinds of sword-fighting. Tao Gan listened absent-mindedly and concentrated on keeping the beakers filled. But when he heard the captain quote some technical terms in Arabic, he looked up and asked:

'You know their lingo?'

'Enough to get along. Picked up Persian too. All in the day's work!' And to Chiao Tai: 'I'd like to show you my collection of foreign swords. What about coming along for a drink at my place? I live over in the east city.'

'Tonight we're rather busy,' Chiao Tai replied. 'Could you make it tomorrow morning?'

The other darted a quick glance at the man at the counter.

'All right,' he said. 'Where are you staying?'

'At the Five Immortals' Inn, near the Moslem mosque.'

The captain started to say something, but changed his mind. He sipped his wine, then asked casually, 'Is your friend staying there too?' When Chiao Tai shook his head, the captain resumed with a shrug, 'Well, you're fully capable of looking after yourself, I dare say. I'll send a litter to fetch you, say about an hour after breakfast.'

Tao Gan paid the bill, and they took their leave of their new acquaintance. The sky had cleared; the river breeze felt pleasantly cool on their flushed faces. The quay now presented an animated scene. Hawkers had set up their night-stalls all along the waterside, lit by strings of coloured lampions. The river was dotted with torches on small boats, moored stem to stern. The breeze wafted the smell of burning firewood to them. The waterfolk were preparing their evening rice.

'Let's rent a litter,' Tao Gan said. 'It's quite a long way to the Governor's Palace.'

Chiao Tai made no reply. He had been surveying the crowd with a preoccupied face. Suddenly he asked:

'Don't you have a feeling that someone is keeping an eye on us?'

Tao Gan quickly looked over his shoulder.

'No, I don't,' he said. 'But your hunches are often right, I admit. Well, since our judge told us to report at six, we still have an hour or so. Let's do some walking, each on his own. That'll give us a better chance to see whether we are being spied upon. And I'll be able to test my memory of the city's layout at the same time.'

'All right. I'll pass by my inn and change, then cut through the Moslem quarter. If I keep to the north-east, I'll sooner or later come to the large street that leads north, won't I?'

'If you behave and keep out of trouble, that is! Do have a look at the Tower of the Water-clock on the main street, it's a famous sight. The exact time is indicated by floaters in a series of brass water vessels, put one above the other, like a flight of stairs. The water drips slowly from the higher into the lower vessels. Quite an ingenious contrivance!'

'Think I need all those gadgets for knowing the time of day?' Chiao Tai asked with a sniff. 'I go by the sun and by my thirst. And at night and on rainy days I make do with my thirst only. See you later, in the palace!'

# II

Chiao Tai turned the corner, crossed the bridge over the moat and entered the city by the Kuei-te Gate.

As he pushed his way through the dense evening crowd, he glanced over his shoulder now and then, but no one seemed to be following him. He passed in front of the high, red-lacquered gate of the Temple of the Five Immortals, entered the first street on his left, and so reached his inn, named after the temple. It was a ramshackle building of two storeys. Over its roof he saw the top of the minaret belonging to the Moslem mosque, rising more than fifteen fathoms up in the air.

Calling out a cheerful good-night to the surly innkeeper, who sat slumped in a bamboo chair in the small lobby, Chiao Tai went straight up to his room on the second floor, at the back. It was hot and stuffy inside, for the shutters of the single window had been closed the whole day. After renting it that morning he had only stayed to put his travelling bundles on the bare plank-bed. With a curse he pushed the shutters wide open. He looked at the minaret, of which he now had a complete view.

'Those foreigners can't even get up a real pagoda,' he muttered with a grin. 'No storeys, no curved roofs, no nothing! Straight as a piece of sugar cane!'

Humming a tune, he changed into a clean shirt, put on his coat of mail again and wrapped his helmet, iron gloves and high military boots in a piece of blue cloth. Then he went downstairs.

Down in the street it was still very hot; the river breeze did not penetrate this far into the city. Chiao Tai was sorry that he could not take off his jacket because of the coat of mail. After a casual glance at the passers-by, he took the alley next to the inn.

The narrow streets were lit by the lampions of the night-stalls, but there were few people about. He saw several Arabs, conspicuous by their white turbans and their quick, long stride. After he had passed the mosque, the streets assumed a foreign aspect. The white-plastered houses had no windows on the ground floor; the only light came from those on the second floor, filtering through screens of intricate latticework. Here and there an arched passage across the street connected the second floors of the houses on either side. Chiao Tai was still in such a cheerful mood after the wine that he forgot to check whether he was being followed.

When he had entered a deserted alley, he suddenly found a bearded Chinese walking by his side, who asked curtly:

'Aren't you a guardsman called Kao or Shao, or something like that, eh?'

Chiao Tai halted. In the uncertain light he scrutinized the stranger's cold face with the long sidewhiskers and greying beard, taking in also his torn brown robe, well-worn cap and mud-covered boots. The fellow looked shabby enough, yet he had the natural poise of a person of consequence, and he had spoken with the unmistakable accent of the capital. He said cautiously:

'My name is Chiao.'

'Ha, of course! Colonel Chiao Tai! Tell me, is your boss, His Excellency Dee, here in Canton too?'

'What if he were?' Chiao Tai asked truculently.

'None of your lip, my man!' the stranger snapped. 'I have to see him, urgently. Take me to him.'

Chiao Tai frowned. The fellow did not seem to be a crook. And if he were, so much the worse for him! He said:

'It so happens that I am on my way to my boss. So you can come along with me right now.'

The stranger quickly looked over his shoulder at the shadows behind him.

'You walk ahead,' he said curtly; 'I'll follow. It's better that we aren't seen together.'

'As you like,' Chiao Tai said, and walked on. He had to be

careful now, for there were many deep holes among the stone flags, and the only light came from an occasional window. There was no one about; the only sound was the heavy tread of the stranger's boots behind him.

After Chiao Tai had turned yet another corner he found himself in a pitch-dark street. He looked up to verify whether he could see the top of the minaret, in order to orientate himself. But the high houses on either side were lurching towards each other; he could see only a narrow strip of starlit sky. He waited till the other had come up behind him, then said over his shoulder:

'Can't see a thing here. We'd better turn back and look for a litter. It's still quite some way along the main street.'

'Ask the people in the house round the corner there,' the stranger said. His voice sounded hoarse.

Chiao Tai peered ahead, and now saw indeed a glimmer in the darkness. 'The old geezer's voice is a bit off, but his eyes are all right!' he muttered, walking towards the faint light. After he had rounded the corner, he saw that it came from a cheap oil lamp, placed in a niche high up in the forbidding blank wall on his left. A little further on he saw a door, embossed with copper ornaments. Over his head was another cross-passage connecting the second floor of the house with the one opposite. He stepped up to the door. As he knocked hard on the shutter of the peephole, he heard his companion behind him stop. Chiao Tai called out to him:

'There's no answer yet, but I'll rouse the bastards!'

He knocked vigorously for some time, then pressed his ear against the wood. He heard nothing. He gave the door a few kicks, then rapped against the peephole till his knuckles hurt.

'Come on!' he shouted angrily at his companion. 'We'll kick this blasted door in! There must be someone at home, else that lamp wouldn't be burning.'

There was no answer.

Chiao Tai turned round. He was all alone in the alley.

'Where could that bastard...' he began perplexedly, then broke

11

off. He saw the stranger's cap lying on the stone flags, under the cross-passage. With an oath Chiao Tai put his bundle on the ground, reached up and took the oil lamp from the niche. As he stepped forward for a closer look at the cap, he suddenly felt a soft tap on his shoulder. He swung round. There was nobody. But then he saw a pair of muddy boots dangling close by his head. With another curse he looked up, holding the oil lamp high. His companion was hanging by his neck from the other side of the cross-passage, head at an unnatural angle, arms stiff by his side. A thin cord ran over the sill of the open passage window.

Chiao Tai turned to the door directly under the passage and gave it a violent kick. It swung inside and crashed against the wall. He quickly climbed the flight of narrow, stone steps that went up at a sharp angle, and so reached the dark, low passage crossing the street. Holding the lamp high, he saw a man clad in an Arab gown sprawling in front of the window. He was lying quite still, clasping a short spear with a long, needle-sharp point in his right hand. One look at his bloated face and protruding tongue sufficed to show that he was dead—strangled. One of his bulging eyes had a cast in it.

Chiao Tai wiped the sweat off his forehead.

'Just the sight for a fellow who has been drinking happily!' he muttered. 'If this isn't the worst way to sober up! It's the bastard I saw in the wine-house. But where's that ugly dwarf?'

He quickly let the light of the lamp fall on the opposite end of the passage. A dark staircase led down from there, but everything was as quiet as the grave. He put the lamp on the floor, stepped over the body of the dead Arab, and began to tug at the thin cord that was fastened to an iron hook under the sill. Slowly he hauled the bearded man up. His horribly distorted face appeared in the window, blood trickling from its grinning mouth.

Chiao Tai dragged the still-warm body inside and laid it on the floor, next to the Arab's. The noose had bitten deeply into its scraggy throat, and the neck appeared to have been broken. He rushed down the steps at the other end of the passage. Half a

CHIAO TAI LOSES A COMPANION

dozen steps down there was a low door. Chiao Tai gave it a thunderous knocking. When there was no answer, he threw himself against it. The old, wormeaten planks broke, and he tumbled into a semi-dark room, amidst a clatter of plates and pots and getting entangled with pieces of wood.

He was on his feet again in a flash. An old Arab hag, huddled in the centre of the small room, looked up at him, her toothless mouth open in speechless fright. The light of a brass oil lamp hanging from age-blackened rafters shone on a young Arab woman squatting in the corner, feeding the baby at her breast. With a piercing scream of terror she covered her bare bosom with part of her ragged cloak. Chiao Tai was about to address them, but then the door opposite swung open and two gaunt Arabs rushed in brandishing curved daggers. They stopped abruptly when Chiao Tai ripped the lapels of his jacket apart, revealing his golden badge.

As the Arabs stood there hesitating, a third one, much younger, pushed them aside and stepped up to Chiao Tai. He asked in halting Chinese:

'What do you mean by forcing your way into our women's quarters, mister officer?'

'Two men were murdered in the passage outside,' Chiao Tai barked. 'Speak up! Who did it?'

The youngster gave the battered door a quick look. Then he said sullenly, 'What happens in that passage across the street is no concern of ours.'

'It connects with your house, you son of a dog!' Chiao Tai growled. 'There are two dead men there, I tell you. Speak up, or I'll have all of you arrested and questioned on the rack!'

'If you would kindly take a closer look, sir,' the young Arab said contemptuously, 'you'll see that the door you battered in hasn't been open for years.'

Chiao Tai turned round. The pieces of wood he had become entangled with were the remains of a high cupboard. One glance at the dusty spot in front of the door-opening and the rusty

14

lock he had shattered, proved that the man was right. The door
leading to the passage had indeed been out of use for a long
time.

'If someone was murdered in the passage over the street,' the
youngster resumed, 'any passer-by could have done it. A staircase
leads up to it from the street on either side, and the doors below
are never locked, as far as I know.'

'What is that passage used for, then?'

'Until six years ago, my father, the merchant Abdallah, also
owned the house opposite. After he had sold it, the door at the
other end was walled up.'

'Did you hear anything?' Chiao Tai asked the young woman.
She made no reply, looking up at him in uncomprehending fear.
As the youngster quickly translated, she shook her head em-
phatically. He said to Chiao Tai:

'The walls are thick, and since the cupboard was standing in
front of that old door...' He raised his hands in an eloquent
gesture.

The two other Arabs had put their daggers back into their belts.
As they began a whispered conversation, the old hag came to life
and began to deliver a long harangue in shrill Arabic, pointing at
the shards on the floor.

'Tell her she'll be compensated!' Chiao Tai said. 'Come along,
you!'

He stooped and passed through the door-opening, followed by
the youngster. When they were standing in the passage, he
pointed at the dead Arab and asked:

'Who is this man?'

The youngster squatted by the dead body. After a casual look at
the distorted face he pried loose the silk scarf that had been
knotted tightly round the dead man's throat. Then he felt with his
nimble fingers in the folds of the turban. Righting himself, he said
slowly:

'He did not carry any money or papers. I have never seen him
before, but he must be from South Arabia, for they are expert

there at throwing the short javelin.' Handing the scarf to Chiao Tai, he went on, 'It was no Arab that killed him, though. Do you see that silver coin tied to the scarf's corner? It weights it, thus enabling the strangler to swing it round the victim's neck from behind. It is a coward's weapon. We Arabs keep to our spears, swords and daggers—for the greater glory of Allah and his Prophet.'

'Amen,' Chiao Tai said sourly. He looked thoughtfully at the two dead bodies. He understood now what had happened. The Arab had meant to murder not only the bearded stranger, but also him. He had been lying in wait for them, at the window. He had let him pass underneath, but when his companion followed and stood waiting there while Chiao Tai knocked, he had thrown the noose over his head and hoisted him up with a fearful jerk. Then he had tied the end of the noose to the hook and taken his javelin. But when he was about to push open the window opposite in order to throw the javelin into his second victim's back, a third person had strangled him from behind with the scarf, then fled.

Chiao pushed the window open and looked down into the street.

'As I was standing there knocking on that blasted door, I must have made a perfect target!' he muttered. 'And that thin point would have gone right through my coat of mail too! I owe my life to that unknown benefactor.' Turning to the young Arab, he said gruffly, 'Tell someone to run to the main street and rent a large litter!'

When the youngster had shouted something through the broken-down door, Chiao Tai searched the corpse of the bearded Chinese. But there was nothing to identify him by. He shook his head disconsolately.

They waited in an uneasy silence till they heard lusty shouts in the street below. Chiao Tai leaned out of the window and saw four litter bearers, carrying smoking torches. Slinging the dead Chinese over his shoulder, he ordered the youngster:

'Stand guard here by the body of your countryman till the constables come to fetch it. You and your entire family will be held responsible if anything should happen to it!'

Carrying his burden, he carefully trudged down the narrow staircase.

## III

Tao Gan had walked back to the custom-house. Having passed underneath its high archway, he watched for a while the clerks who were still busily sorting out piles of bales and boxes. There was a pungent smell of foreign spices. He left by the back door, cast a brief glance at his dismal inn, then entered the city by the south gate.

Strolling along in the teeming crowd, he noticed with satisfaction that he was able to identify most of the larger buildings he passed. Evidently Canton had not changed much in the twenty odd years since he had been there last.

He recognised the large temple that rose on his right; it was dedicated to the God of War. He detached himself from the crowd and walked up the broad marble steps to the high gatehouse, its double doors flanked by two huge stone lions, each crouching on an octagonal pedestal. As usual the male lion on the left scowled down with tightly closed mouth, while the female on the right kept its large head raised, her jaws wide open.

'She can never keep her blasted mouth shut!' Tao Gan muttered sourly. 'Just like that wretched former wife of mine!'

Slowly pulling at his frayed moustache, he reflected wryly that for twenty years he had hardly thought of his adulterous wife. It was revisiting this city where he had lived a few years in his youth, that suddenly brought it all back to him. The wife he had loved had basely deceived him, and had tried to bring about his ruin, so that he had had to flee for his life. He had then sworn off women and, determined to get his own back on a world that disgusted him, had become an itinerant swindler. But later he had met Judge Dee, who had made him reform and had taken him on as his assistant, thus giving him a new interest in life. He had served with Judge Dee in his various posts as district magistrate, and after the judge had been promoted to his present high office in the capital, Tao Gan had been made chief secretary. A twisted smile lit up his long gloomy face as he told the lioness complacently:

'Canton is still the same, but look at me! I am not only a ranking official now, but also a man of means. Of considerable means, I should say!' He adjusted his cap with a jerk, nodded haughtily at the ferocious stone face and entered the temple compound.

Passing the main hall, he cast a quick look inside. In the flickering light of the tall red candles a small group of people were adding new incense sticks to those already in the large bronze burner on the high altar. Through the thick blue smoke he vaguely saw the towering gilt statue of the bearded war god brandishing his long sword. Tao Gan sniffed, for he hardly admired military prowess. He lacked the bulk and strength of his colleague Chiao Tai, and he never carried any arms. But his utter lack of fear and quick wit made him nonetheless a dangerous opponent. He walked on and circled the main hall to the back gate of the compound. Remembering that the city's largest market was directly to the north of the temple, he thought he might as well have a look around there before taking the main street leading up to the Governor's Palace, in the northern part of the city.

The quarter behind the temple consisted of poor wooden houses, noisy with shouting and laughter. A smell of cheap frying fat hung in the air. Further along, however, it suddenly became very quiet. Here stood only abandoned houses, many in ruins. The piles of new bricks and big jars filled with mortar that stood about at regular intervals proved that a building project was in progress. He looked behind him a few times, but he saw no one about. He went on at a sedate pace, keeping his caftan close to his bony body despite the stifling heat.

When he was rounding the corner of another alley, he heard

the noise of the market ahead. At the same time he saw a commotion at the farther end. Under the lantern that hung from a dilapidated doorpost two dishevelled ruffians were attacking a woman. As he quickly ran to them, Tao Gan saw that the one behind her had his arm crooked round the lower half of her face, while his other hand held her arms together behind her back. The second ruffian, standing in front of her, had ripped her robe apart and was now fondling her shapely bare bosom. As he began to tear loose the sash round her waist, she frantically kicked his legs. But the man behind her jerked her head farther back, and the other hit her a hard blow in her exposed midriff.

Tao Gan took quick action. With his right hand he picked up a brick from the nearest pile, and with the other scooped a handful of quicklime from the jar next to it. Tiptoeing up to the men, he struck the one holding the girl a sharp blow on the shoulder with the edge of the heavy brick. The man let go of her and clasped his crushed shoulder with an agonized cry. The other ruffian turned on Tao Gan, groping for the dagger in his belt. But Tao Gan threw the quicklime into his eyes, and the man put his hands to his face, howling with pain.

'Arrest the bastards, men !' Tao Gan shouted.

The ruffian with the crushed shoulder grabbed his yelping comrade's arm. Dragging him along, he ran down the alley as fast as he could.

The girl was pulling her robe close to her, gasping for air. He vaguely saw that she was quite handsome; her hair was gathered at the nape of her neck in two coils, the hair-do of an unmarried girl. He put her age at about twenty-five.

'Come along to the market, quick !' he addressed her gruffly in Cantonese, 'before those two fellows discover I bluffed them.'

As she seemed to hesitate, he took her sleeve and pulled her along towards the noise of the market.

'Walking alone in such a deserted quarter is asking for trouble, miss,' he said reprovingly. 'Or did you know those two scoundrels?'

'No, they must be vagrant bullies,' she replied in a soft cultured voice. 'Coming from the market, I took this short cut to the Temple of the War God, and met those men. They let me pass, then suddenly grabbed me from behind. Thanks very much for your timely help!'

'Thank your lucky star!' Tao Gan growled. When they had stepped out on the crowded street that ran along the south side of the brilliantly lit market place, he added, 'Better postpone your visit to the temple till broad daylight! Good-bye.'

He wanted to enter the narrow passage between the market stalls, but she laid her hand on his arm and asked timidly:

'Please tell me the name of the shop in front of us. It must be a fruit shop, for I can smell the tangerines. If I know where we are, I can find the way by myself.'

So speaking, she took a thin bamboo tube from her sleeve and shook several thinner joints from it. It was a collapsible walking-stick.

Tao Gan quickly looked at her eyes. They were a dead, opaque grey.

'I'll see you home, of course,' he said contritely.

'That's quite unnecessary, sir. I am thoroughly familiar with the quarter. I only need a starting point.'

'I should have killed those cowardly bastards!' Tao Gan muttered angrily. And to the girl, 'Here, this is the tip of my sleeve. If I guide you, you'll get there quicker. Where do you live?'

'You are very thoughtful, sir. I live near the north-east corner of the market.'

They walked along, Tao Gan pushing his way with his bony elbows. After a while she asked:

'You are an officer temporarily attached to the city administration, aren't you?'

'Oh no! I am just a merchant, from the west city,' Tao Gan replied quickly.

'Of course. Excuse me!' she said meekly.

'What made you think I am an officer?' Tao Gan asked, curious.

She hesitated for a moment, then replied:

'Well, your Cantonese is fluent, but my sense of hearing is very acute, and I detect the accent from the capital. Secondly, when you were bluffing those two men, your voice had the genuine ring of authority. Thirdly, in this city everybody strictly minds his own business. No ordinary citizen would dream of tackling alone two ruffians who assault a woman. I may add I have a distinct feeling that you are a kind and considerate man.'

'Good reasoning,' Tao Gan commented dryly. 'Except for your last statement, which is wide of the mark indeed!'

Giving her a sidelong glance, he saw that a slow smile lit up her still face. Her wide-set eyes and full mouth gave her a slightly outlandish appearance, yet he found her uncommonly attractive. They walked on in silence. When they had arrived at the north east corner of the market, she said:

'I live in the fourth alley, on the right. From now on you'd better let me guide you.'

The narrow street became very dark as they went on, the girl lightly tapping the cobblestones with her stick. On either side stood decrepit, two-storeyed wooden houses. When they had entered the fourth side street, everything was pitch-dark. Tao Gan had to tread warily so as not to stumble on the uneven, slippery ground.

'In the tenement houses here live several families of market vendors,' she said. 'They don't come home till late at night, that's why it's so quiet here. Well, here we are. Mind the stairs, they are very steep.'

This was the moment to say good-bye, but he told himself that since he had come as far as this, he might as well find out more about this strange girl. Thus he followed her up the creaking, dark staircase. On the landing she guided him to a door, pushed it open and said:

'You'll find a candle on the table directly to your right.'

Tao Gan lit it with his tinderbox and surveyed the small, bare room. The floor consisted of wooden boards; three walls were

22

covered with cracked plaster, but the front was open. There only a bamboo balustrade divided the room from the flat roof of the adjoining house. In the distance the curved roofs of higher buildings stood out against the evening sky. The room was scrupulously clean, and a faint breeze had dispelled the stifling heat that still hung about in the streets. Next to the candle stood a cheap tea-basket, a cup of earthenware, and a platter bearing a few slices of cucumber and a long, thin knife. In front of the table was a low stool of plain wood, and against the side wall a narrow bench. At the rear he saw a high bamboo screen.

'I haven't much to offer, as you see,' she said gravely. 'I took you here because there's nothing I hate more than incurring debts. I am young, and not too bad-looking. If you want to sleep with me, you may do so. My bed is behind that screen.' As he stared at her in speechless astonishment, she added placidly, 'You need have no qualms, for I am not a virgin. I was raped by four drunken soldiers last year, you see.'

Tao Gan looked sharply at her still, pale face. He said slowly:

'You are either thoroughly depraved, or else utterly, unbelievably sincere. Whatever it is, I am not interested in your offer. I am interested, however, in human types, and yours is a new one to me. So a brief talk and a cup of tea will nicely settle the debt you think you owe me.'

She smiled faintly.

'Sit down! I'll change this torn robe.'

She disappeared behind the screen. Tao Gan poured himself a cup from the pot in the basket. Sipping his tea, he looked curiously at the row of small boxes that hung by bamboo hooks on a pole suspended under the eaves. There were about a dozen of them, each of different size and shape. Turning round, he saw on the shelf above the bench four large pots of green earthenware, with tight-fitting covers of woven bamboo. He listened intently, with a perplexed frown. Above the confused noise of the city he heard a persistent, whirring sound that he couldn't place at all. It seemed to come from the small boxes.

23

He rose and went to stand by the balustrade, scrutinizing them. Every box was perforated with small holes, and the noise came from there. He suddenly understood. They contained crickets. He himself was not particularly interested in those insects, but he knew that many people love to listen to their chirruping, and keep a few of them about the house, often in costly small cages of carved ivory or silver wire. Others are addicted to cricket-fighting. They match their champions in wine-houses and in the market place, putting a pair of these bellicose insects in a tube of carved bamboo and tickling them with thin straws to urge them on. Considerable bets were laid on these fights. He now noticed that each cricket made a slightly different sound. All were dominated, however, by the clear, sustained note coming from a tiny calabash hanging at the end of the row. It began low, then gradually rose to a high pitch of astonishing clarity. He took the calabash down and held it close to his ear. Suddenly the vibrating note changed into a low buzz.

The girl came out from behind the screen, now dressed in a simple, olive-green robe with black borders and a thin black belt. She came up to him quickly and frantically groped in the air for the small cage.

'Be careful with my Golden Bell!' she cried out.

Tao Gan put the calabash into her hands.

'I was just listening to its nice sound,' he said. 'Do you sell these insects?'

'Yes,' she replied, hanging the calabash back on the pole again. 'I sell them either on the market, or directly to good customers. This is my best one; it's very rare, especially here in the south. The experts call it the "Golden Bell".' Sitting down on the bench and folding her slender hands in her lap, she added, 'In the pots on the shelf behind me I keep a few fighting-crickets. They are rather pitiful; I hate to think of their sturdy legs and beautiful long feelers getting broken in fights. But I have to keep them in stock, for there's a steady demand for them.'

'How do you catch them?'

24

TAO GAN MEETS THE GOLDEN BELL

'I just walk at random along the outer walls of gardens and old buildings. I recognize good crickets by their song and use sliced fruit as bait. The tiny creatures are very clever; I even think they know me. When I let them loose in this room, they always come back to their boxes as soon as I call them.'

'Is no one looking after you?'

'I don't need anyone, I can look after myself quite well.'

Tao Gan nodded. Then he looked up sharply. He thought he had heard the stairs creak outside.

'Didn't you say that your neighbours here come home only late at night?'

'They do indeed,' she replied.

He listened intently. But now he only heard the singing of the crickets. He must have been mistaken. He asked dubiously:

'Is it all right for you to be all alone in this building most of the time?'

'Oh yes! You can speak your own language, by the way. I am quite familiar with it.'

'No, I much prefer to practise my Cantonese. Do you have no family here in the city?'

'I have. But after the accident with my eyes I left the house. My name is Lan-lee, by the way. And I still think you are an officer.'

'Yes, you are right. I am a sort of clerk, a member of the suite of an official from the capital. My name is Tao. Do you earn enough from these crickets for your daily needs?'

'Enough and to spare! I only need money for an oil-cake in the morning and at night, and for a bowl of noodles at noon. The crickets cost me nothing, and they sell at a good price. Take that Golden Bell, for instance. He is worth one silver piece, you know! Not that I'd ever think of selling him, though! I was so happy this morning when I woke up and heard him sing.' She smiled, then went on, 'I got him only last night, you see. It was a wonderful piece of luck. I happened to walk along the west wall of the Hwa-ta ... do you know that Buddhist temple?'

26

'Of course. The Temple of the Flowery Pagoda, in the west quarter.'

'Exactly. Well, I suddenly heard his voice there; it sounded frightened. I put a slice of cucumber at the foot of the wall and called him, like this.' She pursed her lips and made a sound that curiously resembled the chirruping of a cricket. 'Then I squatted down, waiting. At last he came; I heard him munching the cucumber. When he had eaten his fill and was quite happy, I coaxed him into that hollowed-out calabash I always carry in my sleeve.' Raising her head, she said, 'Listen! Now he sings very nicely again, doesn't he?'

'He certainly does!'

'I think that you too might become fond of them, in course of time. Your voice sounds kind; you can't be a bully. What did you do to those two men who assaulted me? They seemed to be in great pain.'

'Well, I am not a fighter. I am an elderly man, you know. About twice your age. But I have been around a lot and have learned how to take care of myself. I hope you'll learn to do so too, Lan-lee, from now on. The world is full of nasty persons who are out to take advantage of a girl like you.'

'Do you really think so? No, I have found people rather kind-hearted, on the whole. And if they are nasty, it's mainly because they are unhappy or lonely, or can't get the things they want; or have got too many of the things they want, perhaps. Anyway, I'll wager that those two men didn't even have enough to buy themselves a square meal, let alone a woman! They frightened me, because I thought they'd beat me senseless after they were through with me. But now I realize that they wouldn't have done that after all, because they'd know that I, being blind, could never denounce them.'

'Next time I meet them,' Tao Gan said crossly, 'I'll present each with a silver piece, as a reward for their kind intentions!' He emptied his cup, then resumed with a contented grin, 'Speaking about silver, they'll need that badly, I suppose! For one will never use his right arm again, and the other will try to wash the lime from his eyes and be crippled for life!'

She sprang up.

'What horrible things you did!' she exclaimed angrily. 'And you seem to take delight in it too! You are a nasty, cruel man!'

'And you a very foolish young woman!' Tao Gan retorted. Getting up and making for the door, he added sourly, 'Thanks for the tea!'

She groped for the candle and stepped out on the landing after him, holding it high.

'Be careful,' she said quietly, 'those steps are slippery.'

Tao Gan muttered something and went down.

When he was standing in the alley, he strained his eyes to get a good look at the house. Just from habit, he told himself; I haven't the slightest inclination ever to come back here, of course. I have no use for women, let alone for that silly bit of skirt with her crickets! He walked on, considerably annoyed.

## IV

The main thoroughfare that crossed the city from north to south was brilliantly lit by the gaudy lampions of shops, restaurants and wine-houses. Moving along with the motley crowd and hearing fragments of bitter quarrels and spirited altercations, Tao Gan's temper improved. He was smiling his accustomed sarcastic smile again when the high outer walls of the Governor's Palace came into sight.

Here there were fewer shops, and the traffic grew less. He now saw mainly high buildings, their gates guarded by armed sentries. Those on the left housed the various offices of the city tribunal, on the right was the garrison headquarters. Tao Gan passed by the broad marble steps leading up to the magnificent red-lacquered palace gate. Following the forbidding, crenelated wall, he knocked on the peephole of a smaller gate at the east corner of the compound. He explained to the sentry who he was. The door swung open and he walked through the long, echoing marble corridor to the separate courtyard in the east wing, where Judge Dee had taken up residence.

In the anteroom the smartly uniformed majordomo scrutinized the dishevelled visitor with raised eyebrows. Tao Gan calmly took off his goatskin caftan. Underneath he wore a dark-brown robe, with the gold-embroidered collar and cuffs that indicated his secretarial rank. The majordomo quickly made a low bow, and respectfully took the shabby garment from him. Then he pushed the high double door open.

The vast, empty hall was dimly lit by a dozen silver candelabras, standing in between the thick, red-lacquered pillars that formed two stately rows all along the side walls. On the left stood a broad couch of carved sandalwood and a table with a tall bronze flower vase, while the centre of the hall was just a vast expanse of dark-blue carpet. At the far end Tao Gan saw an enormous desk, standing in front of a gilded wall screen. Judge Dee sat behind it, Chiao Tai on one of the low chairs opposite. It was cool in the hall, and very quiet. As Tao Gan walked to the rear, he noticed the faint fragrance of sandalwood and of wilting jasmine flowers.

Judge Dee wore a purple robe with gold-embroidered rims, and his high, winged cap with the golden insignia indicating a Counsellor of State. He was leaning back in a capacious armchair, his arms folded in his wide sleeves. Chiao Tai seemed deep in thought too; he was staring at the antique bronzes on the desk, his broad shoulders hunched. It struck Tao Gan again that the judge had aged considerably these last four years. His face had grown thinner, and there were many deep lines round his eyes and mouth. His tufted eyebrows were still jet-black, but his long beard, moustache and sidewhiskers were streaked with grey.

When Tao Gan came up to the desk and made his bow, Judge Dee looked up. He righted himself, shook out his long sleeves, and spoke in his deep, resonant voice:

'Sit down there, next to Chiao Tai. There is bad news, Tao Gan. I was right in sending you two in disguise to the quay, for that set things moving. Fast.' And to the majordomo who had remained standing there: 'Bring fresh tea!'

After the majordomo had left, the judge placed his elbows on the desk, regarded his two lieutenants for a while, then resumed with a bleak smile:

'It's good to be among ourselves again for once, my friends! After our arrival in the capital, each of us was kept so busy there by his own particular duties that there was but rarely an occasion for an informal discussion, as we used to have nearly daily when I was still a district magistrate. Those were good days, when old Sergeant Hoong was still with us and...' He passed his hand over his face in a tired gesture. Then he took hold of himself and sat up straight. He opened his folding fan, and said briskly to Tao Gan, 'Just now Chiao Tai witnessed a particularly nasty murder. Before I let him tell you about it, however, I would like to hear your impressions of this city.'

He nodded to the thin man, leaned back in his chair and began to fan himself. Tao Gan shifted in his chair, then began quietly:

'After Chiao Tai and I had escorted Your Honour to the palace here, we went in a litter to the south city, looking for lodgings near the Arab Quarter, as you had ordered, sir. Brother Chiao chose an inn near the Moslem mosque, I one just outside the south gate, on the quay. We met again in a small eating-house for our noon rice, and passed the entire afternoon strolling about all along the river front. We saw many Arabs about; I heard that about a thousand of them have settled down in the city, and there are another thousand on the ships they have in port. They keep very much to themselves, however, and don't seem to mix much with the Chinese. Some Arab sailors got nasty when a custom-guard hit one of them, but they soon calmed down when the soldiers had marched out and after one of their leaders had reprimanded them.' He pensively stroked his moustache and resumed, 'Canton is the wealthiest city in the entire south, sir, famous for its gay night-life, especially on the flowerboats in the Pearl River. Life moves here at a feverish pace: merchants who are rich today may be beggars tomorrow, and at the gaming tables fortunes are made and lost every night. It goes without saying that this is a veritable paradise for all kinds of racketeers and swindlers, big and small, and that there's a considerable amount of financial juggling going on. But the Cantonese are businessmen first and foremost, they don't bother much with politics. If they grumble a bit now and then about the central government, it's only because, just as most businessmen, they resent official interference with their trade. But I found no signs of any real discontent, and I just can't see how a handful of Arabs could ever stir up real trouble here.'

As Judge Dee remained silent, Tao Gan pursued:

'Before leaving the quay, we made, in a wine-house, the acquaintance of a sea captain called Nee, rather a nice fellow who speaks Arabic and Persian, and used to trade to the Persian Gulf.

31

Since he may prove a useful connection, Chiao Tai accepted his invitation to visit him tomorrow.' He gave the judge a diffident look, then asked, 'Why are you so interested in those black barbarians, sir?'

'Because, Tao Gan, they represent our only hope of obtaining a clue to the whereabouts of a very important man who has disappeared in this city.' The judge waited till the two servants had placed a tea-tray loaded with exquisite antique porcelain on the desk, under the watchful eye of the majordomo. After the latter had poured the tea, Judge Dee told him, 'You may go and wait outside.' Then he resumed, looking steadily at his two lieutenants:

'Ever since His Majesty fell ill, contending groups have been forming at court. Some support the Crown Prince, the rightful heir to the throne, others the Empress, who wants to replace him by a member of her own family; still others are uniting in a powerful combination that favours a Regency, after the Great Demise. The man who holds the balance of power is the Imperial Censor Lew. I don't think you have ever met him, but you have heard about him, of course. A young, but extremely capable man, dedicated to the interests of our great Empire. I have been maintaining close contact with him, for I have a high regard for his integrity and his great talents. If a crisis should develop, I shall give him all my support.'

Judge Dee sipped his tea. He considered for a while, and resumed:

'About six weeks ago Censor Lew travelled here to Canton, accompanied by his trusted adviser Dr Soo and a number of military experts. The Grand Council had ordered him to check the preparations for our naval expedition to Annam. He returned to the capital and handed in a favourable report, praising the work of Weng Kien, the Governor of the Southern Region, whose guest I am now.

'Last week the Censor suddenly came back to Canton, this time accompanied only by Dr Soo. He had no orders to do so, and nobody knows the purpose of this second visit. He did not notify the Governor of his arrival and did not present himself in the palace here; evidently he wanted to remain incognito. But a special agent of the Governor once happened to see the Censor and Dr Soo near the Arab quarter, on foot and rather poorly dressed. After the Governor had reported this to the capital, the Grand Council instructed him to trace the Censor's whereabouts, and to apprise the Censor that the Council had ordered him to return to the capital without delay, for his presence was urgently required at court. The Governor mobilized all his investigators, special agents, and so on. They combed out the city, but their efforts were of no avail. The Censor and Dr Soo had disappeared completely.'

The judge heaved a sigh. He shook his head and continued:

'The matter had to be kept a closely guarded official secret, for the Censor's prolonged absence from the capital might have serious political consequences. The Council suspected that something was seriously amiss here, and therefore informed the Governor that the matter had been disposed of, ordering him to call off the search. At the same time, however, the Council instructed me to go to Canton and institute a secret investigation, on the pretext of gathering information on foreign trade in connection with a query from the Board of Finance. In fact, however, our task is to establish contact with the Censor, find out from him why he came to Canton, and what is keeping him here. For Dr Soo we need not look any more. His dead body is lying in the side hall. Tell him what happened, Chiao Tai!'

Chiao Tai gave his astonished colleague a brief account of the double murder in the Arab quarter. When he had finished, Judge Dee said:

'I recognized the body brought here by Chiao Tai at once as that of Dr Soo. The doctor must have spotted Chiao Tai when you two were walking about on the quay, but he did not want to accost Chiao Tai as long as you, Tao Gan, were still with him, because he had never seen you before. So he followed you two to the wine-house, and after you had separated he spoke to Chiao Tai. However, Dr Soo himself had been followed by the Arab

33

assassin and the mysterious dwarf. Those two must have seen Dr Soo accosting Chiao Tai, and they took quick action. Since the Arab quarter is a rabbit warren of crooked alleys and unsuspected shortcuts, they and their accomplices could run ahead and post themselves in the two or three alleys Chiao Tai and Dr Soo would have to pass through. The Arab assassin was partly successful, for he murdered Dr Soo. He had planned to kill Chiao Tai too, but then a third, unknown party intervened, and strangled him. Thus we have to reckon with two well-organized groups, equally ruthless in their methods, but pursuing conflicting aims. Which proves that the Censor is in very serious trouble indeed.'

'Is there no indication at all regarding the nature of that trouble, sir?' Tao Gan asked.

'None but his evident interest in the Arabs here. After you had left this morning to look for a lodging, the Governor showed me over my quarters here in the east wing. I told him to send me the secret dossiers on the provincial and city administration of the last year, for my general orientation. I devoted the morning to a careful study of these. However, I found only routine problems, nothing connected with the Arabs here, and nothing that could conceivably rouse the Censor's special interest. I did find, however, the report of the agent who had got a glimpse of the Censor and Dr Soo. In it he states that both of them were dressed rather poorly, and looked wan and worried. The Censor was accosting a passing Arab. Just when the agent was stepping up to them to confirm their identity, the three men disappeared among the crowd. The agent then hurried to the palace and reported to the Governor what he had seen.' The judge emptied his teacup and went on, 'Before leaving the capital, I made a study of the affairs the Censor had been working on, but I failed to discover a single reference to Canton or to the Arabs here. As for his private life I know nothing beyond the fact that he is a man of considerable means but still unmarried, and that besides Dr Soo he has no close friends.' Giving his two lieutenants a sharp look, he added, 'The Governor must be kept ignorant of all this, mind you! When I had tea with him just now, I told him that Dr Soo was a dubious character from the capital who had got mixed up here with Arab hooligans. The Governor must be left under the impression that we are here only to investigate foreign trade.'

'Why, sir?' Chiao Tai asked. 'Since he is the highest local authority, he might help us in ...'

The judge shook his head emphatically.

'You must remember,' he said, 'that the Censor did not apprise the Governor of his second visit to Canton. That may mean that the Censor's business here is so secret that he doesn't dare to take even the Governor into his confidence. It may mean also, however, that the Censor doesn't trust the Governor, and suspects him of being implicated in whatever mysterious business the Censor is tracing here. In either case we must abide by the Censor's policy of utter secrecy—at least until we know more about what is going on here. Therefore we can not avail ourselves of the facilities the local authorities could supply us with. After I had taken my noon rice, however, I did summon the head of the special branch of the military police, and he selected four secret agents who will assist us with the routine side of our investigation. As you know, the special branch is entirely independent; the local military authorities have no say over them, and they report directly to the capital.' He sighed and resumed, 'So you see we are confronted with a particularly difficult task. On one hand we must feign to collaborate closely with the Governor for a fictitious purpose, and on the other conduct our own investigation with the utmost discretion.'

'And with an unknown opponent closely watching us too!' Tao Gan remarked.

'Not us, but the Censor and Dr Soo,' Judge Dee corrected. 'For that person, or persons, can not possibly know the real purpose of our visit here; that is a secret of state, known only to the Supreme Council. They watch Dr Soo, and presumably also the Censor, because they do not want them to communicate with outsiders. And since they don't shrink from murder, the Censor may be in considerable danger.'

'Are there any grounds for suspecting the Governor, sir?' Chiao Tai asked.

'None that I know of. Before leaving the capital I looked up his record at the Board of Personnel. He is described as a diligent and capable official, a brilliant young man already twenty years ago, when he was a junior assistant in the local tribunal here. Thereafter he served with distinction as magistrate in several districts, and was promoted to Prefect. Two years ago he was again sent to Canton, this time as Governor of the entire southern region. His family life is exemplary; he has three sons and one daughter. The only critical remark I found was that he is devoured by ambition, and fervently hopes for the post of Metropolitan Governor. Well, after I had given him the rigmarole about Dr Soo's murder, I ordered him to summon for a conference half an hour before the evening meal, the best experts on foreign trade. Thus I hope to gather some general information on Arab affairs, under the cloak of orientating myself on foreign trade in general.' Rising he added, 'Let's go to the Council Hall now; they'll be waiting for us.'

As they were walking to the door, Tao Gan asked:

'What could an Imperial Censor have to do with the paltry affairs of those black barbarians, sir?'

'Well, one never knows,' Judge Dee said cautiously. 'It seems that the Arab tribes have united themselves under a kind of chieftain whom they call the Khalif, whose armed hordes have overrun most of those barren western regions. What happens in those benighted lands on the periphery of our civilized world does not concern us, of course; that Khalif has not even become important enough to dare send tribute-bearing envoys begging His Imperial Majesty to grant him the status of vassal. Yet there is the possibility that some time he may establish contact with our arch-enemies, the Tartars, beyond our north-western frontier. Also, the Arab ships here in the south might supply arms to the rebels in Annam—just to mention two possibilities that come to mind. But let us not indulge in irrelevant speculation. Come along!'

# V

The majordomo led the judge and his two assistants ceremoniously through a veritable maze of covered corridors. After they had crossed the central courtyard where clerks, messengers and guards were bustling about in the light of the coloured lampions, he took them through an imposing gate and ushered them into the sumptuous Council Hall, brilliantly lit by dozens of man-high candelabras.

The Governor, a tall, bearded man with broad, round shoulders, received the judge with a low bow that made the sleeves of his gorgeous robe of shimmering green brocade sweep the marble floor. The golden insignia attached to the quivering wings of his high cap made a tinkling sound. He acknowledged Judge Dee's introduction of Colonel Chiao and Chief-Secretary Tao with another, now rather perfunctory bow. Then he presented the thin, elderly man who was kneeling by his side at Pao Kwan, Prefect of Canton, in charge of the city administration. The Prefect touched the floor with his forehead.

Judge Dee told the Prefect to rise. After a casual glance at the old man's deeply-lined, worried face, he followed the Governor, who conducted him to a throne-like seat in the rear. Then the Governor stood himself respectfully in front of the dais; for although he was the highest authority in the Southern Region, he was still several ranks below Judge Dee, now President of the Metropolitan Court, and for two years concurrently Counsellor of State.

The judge sat down, and Chiao Tai and Tao Gan went to stand somewhat apart, on either side of the dais. Tao Gan looked quite dignified in his long brown robe and high gauze cap. Chiao Tai had put on his spiked helmet and had taken a sword from the armoury of the palace. The close-fitting coat of mail revealed his wide, bulging shoulders and muscular arms.

The Governor made a bow, then spoke formally:

'In accordance with Your Excellency's instructions, I have summoned here Mr Liang Foo and Mr Yau Tai-kai. Mr Liang is one of the wealthiest merchants of this city, he...'

'Is he a member of the clan of Liang that was nearly decimated by that infamous ninefold murder?' the judge interrupted. 'I dealt with that case fourteen years ago, when I was magistrate of Pooyang.'

'One of Your Excellency's most famous cases!' the Governor said suavely. 'It is still talked about here in Canton, with gratitude and admiration! No, this Mr Liang belongs to quite a different clan. He is the only son of the late Admiral Liang.'

'An illustrious family,' Judge Dee remarked. Unfolding his fan, he went on, 'The Admiral was a valorous soldier and a great strategist. The "Subduer of the South Seas", he was called. I met him only once, but I well remember his extraordinary appearance. A squat, broad-shouldered man, with a flat, rather ugly face—a low forehead and high cheekbones. But once you had seen those piercing eyes you knew that you were in the presence of a truly great man!' He tugged at his moustache, then asked, 'Why didn't his son continue the family tradition?'

'Bad health made him unfit for a military career, sir. Which is a pity, for he has inherited his father's strategical talents, as evinced by his acumen in administering his vast commercial interests. And, in a minor manner, by his rare skill in the game of chess! Mr Liang is the chess champion of this province.' The Governor coughed behind his hand and continued, 'Of course a man of Mr Liang's breeding doesn't stoop to direct ah ... association with the barbarian traders. But he keeps himself informed about all the broader issues. Mr Yau Tai-kai, on the other hand, has close contacts with the foreign merchants, mainly Arabs and Persians. He doesn't mind; he comes from a rather er ... modest family, and is a broadminded, easy-going fellow. I thought that Mr Liang and Mr Yau would be able to present to Your Excellency a reasonably complete picture of the trade situation in my territory.'

'It's a big city,' the judge remarked casually. 'One would think that it harboured more experts on foreign trade than just these two.'

The Governor darted a quick look at him. He said quietly:

'Foreign trade is highly organized, sir. Has to be, seeing that it is partly state controlled. It's these two gentlemen who pull the strings.'

Chiao Tai came forward and said: 'I heard that a sea captain called Nee also is considered an expert in this field. His ships ply between Canton and Arab ports.'

'Nee?' the Governor asked. He cast a questioning look at the Prefect. Pao slowly pulled at his wispy goatee, then said vaguely:

'Oh yes! The captain is well known in shipping circles. But it seems that he has been staying ashore the last three years or so, and is leading a rather er ... dissolute life.'

'I see,' Judge Dee said. And to the Governor, 'Well, let the two gentlemen you mentioned come in.'

The Governor gave an order to the Prefect, then ascended the dais and stood at Judge Dee's right hand. Pao came back leading two men across the hall, one of small stature, very thin, the other tall, with a large paunch. When they were kneeling in front of the dais the Prefect introduced the first as the merchant Liang Foo, his portly companion as Mr Yau Tai-kai.

The judge told them to rise. He saw that Liang Foo had a pale, rather cold face with a jet-black, silky moustache and thin goatee. His curved eyebrows and unusually long lashes gave the upper half of his face a nearly feminine air. He wore a long, olive-green robe; on his head a black gauze cap indicated that he possessed a literary degree. Mr Yau evidently was quite a different type; he had a cheerful round face, adorned by a bristling moustache and a neatly trimmed ring-beard. Tiny wrinkles surrounded his large bovine eyes. He was puffing slightly, and perspiration pearled on

PREFECT PAO PRESENTS YAU AND LIANG TO JUDGE DEE

his florid face. His ceremonial dress of heavy brown brocade was apparently bothering him.

Judge Dee said a few polite words, then began to question Liang Foo on the trade situation. Liang spoke excellent standard Chinese and his answers were very much to the point. He seemed unusually clever and displayed the easy poise of a born gentleman. Judge Dee learned to his dismay that the Arab colony in Canton was larger than he had thought; Liang said that there were about ten thousand of them spread over the city and suburbs. He added, however, that their number fluctuated with the season, for both Arab and Chinese captains had to wait in Canton for the winter monsoon before taking their ships to Annam and Malaya. Then they went on to Ceylon, and from there sailed across the Indian Ocean to the Persian Gulf. Mr Liang said that the Arab and Persian junks were capable of carrying five hundred men, the Chinese vessels even more.

Then it was Mr Yau's turn. He seemed overawed by the exalted company, and at first tended to bluster. But when he came to a description of his business, Judge Dee soon understood that he was an uncommonly shrewd man with a good grasp of financial problems. When Yau had completed a list of the products imported by various Arab merchants, the judge remarked:

'I can't understand how you manage to tell all those foreigners apart. To me they all look alike! It must be rather distressing to associate daily with those uncultured barbarians!'

Yau shrugged his round shoulders.

'In business one has to take things as one finds them, Excellency! And a few Arabs have acquired a smattering of Chinese culture. Take Mansur, the leader of the Arab community, for instance. He speaks our language fluently, and he entertains well. I have an early dinner appointment at his place tonight, as a matter of fact.'

The judge noticed that he shifted uneasily on his feet, and seemed eager to take his leave. He said:

'Many thanks for your valuable information, Mr Yau. You may go now. Take Colonel Chiao with you to that Arab party; it will be an interesting experience for him.' He beckoned Chiao Tai and told him in an undertone, 'Find out how the Arabs are distributed over the city, and keep your ears and eyes open!'

After an adjutant had conducted Chiao Tai and Mr Yau to the door, Judge Dee talked for a while with Mr Liang about the naval campaigns of his late father, and then dismissed him too. He fanned himself for a while in silence. Suddenly he addressed the Governor:

'We are a long way from the capital here, and the Cantonese are reputedly rather headstrong, and very independent by nature. If one adds thereto the presence of all those foreigners, one would suppose that preserving the peace in this city is not an easy task.'

'I can't complain, sir. Prefect Pao here is a capable administrator and has an experienced staff, and our garrison consists of seasoned soldiers from up north. It is true that the local population is a bit surly at times, but they are a law-abiding lot, on the whole, and with a little tact...'

The Governor shrugged his shoulders. Prefect Pao started to say something, but apparently changed his mind.

Judge Dee closed his fan with a snap and rose. The Governor took the judge and Tao Gan to the door, and the majordomo led them back to Judge Dee's own wing.

The judge made him take them to a pavilion in a small, moonlit back garden. An artificial goldfish pond afforded some coolness there. When they were seated at the small tea-table by the carved marble balustrade, Judge Dee dismissed the majordomo. He said slowly:

'Quite an interesting session. But except for the fact that we now know there are even more Arabs here than we expected, it didn't help us much. Or did I miss something?'

Tao Gan gloomily shook his head. After a while he said:

'You told us that the Censor's public life is impeccable, sir. But what about his private interests? In the case of an unmarried young man...'

'I too thought of that. Since as President of the Court I have all

42

kinds of special facilities, checking on his private life was an easy matter. Although he is a handsome fellow, he never shows the slightest interest in women. Many a prominent family in the capital has tried to make him their son-in-law, but in vain. Neither does he cultivate any of the charming courtesans who assist at the parties a man in his position has to attend nearly every night. This lack of interest is not rooted in an innate aversion to women—a trait not uncommon in handsome young men, as you know. The reason for his abstention is simply that he is completely engrossed in his work.'

'Does he have no hobby at all, sir?'

'No, except for a great interest in crickets. Has a fine collection, both singing and fighting ones. The subject came up during the last conversation I had with him. I noticed a chirruping sound coming from his sleeve, and he produced a cricket in a small cage of silver thread. Said he always carried it with him, a rare specimen called a Golden Bell, if I remember correctly. He...' He broke off and looked at Tao Gan's startled face. 'What is wrong with that?' he asked, astonished.

'Well,' Tao Gan replied slowly, 'it so happened that on my way here I met a blind girl selling crickets who caught a stray Golden Bell last night. It must be a coincidence, of course, but since she told me also that it is of great rarity, especially here in the south, it might...'

'It all depends on how and where she got it,' Judge Dee said curtly. 'Tell me more about this meeting!'

'I ran into her by accident near the market place, sir. She catches them herself, recognizing good specimens by their singing. While passing by the west wall of the Flowery Pagoda, a famous temple in the west city, she heard the peculiar noise produced by the Golden Bell. It must have been hiding in a crack in the wall; its voice sounded frightened, she said. She laid a bait, and coaxed the cricket into a small calabash.'

Judge Dee made no comment. He tugged at his moustache for a while, then said pensively:

43

'It's a long chance, of course. Yet we may not rule out the possibility that it is indeed the Censor's Golden Bell that escaped from its cage while he was in that neighbourhood. While Chiao Tai is gathering information at Mansur's party, we may as well have a look at the temple and see whether we can't obtain a clue to the Censor's whereabouts there. Anyway, it is one of the historical sights of the city, I am told. We can take our evening rice in some small place on the way.'

'You can't do that, sir!' Tao Gan protested, aghast. 'Formerly, when you were still a local magistrate, there was no harm in making the rounds of the city incognito, on occasion. But now, as one of the highest officials in the Empire, you really can't...'

'I can and I will!' the judge cut him short. 'In the capital I have to adopt all the pomp and circumstance belonging to my office—that can't be helped. But we aren't in the capital now, we are in Canton. I am certainly not going to let slip this welcome opportunity for getting out of myself!' Forestalling all further protests by rising abruptly, he added, 'I shall meet you in the anteroom, when I have changed.'

# VI

After Chiao Tai and Mr Yau had left the Council Hall, the former quickly went to the armoury, doffed his martial dress, and put on a light robe of thin grey cotton and a cap of black gauze. Then he joined Mr Yau in the gatehouse of the palace. Yau proposed that they call at his own house, for he too wanted to change before going to the party. They were carried in Yau's comfortable well-cushioned palankeen to his mansion, a large building to the west of the palace, near the Kwang-Siao Temple.

While Chiao Tai was waiting for Yau in the spacious reception room, he looked dubiously at the vulgar luxury displayed there. The wall tables were loaded with glittering silver vases filled with artificial flowers made of wax, and red scrolls inscribed with texts extolling Yau's wealth and importance decorated the walls. The maidservant who brought him his tea was sedately dressed, but her heavy make-up and the frankly appraising look she gave him indicated a former dancing-girl.

Soon Yau came to fetch him. He had put on a thin blue robe, and he wore his simple black cap at a jaunty angle. 'Let's get along!' he said briskly. 'I am rather busy tonight, you know. After dinner I have an urgent affair to attend to. Fortunately these Arab parties end rather early.'

'What do we get there?' Chiao Tai asked, as their palankeen was carried down the street.

'Rather simple fare, but quite appetizing in its own way. Not a patch on our Chinese kitchen, needless to say. Have you tried our Cantonese stewed octopus yet? Or eels?'

He started with a detailed explanation of these dishes that made Chiao Tai's mouth water, then gave an eloquent discourse on the

45

local wine and liqueur. Evidently he does himself well, Chiao Tai thought. Although Yau was a rather vulgar upstart, he was a pleasant fellow all the same.

When they were descending from the palankeen in front of a plain whitewashed gatehouse, Chiao Tai exclaimed:

'I had my noon rice early today, and your talk has made me ravenous! I could devour a whole roasted pig, I tell you!'

'Hush!' Yau warned quickly, 'don't mention pork! The Moslems aren't allowed to even touch it; the meat is considered unclean. They aren't allowed to drink wine either, but they have another liquor that tastes rather nice.' So speaking, he knocked on the door, which was decorated with iron bosses shaped like fishes.

It was opened by an old Arab hunchback with a striped turban. He led them through a small courtyard to a rectangular garden, planted with low flowering shrubs in an unusual pattern. A tall lean man came to meet them. His turban and flowing long gown were very white in the moonlight. Chiao Tai recognized him. It was the same man he had seen scolding the Arab sailors on the quay.

'Peace on you, Mansur!' Yau exclaimed jovially. 'I took the liberty of bringing a friend, Colonel Chiao, from our capital.'

The Arab fixed his large, flashing eyes on Chiao Tai. The whites of them stood out clearly against his dark-brown skin. He spoke in a sonorous voice, in slow but good Chinese:

'Peace on all true believers!'

Chiao Tai reasoned that if the salutation was limited to Moslems, it did not include Yau and himself and thus was rather rude. But by the time he had thought this out, the Arab and Yau, bent over a shrub, were already deep in a discussion on raising plants.

'The noble Mansur is a great lover of flowers, just like me,' Yau explained as he righted himself. 'These fragrant plants he brought along all the way from his own country.'

Chiao Tai noticed the delicate scent drifting about in the garden, but what with the insolent greeting and his empty stomach he was not in the proper mood for flowers. He sourly surveyed the low house in the rear. Seeing behind it the minaret of the mosque outlined against the moonlit sky, he concluded that Mansur's house could not be far from his inn.

At last Mansur led his two guests into the large airy room at the back of the garden. Its façade consisted of a row of high open arches of a quaint, pointed shape. Upon entering, Chiao Tai noticed to his dismay that there was no furniture at all, let alone a dining-table. The floor was covered by a thick blue pile carpet, and in the corners lay a few stuffed silken pillows. From the ceiling hung a brass lamp with eight wicks. All across the back wall ran a curtain of a type he had never seen before: it was attached with brass rings to a pole close to the ceiling, instead of being sewn to a bamboo stick, as it should be.

Mansur and Yau sat down cross-legged on the floor, and after some hesitation Chiao Tai followed their example. Apparently Mansur had seen his annoyed look, for he now addressed him in his measured voice:

'I trust the honoured guest doesn't object to sitting on the floor, instead of in a chair.'

'As a soldier,' Chiao Tai said gruffly, 'I am accustomed to roughing it.'

'We consider our manner of living quite comfortable,' his host remarked coldly.

Chiao Tai instinctively disliked the man, but he had to admit that he was an impressive figure. He had a regular, clean-cut face, with a thin beaked nose, and a long moustache, the ends of which curled up in foreign fashion. He carried his shoulders very straight, and flat muscles rippled smoothly under his thin white gown. Evidently he was a man capable of great feats of endurance.

To break the awkward silence, Chiao Tai pointed at the band of intricate design that ran all along the top of the wall and asked:

'What do those curlicues mean?'

'It's Arab writing,' Yau explained hastily. 'It's a holy text.'

'How many letters do you have?' Chiao Tai asked Mansur.

'Twenty-eight,' he replied curtly.

47

'Holy heaven!' Chiao Tai exclaimed. 'Is that all? We have more than twenty thousand, you know!'

Mansur's lips curved in a contemptuous smile. He turned round and clapped his hands.

'How in hell can they express their thoughts in only twenty-eight letters?' Chiao Tai asked Yau in an undertone.

'They haven't got so many thoughts to express!' Yau whispered with a thin smile. 'Here comes the food!'

An Arab youth entered carrying a large round tray of engraved brass. On it lay several fried chickens, and a jug and three goblets of coloured enamel. After the boy had poured out a colourless liquor, he withdrew. Mansur lifted his goblet and said gravely:

'Welcome to my house!'

Chiao Tai drank and found the strong liquor flavoured with aniseed rather good. The chickens smelled nice, but he was at a loss how to eat them, for he saw no chopsticks. After a few more rounds, Mansur and Yau tore a chicken apart with their fingers, and he followed their example. He took a bite from the leg and found it excellent. After the chicken came a platter heaped with saffron rice, fried with sliced lamb, raisins and almonds. Chiao Tai liked that too; he ate it as the others did, kneading the rice into lumps with his fingers. After he had washed his hands in scented water from the basin that the servant presented to him, he leaned back against the pillow and said with a contented grin:

'Very good indeed! Let's have another round!' After they had emptied their goblets, he said to Mansur:

'We are neighbours, you know! I am staying in the Five Immortals' Inn. Tell me, are all your countrymen living in this particular quarter?'

'Most of them do. We like to be near our place of worship. Our prayers are announced from the top of the minaret, and when one of our ships enters the estuary, we light a beacon fire there and say prayers for a safe landing.' He took a long draught, then went on: 'About fifty years ago a relative of our Prophet—the peace of Allah be upon him!—came to this city and died in his abode outside the north-east gate. Many true believers settled down in that holy place, to tend to his tomb. Further, our sailors live as a rule in the six large hostels, not far from the custom-house.'

'I met here a Chinese sea captain,' Chiao Tai resumed, 'who speaks your language. Fellow called Nee.'

Mansur gave him a wary look. He said in a level voice:

'Nee's father was a Chinese, but his mother a Persian. The Persians are no good. Our valiant warriors, led by our great Khalif, made mincemeat out of them. Forty years ago, at the battle of Nehavent.'

Yau proposed another round, then asked:

'Is it true that to the west of the Khalif's domain there live white-skinned people, with blue eyes and yellow hair?'

'There can't be real men like that!' Chiao Tai protested. 'Must be ghosts or devils!'

'They do indeed exist,' Mansur said gravely. 'They fight well, too. They can even write, but the wrong way round, from left to right.'

'That clinches it!' Chiao Tai said with satisfaction. 'They are ghosts! In the Nether World everything is done exactly the other way round as in the world of men.'

Mansur emptied his goblet.

'Some have red hair,' he remarked.

Chiao Tai gave him a searching look. Since the man was talking such arrant nonsense, he must be getting very drunk.

'What about some Arab dances now, eh Mansur?' Yau asked with a broad grin. And to Chiao Tai, 'Ever seen Arab dancing girls, colonel?'

'Never! Do they dance as well as ours?'

Mansur sat up.

'By Allah!' he exclaimed. 'Your question betrays your ignorance!' He clapped his hands, and barked an order at the servant in Arabic.

'Watch the curtain!' Yau whispered excitedly. 'If we are lucky, it'll be a real treat!'

49

A woman appeared in the curtain opening. She was just over medium height, and naked but for a narrow fringed black band round her hips. It hung so low that it left her belly completely bare, and its smooth rounded surface set off with disconcerting clarity the glittering emerald inserted into her navel. Her slender waist made her round breasts seem very large, her voluptuous thighs too heavy. She had a beautiful, golden-brown skin, but her face, though very expressive, did not correspond to Chinese standards of feminine beauty. Her eyes with their kohl-tinted rims seemed too wide, her scarlet lips too full, and there were curious kinks in her shiny blue-black hair. These un-Chinese features repelled but, at the same time, strangely fascinated Chiao Tai. As she was standing there observing the company with slightly raised eyebrows, her large, moist eyes suddenly reminded Chiao Tai of those of a doe he had killed by mistake while hunting, many years ago.

She stepped into the room, her golden ankle-rings making a faint, tinkling sound. Completely unconcerned about her nakedness, she made a bow in front of Mansur, touching her breast briefly with her right hand, then inclined her head to Yau and Chiao Tai. She kneeled facing Mansur, keeping her knees close together. When she folded her slender hands in her lap, Chiao Tai noticed with astonishment that her palms and nails had been painted with a bright red pigment.

Seeing Chiao Tai's admiring stare, Mansur's lips curved in a satisfied smile.

'This is Zumurrud, the Smaragdine dancer,' he said quietly. 'She will now show you a dance of our country.'

Again he clapped his hands. Two Arabs clad in wide gowns came from behind the curtain and squatted down in the farthest corner. One began to thumb a large wooden drum, the other tuned his fiddle, drawing the long curved rattan bow across the strings.

Mansur looked at the woman fixedly with his large, smouldering eyes. After a casual glance at him she half-turned on her

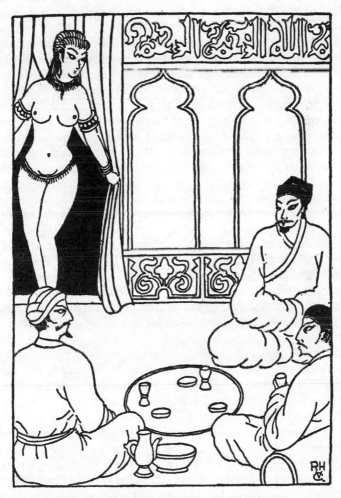

MANSUR ENTERTAINS HIS GUESTS

knees, and surveyed Yau and Chiao Tai with an insolent stare. When Mansur saw that she was about to address Mr Yau, he shouted an order at the musicians.

As the fiddle started upon a low, wailing tune, Zumurrud folded her hands behind her head, and began to sway her torso to the slow rhythm. While doing so she leaned backwards, lower and lower, till her head was resting against the floor, on her folded arms. Her breasts pointed upward, nipples taut, while her curly locks spilled out over her shapely arms. She closed her eyes, the lashes forming two long fringes across her smooth cheeks.

The fiddler now moved his bow in a quicker rhythm; dull beats of the drum accentuated the melody. Chiao Tai expected her to get up now and commence her dance, but she remained motionless. Suddenly he noticed with a start that the emerald in the centre of her bare belly was moving slowly to and fro. The rest of her arched body remained completely still; only her belly moved, up and down, left and right, in a strange, staccato movement. The drumbeat quickened: now the emerald began to describe circles, which gradually became larger. Chiao Tai's eyes were riveted upon the green stone which glittered viciously in the lamplight. The blood pounded heavily inside him; his throat felt constricted. Perspiration came streaming down his face, but he did not notice it.

He woke up from his trance when the drum stopped suddenly. The fiddle ended with a few strident notes. In the dead silence that followed, the dancer raised herself to a kneeling position with the lithe grace of a wild animal and put her hair in order with a few deft gestures. Her bosom was heaving; a thin film of moisture covered her naked body. Chiao Tai now noticed the strong musk perfume she used; it was mixed with a strange, slightly pungent body-smell. Although he told himself that it was repugnant, at the same time it stirred some elemental feeling deep inside him, made him remember certain wild, animal smells of hunting, of sweating horses and red, hot blood at the height of battle.

52

'Mashallah!' Mansur cried out admiringly. He took a foreign gold coin from his belt and placed it on the floor in front of the kneeling woman. She picked it up and without giving it a second glance threw it across the room towards the two musicians. Then she turned round on her knees and asked Chiao Tai in fluent Chinese:

'Has the stranger come from afar?'

Chiao Tai swallowed; his throat felt tight. He hastily took a sip from the goblet, and replied as casually as he could:

'I am from the capital. My name is Chiao Tai.'

She gave him a long look from her large liquid eyes. Then she turned to his neighbour and said listlessly:

'You are looking well, Mr Yau.'

The merchant smiled broadly. He said, imitating the Arab custom:

'I am in good health, praise be to Allah!' Staring at her bosom, he said with a leer to Mansur, 'As one of our Chinese poets put it: The tree bends under the weight of the ripe fruit!'

Mansur's face fell. He watched Zumurrud sharply as she refilled Yau's and Chiao Tai's goblets. When she leaned forward to Chiao Tai, her strong, nearly animal smell gave him a tense feeling in the pit of his stomach. He clenched his large fists in an effort to control his surging blood. She bent her head close to him, a slow smile revealing her perfect teeth, and said in an undertone:

'I live on the first boat in the fourth row.'

'Come here!' Mansur shouted.

As she turned to him, he hissed something at her in Arabic.

She languidly raised her eyebrows, then replied haughtily in Chinese:

'I converse with whom I please, oh master of many ships.'

Mansur's face contorted in an angry scowl. The whites of his eyes flashed as he barked:

'Bow and apologize for your insulting remark!'

She spat on the floor, right in front of him.

Mansur uttered an oath. He sprang up, grabbed her hair with

one hand and pulled her roughly to her feet. Ripping off with the other the fringed band from her hips, he turned her round so that she faced his two guests and shouted in a strangled voice:

'Have a good look at the harlot's charms! They are for sale!'

She tried to shake herself loose, but he swung her round again with a savage jerk. Forcing her down on her knees and pressing her head to the floor, he barked an order at the musicians. The man with the fiddle rose quickly and handed Mansur the long rattan bow.

Chiao Tai averted his eyes from the crouching woman. He addressed Mansur coldly:

'Better settle your squabbles in private, Mansur. You are embarrassing your guests.'

Mansur gave him a furious look. He opened his mouth, then checked himself. Biting his lips, he lowered the raised rattan and let go of the woman's hair. He sat down again, muttering something under his breath.

The dancer came to her feet. She picked up the torn fringe, then turned to Chiao Tai and Yau and hissed with blazing eyes:

'Mark what he said. I am available to the highest bidder!'

Tossing back her head, she went to the curtain and disappeared. The two musicians hurriedly followed her.

'Spirited wench!' Yau said with a grin to Mansur. 'Quite a handful, I dare say!' He refilled Mansur's goblet, and added as he raised his own, 'Many thanks for this lavish entertainment!'

Mansur silently inclined his head. Yau got up and Chiao Tai followed his example. He wanted to say a few words of thanks too, but thought better of it when he saw the burning hatred in Mansur's eyes. Their host led them across the scented garden to the gate, and took leave of them with a few barely audible phrases.

Yau's palankeen bearers scrambled to their feet, but Chiao Tai shook his head at them.

'Let's walk a little,' he said to Yau. 'The air was very close in there and that foreign liquor has gone to my head.'

54

'I am a well-known man,' the fat merchant said doubtfully. 'I am not really supposed to move about on foot.'

'Neither is a colonel of the guard,' Chiao Tai said dryly. 'Since the streets are deserted, no one'll see us. Come along!'

They walked towards the corner, the palankeen bearers following at some distance.

'The food was good,' Chiao Tai muttered, 'but the fellow shouldn't have made that disgraceful scene.'

'What can you expect from barbarians?' Yau said with a shrug. 'It was a pity you stopped him, though. She's giving herself airs, nowadays, and a sore bottom would have done her good. She's not a pure Arab, you know. Her mother belonged to the Tanka, the waterfolk, and that makes her doubly savage. Anyway he wouldn't have dared to give her a real good whipping, one that draws blood and leaves scars.'

He wetted his lips with the tip of his tongue. Chiao Tai gave him a sour look. He revised his former favourable opinion. The fellow had a nasty streak in him. He said coldly:

'Mansur seemed fully intent on doing just that. And why shouldn't he dare to mark her?'

The question apparently embarrassed Yau. He hesitated for a while before he replied:

'Well, Mansur doesn't own her—as far as I know, that is. I assume that she has a powerful patron, somewhere. And although such fellows don't mind their women earning a little pin-money by dancing at parties, they don't like to get 'em back with a broken skin.'

'But Mansur said she was for sale!'

'Oh, that was only to humiliate her. Don't let that give you ideas, colonel! I wouldn't recommend those black women, anyway. They are rather crude in their ways, you know, like beasts of the field. Well, I'd like to take my palankeen now, if you don't mind. I have to keep an appointment in a er ... private establishment of mine.'

'Don't miss it!' Chiao Tai said gruffly. 'I'll manage.'

Yau looked at him askance; he seemed to have noticed the change in his companion's attitude. He laid his podgy hand on Chiao Tai's arm and said with an ingratiating grin:

'I'll take you there some other night, colonel! The lady I put in charge is very discreet, and the amenities are er ... exceptional. I go there regularly—for the sake of variety, you understand! It's not that I am not served well at home. Very well, I may say. Ought to be, seeing the amount of money I spend on my wives and concubines. That cosy little place of mine is conveniently located, not too far from my residence. On the corner of the second street south of the Kwang-siao Temple, as a matter of fact. I'd take you there right now, only the lady I am due to meet there is rather shy, you see.... Not so easy to get! We have a hobby in common and that'll help, I trust, but if she saw me coming with a stranger, she might...'

'Quite,' Chiao Tai interrupted him. 'Don't keep her waiting, she might run away!' Walking on, he muttered to himself, 'Would be the wisest thing for her to do, too, I think!'

In the next street he hailed a litter and told the bearers to take him to the palace. As the men trotted off, he leaned back in the seat and tried to get a brief nap. But as soon as he had closed his eyes he saw the sinuous figure of the Arab dancer, and remembered again that heady smell.

## VII

Judge Dee and Tao Gan had left the palace by a small side gate, and were strolling down the main thoroughfare. They now looked like two elderly gentlemen of letters. The judge had put on a dark-blue cotton robe with a black sash round his waist. On his head he had a skull-cap of black silk. Tao Gan wore a faded brown gown, and his inseparable old velvet cap.

After they had passed the buildings of the city administration, they entered the first restaurant they saw. Judge Dee chose a table in the rear, where he had a good view of the motley crowd of customers. 'You order!' he told Tao Gan. 'You speak the language. Make it a large bowl of soup with dumplings. I am told that is particularly good here in this city. Add a crab omelette, another local speciality.'

'Let's also try a jug of the local wine,' Tao Gan proposed.

'You used to be rather abstemious,' the judge remarked with a smile. 'I fear that Chiao Tai has a bad influence on you!'

'Chiao Tai and I see much of each other,' Tao Gan said. 'Ever since his blood-brother Ma Joong became such a stay-at-home!'

'That's why I didn't take Ma Joong along on this trip. I am happy that he has settled down to family life at last. I wouldn't like to get him involved in all kinds of adventures that might tempt him to revert to his old ways! We'll find the Censor all right among the three of us!'

'Does he have any special marks or mannerisms, sir? Things we might mention while inquiring about him in the temple later?'

Judge Dee pensively stroked his sidewhiskers.

'Well, he is a handsome fellow, of course, and he has all the self-assured poise of a high official moving in court circles. Then his language might also provide a clue. He speaks as a typical courtier, with all their latest mannerisms. Ha, this soup smells very good indeed!' Picking a dumpling from the bowl with his chopsticks, he added, 'Cheer up, Tao Gan, we have solved harder problems together!'

Tao Gan grinned and fell to with gusto. When they had finished the simple but substantial meal, they had a cup of strong Fukien tea, then paid and left.

There were less people about in the dark streets, for it was now time for the evening rice. When they were in the west quarter, however, they saw more people, and upon entering the street that led to the Temple of the Flowery Pagoda, they found themselves in the midst of a gay crowd, young and old dressed in their best clothes, and all moving in the same direction. Judge Dee counted on his fingers, and said:

'Today is the birthday of Kwan Yin, the Goddess of Mercy. The temple will be crowded with visitors.'

As soon as they had passed through the outer gate, they saw that the temple compound resembled indeed a night-fair. The stone-paved pathway leading to the high marble staircase of the monumental front hall was lined with temporary lamp posts, connected by gaily coloured garlands of lampions. On either side was a row of stalls offering a great variety of merchandise: holy books as well as children's toys, sweetmeats as well as rosaries. Hawkers of oil-cakes pushed their way through the throng, praising their wares in strident voices.

Judge Dee looked at the teeming crowd.

'Bad luck!' he said peevishly to Tao Gan. 'How could one locate a man in this awful throng? And where is this famous pagoda?'

Tao Gan pointed at the sky. Beyond the main building rose the nine storeys of the Flowery Pagoda, nearly three hundred feet high. The golden globe crowning its spire shone in the moonlight. Judge Dee could hear faintly the tinkling of the small silver bells suspended all along the curved roofs of every storey.

'Beautiful construction!' the judge remarked with satisfaction.

As he walked on, he cast a casual glance at the tea-pavilion on his right, under a cluster of tall bamboos. The pavilion was empty; people were so busy admiring the sights that they had no time for a leisurely cup of tea. In front of the gate stood two gaudily dressed women, under the watchful eye of an old hag who was leaning against the doorpost, picking her teeth. Judge Dee suddenly halted in his steps.

'You go ahead and have a look around,' he told Tao Gan; 'I'll follow presently.'

Then he stepped up to the pavilion. The smaller girl was young and not unattractive, but the taller one looked about thirty, and the thick layer of powder and rouge on her face could not conceal the ravage caused by her profession. The old hag quickly pushed the girls aside and with an ingratiating smirk addressed the judge in Cantonese.

'I'd like to talk a bit with your girls,' he cut her unintelligible harangue short. 'Do they understand the northern language?'

'Talk? Nonsense! You either do business, or nothing!' the hag rasped in atrocious northern Chinese. 'Sixty coppers. The house is back of the temple.'

The elder girl, who had been looking at the judge with a listless air, now beckoned him and said eagerly in pure northern dialect:

'Please take me, sir!'

'The scarecrow you can get for thirty!' the hag remarked with a sneer. 'But why not pay sixty and have yourself this nice young chicken?'

He took a handful of coppers from his sleeve and gave them to the old woman.

'I'll take the tall one,' he said curtly. 'But I want to talk a bit with her first. I am fastidious.'

'I don't get that word, but for this money you can do with her whatever you like! It's getting so that she costs more money than she brings in!'

The judge motioned the girl to follow him inside the pavilion. They sat down at a small table, and he ordered from the sneering

A MEETING AT THE TEMPLE FAIR

waiter a pot of tea and a platter of dried melon seeds and sweet-meats.

'What is all this supposed to lead up to?' she asked suspiciously.

'I just want to talk my own language, for a change. Tell me, how did you come so far south?'

'Not the kind of story that'd interest you,' she said sullenly.

'Let me be the judge of that. Here, have a cup.'

She drank avidly, tasted the sweetmeats, then said gruffly:

'I was foolish, and unlucky to boot. Ten years ago I fell in love with a travelling silk merchant from Kiangsu, who used to eat in my father's noodle stall, and I went off with him. It was all right, for a couple of years. I like travelling about, and he treated me well. But when his business took him here to Canton, I bore him a daughter. Of course he was very angry that it wasn't a boy, and drowned the child. Then he got interested in a local girl and wanted to get rid of me. But it's hard to sell an unskilled northern woman here. The larger flowerboats employ only Cantonese women, or northerners who are really good at singing and dancing. So he sold me for a trifle to the Tanka.'

'Tanka? Who are they?' the judge asked, curious.

She quickly stuffed a whole sweetmeat into her mouth, then mumbled:

'They are also called simply the "waterfolk", quite a different people, you see. The Cantonese despise them. They say they are descended from the savages who lived here more than a thousand years ago, before we Chinese came south. They must stay on their boats moored on the river near the custom-house. It's there that they are born, copulate and die. They are not allowed to dwell on land, or to intermarry with Chinese.

Judge Dee nodded. He now remembered that the Tanka were a class of outcasts, subject to special laws severely restricting their activities.

'I had to work in one of their floating brothels,' she went on, now completely at ease. 'The bastards speak a queer language all

61                                                                      c*

of their own, jabbering like monkeys. You should hear them! And their women are always messing about with all kinds of dirty drugs and poisons. Those people vented their resentment against the Chinese on me; for food I got left-overs, for clothing nothing but a dirty loin cloth. The main customers were foreign sailors, for no Chinese brothel would admit them, of course. So you can imagine the kind of life I had there!' She sniffed, and took another sweetmeat.

'The Tanka are afraid of their own women because half of them are witches, but me they treated like the lowest of slaves. At their drunken orgies I had to do disgusting dances for them stark naked, for hours on end, getting my behind smacked with a paddle every time I wanted to rest. And their women shouted insults at me all the time, saying that all Chinese girls are sluts, and that Chinese men prefer Tanka women. Their favourite boast was that eighty years ago a Chinese of mark had married secretly a Tanka woman, and that their son had become a famous warrior who addressed the Emperor as "uncle". Can you beat that? Well, it was a relief when I was sold to a city-brothel, not exactly high-class, but at least Chinese! That's where I've been working these last five years. But I don't complain, mind you! I've had three happy years, and that's more than many a woman can say!'

Judge Dee thought that now that he had gained her confidence, he could broach the subject he had had in mind when accosting her.

'Listen,' he said, 'I am in rather a quandary. I was to have met here a friend of mine from up north, a couple of days ago. But I was detained up river, and arrived only this afternoon. I don't know where he's staying, but it must be nearby, for it was he who suggested this temple as meeting place. If he hasn't left the city, he must be around hereabouts. Since it's your job to pay special attention to the men who pass here, you may have seen him. A tall, good-looking fellow of about thirty, with a kind of haughty air. A small moustache, no beard or whiskers.'

'You are just one day late!' she said. 'He came here last night, you see, at about the same time as now. Walking about as if he was looking for someone.'

'Did you speak to him?'

'You bet I did! I always keep on the look-out for northerners. And he was handsome, just as you said. Dressed rather poorly though, I must say. I stepped up to him, regardless. He could've had me for half the price. But no such luck, he walked on to the temple, without giving me a second look. Snooty bastard! You are quite different; you are nice! I knew that as soon as...'

'Did you see him again today?' the judge interrupted.

'No, I didn't. That's why I told you you are too late. Well, you've still got me! Shall we go to my house now? I could do some of those Tanka dances for you, if you like that kind of thing.'

'Not now. I want to have a look for my friend in the temple, anyway. Tell me your name and address; I may visit you later on. This is my payment in advance.'

Smiling happily, she told him the name of the street where she lived. Judge Dee went to the counter, borrowed a writing-brush from the waiter and jotted down the address on a scrap of paper. Then he paid the bill, took leave of her and walked to the temple.

When he was about to ascend the marble stairs, Tao Gan came down to meet him.

'I had a quick look around, sir,' he said dejectedly. 'I saw no man answering the Censor's description.'

'He came here last night,' the judge told him. 'In disguise, apparently, just as when the agent saw him and Dr Soo. Let's have a look inside together!' As his eye fell on the large palankeen standing by the side of the steps, with half a dozen neatly uniformed bearers squatting by it, he asked, 'Is an important person visiting the temple?'

'It's Mr Liang Foo, sir. A monk told me that he comes here regularly to play chess with the abbot. I met Mr Liang in the corridor and tried to slip by him, but the fellow has sharp eyes. He recognized me at once and asked me whether he could be of any assistance. I told him that I was just sightseeing.'

63

'I see. Well, we have to be doubly careful, Tao Gan. For the Censor is evidently conducting a secret investigation here, and we mustn't give him away by inquiring too openly about him.' He told him what the prostitute had said. 'We'll just walk about, and try to discover him by ourselves.'

They soon realized, however, that their task was even more difficult than they had imagined. The temple compound counted numerous separate buildings and chapels, connected by a network of narrow corridors and passages. Monks and novices were about everywhere, mixing with the laymen from the country who were gaping at the large gilded statues and the gorgeous paintings on the walls. They saw no one who resembled the Censor.

After they had admired the larger than life-size statue of the Goddess of Mercy in the main hall, they went to explore the buildings at the back of the compound. At last they came to a large hall where a memorial service was in progress. In front of the altar, piled with offerings, six monks were sitting on their round prayer cushions intoning prayers. Near the entrance knelt a small group of neatly dressed men and women, evidently the relatives of the deceased. Behind them stood an elderly monk, who was watching the proceedings with a bored air.

Judge Dee decided that they would have to ask about the Censor, after all. They now had looked everywhere, except in the pagoda which was hermetically closed, because formerly someone had committed suicide by jumping down from the top storey. He walked up to the elderly monk and gave him a description of the Censor.

'No, I haven't seen him, sir. And I am practically certain that no one of that description visited the temple tonight, for till the service here began I was about in the gatehouse all the time, and I wouldn't have missed a man of such striking appearance. Well, you'll kindly excuse me now, for I am supposed to supervise this memorial service. They bring in good money, you know.' Then he went on hurriedly, 'A large portion of the proceeds is used for defraying the costs of the ceremonial burning of dead beggars and vagrants who leave no relations behind and don't belong to a guild. And that is only one of the many charitable undertakings the temple engages in. Hey, that reminds me! Yesterday night they brought in a dead vagabond who looked like your friend! It wasn't him, of course, for he was clad in rags!'

The judge gave Tao Gan a startled look. He told the monk curtly:

'I am an officer of the tribunal, and the man I was to meet here is a special agent, who may have disguised himself as a beggar. I want to see the body, at once.'

The monk looked frightened. He stammered:

'It's in the mortuary, in the west wing, sir. Due to be incinerated after midnight. Not on this auspicious day, of course.' He beckoned a novice and said, 'Take these two gentlemen to the mortuary.'

The youngster led them to a small, deserted yard. On the other side stood a low, dark building, close to the high outer wall of the temple compound.

The novice pushed the heavy door open and lit the candle on the window sill. On a trestle table of plain boards were lying two human shapes, wrapped from head to feet in sheets of cheap canvas.

The novice sniffed the air with a sour face.

'Good that they'll be burned tonight!' he muttered. 'For in this hot weather...'

Judge Dee had not heard him. He lifted the end of the canvas covering the shape nearest him. The bloated face of a bearded man was revealed. He quickly covered it up again, then bared the head of the other corpse. He stood stock-still. Tao Gan grabbed the candle from the novice, came up to the table and let its light fall on the smooth, pale face. The topknot had got loose, thin strings of wet hair were clinging to the high forehead, but even in death the face retained its calm, haughty expression. Judge Dee swung round to the novice and barked:

'Get the abbot and the prior, at once! Here, give them this!'

He groped in his sleeve, and gave the astonished youngster one of his large red visiting cards, inscribed with his full name and rank. The novice scurried away. Judge Dee bent over the head of the dead man and carefully examined the skull. Righting himself, he said to Tao Gan: 'I can't find any wound, not even a bruised spot. Let me hold the candle! You have a look at the body.'

Tao Gan loosened the canvas, then took off the dead man's ragged jacket and clumsily patched trousers. Besides these he had worn nothing. Tao Gan studied the smooth-skinned, well-made body. Judge Dee looked on in silence, holding the candle high. After Tao Gan had turned the corpse over and examined the back, he shook his head.

'No,' he said, 'there are no signs of violence, no discoloured spots, no abrasions. I'll search his clothes.'

After he had covered up the corpse again, he went through the sleeves of the tattered jacket. 'What have we got here?' he exclaimed. He took from the sleeve a small cage of silver wire, about one inch square. Its side was crushed, the small door hanging loose.

'That is the cage the Censor kept his cricket in,' the judge said hoarsely. 'Is there nothing else?'

Tao Gan looked again. 'Nothing at all!' he muttered.

Voices sounded outside. The door was pushed open by a monk who ushered in respectfully a heavily built, imposing figure in a long saffron robe. A purple stole was draped over his shoulders. As he made a low bow, the light of the candle shone on his round, closely shaved head. The prior knelt down by the abbot's side.

As Judge Dee saw by the door a group of other monks trying to peer inside, he snapped at the abbot:

'I said you and your prior, didn't I? Send all those other fellows away!'

The frightened abbot opened his mouth but brought out only incoherent sounds. It was the prior who turned round and shouted at the monks to make themselves scarce.

'Close the door!' Judge Dee ordered. And to the abbot, 'Calm yourself, man!' Pointing at the corpse, he asked, 'How did this man die?'

The abbot recollected himself. He replied in a trembling voice:

'We ... we are completely ignorant of the cause of death, Excellency! These poor men are brought here dead, we have them burned as a charitable...'

'You are supposed to know the law,' the judge cut him short. 'You are not allowed to incinerate any corpse, gratis or otherwise, without having checked the death certificate and submitted it to the tribunal for inspection.'

'But the tribunal sent the corpse here, Excellency!' the prior wailed. 'Two constables brought it last night, on a stretcher. They said it was a dead vagrant of unknown identity. I myself signed the receipt!'

'That's different,' Judge Dee said curtly. 'You two may leave now. Stay in your quarters. I may want to question you again, later tonight.'

When they had scrambled to their feet and left, the judge said to Tao Gan:

'I must know where and how the constables found him, and I also want to see the coroner's report. Strange that the constables left that silver cage in his sleeve; it's a valuable antique piece. Go to the tribunal at once, Tao Gan, and question the Prefect, his coroner, and the men who found the body. Tell them to have the body removed to the palace. Just say that the dead man was a secret investigator from the capital, sent here on my orders. I'll go back to the palace after I have had another look around here.'

# VIII

When Chiao Tai's litter was set down at the side gate of the palace, it was already one hour before midnight. He had told the bearers to bring him there by a round about way, hoping that the night air would cool his brain. It had been a forlorn hope.

He found Judge Dee sitting all alone at his large desk. His chin in his cupped hands, he was studying the large city map spread out before him. When Chiao Tai had greeted him, the judge said in a tired voice:

'Sit down! We have found the Censor. Murdered.'

He told Chiao Tai about Tao Gan's talk with the blind girl, and how the clue of the Golden Bell had made them discover the Censor's dead body in the temple. Cutting short Chiao Tai's excited questions, he pursued:

'After the dead body had been brought here, I had the Governor's physician perform a thorough autopsy. He found that the Censor had been poisoned, by an insidious drug that is not mentioned in our medical books. For the only people who know how to prepare it are the Tanka, who inhabit the river boats. If administered in a large dose, the victim dies practically at once; a small dose causes only a general fatigue, but death ensues in a couple of weeks. It can only be traced by examining the condition of the throat. If the Governor's physician hadn't happened to have treated a case recently among the Tanka, he would never have traced the poison, and death would have been ascribed to a heart attack.'

'That explains why the coroner of the tribunal failed to discover it!' Chiao Tai observed.

'The coroner never saw the body,' Judge Dee said wearily. 'Tao

Gan came back here an hour ago, with the Prefect. Together they had questioned the entire personnel of the tribunal, but nobody knew anything about the body of a vagrant sent to the temple last night.'

'Holy heaven!' Chiao Tai exclaimed. 'So those two constables who took it there were impostors!'

'They were. I had the prior summoned at once, but he couldn't give a good description of the two self-styled constables. They were just ordinary fellows and wore the regular uniform, leather jackets and black-lacquered helmets. Everything seemed perfectly in order. We can't blame the prior for not taking a closer look at them.' He heaved a sigh and went on, 'The fact that the Censor was seen in the temple earlier on the night of his murder, and the clue of the cricket, point to the deed having been done somewhere in that same neighbourhood. Since the uniforms of the constables must have been prepared beforehand, it must have been a premeditated murder. And since the Censor's body did not show any signs of violence and his face was calm, he must have been lured into a trap by a person or persons he knew well. Those are the facts we have to work with.'

'That blind girl must know more about what happened, sir! You said she told Tao Gan that she had been squatting by the wall a long time before she caught the cricket; therefore she may have heard something. Blind people have a very acute sense of hearing.'

'I have some very pertinent questions to ask that girl,' Judge Dee said grimly. 'I had a good look at the wall against which the mortuary is built. It has been repaired recently, and there is not a single crack between the bricks. Yes, I certainly want to meet that girl! I have sent Tao Gan to her house to fetch her. I am expecting them any moment now, for he has been gone quite some time. Well, did you have a good dinner at that Arab's place?'

'Food and drink were all right, sir, but I must confess I don't like that fellow Mansur. He's as proud as the devil, and not too favourably disposed towards us. When the liquor had loosened his tongue a bit, I asked him about the Arab colony here, as you

69

ordered.' Rising, he bent over the map on the desk and went on, pointing with his forefinger, 'This here is the mosque; Mansur and most of the other Moslems live in this neighbourhood. The inn where I am staying is close by. Outside the north-east gate there's a smaller colony, near the tomb of one of their saints. All these Arabs have settled down here for some time. The sailors who are here temporarily, waiting for the monsoon, live in these hostels here, on the riverfront.'

When Chiao Tai had resumed his seat, the judge said annoyed:

'I don't like this at all! How can we ever keep an eye on these foreigners that way! I shall speak to the Governor about it. All those Arabs, Persians and what not must be brought together in one quarter, surrounded by a high wall with only one gate that is closed between sunset and dawn. Then we shall appoint an Arab as warden, responsible to us for all that happens inside. Thus we shall keep them under control, while they can observe their own uncouth customs there without offending their Chinese co-citizens.'

The door at the other end of the hall opened and Tao Gan came in. While he was taking the other chair in front of the desk, Judge Dee cast a quick glance at his worried face and asked:

'Didn't you bring that blind girl with you?'

'Heaven knows what's going on here, sir!' Tao Gan exclaimed, wiping his perspiring brow. 'She has disappeared! And all her crickets have gone too!'

'Have a cup of tea, Tao Gan,' the judge said calmly. 'Then tell me the entire story. How did you happen to meet her, to begin with?'

Tao Gan gulped down the tea Chiao Tai had poured for him and replied:

'I saw two ruffians assaulting her in a deserted street, sir. Near the market place. When I had shooed away those fellows and realized she was blind, I took her home. She lives in a tenement house over on the other side of the market. I had a cup of tea up in her room, and she told me how she had caught the Golden Bell.

She lives alone in that room. When I went back there just now, the dozen or so small cages with crickets which had been hanging on a pole there were gone, and so were a few pots with fighting-crickets, and her tea-basket. I looked behind the screen that partitions the room, and only saw a bare couch—the bedding had gone!' He took another sip, and went on, 'I asked the market vendor who lives on the same floor about her. He had met the girl once or twice on the landing, but had never even spoken to her. Then I went to the market, and had the supervisor show me his register. Several stalls rented to cricket dealers were listed there, but none under the name of Lan-lee. Since he told me that some people are allowed to put up small temporary stalls rent-free, I accosted a regular cricket dealer. He said he had heard about a blind girl dealing in crickets, but never actually met her. That was all!'

'It was just another hoax!' Chiao Tai muttered. 'The wench fooled you, brother Tao!'

'Nonsense!' Tao Gan said crossly. 'The assault could never have been arranged beforehand, for my benefit. Even if someone had been following me, how could he have known I would be taking that particular alley? I was walking at random. I could have taken a dozen other turns!'

'I think,' Judge Dee said, 'that you were spotted when you were taking the girl home. You two must have made a conspicuous couple.'

'That's it, of course!' Tao Gan exclaimed. 'While we were talking, I heard the stairs creak! Some people must have eavesdropped on our conversation. When they overheard her telling me where she had caught the Golden Bell, they decided to abduct her!'

'If she didn't disappear of her own free will, that is,' the judge remarked dryly. 'For I don't believe a word of her story of how she got the cricket. She picked it up when the Censor was being murdered, of course. On the other hand, the fact that she gave you a clue to the temple would seem to prove that she belongs to a group opposing the Censor's murderers, like the man who

71

strangled Chiao Tai's prospective killer. Anyway, we are faced with a disgusting situation! Some persons apparently know exactly what we are doing, while we haven't got the faintest idea who they are or what they are after!' He angrily tugged at his beard, then went on in a calmer voice, 'The prostitute who saw the Censor in the temple told me that the Tanka boats lie close to the custom-house, which means they're not far from the Moslem quarter inside the Kuei-te city gate. It is possible, therefore, that it was not Arab affairs which made the Censor frequent their neighbourhood, but rather something going on among the people of the floating brothels. And the two self-styled constables who took the Censor's body to the temple were Chinese. All the more reason for not staring ourselves blind at the Arab aspect of our problems.'

'Yet Dr Soo was killed by an Arab hooligan, sir,' Chiao Tai remarked.

'Arabs are the main customers of the Tanka harlots, I'm told,' the judge said, 'so the hooligan could well have been recruited in a Tanka brothel. I would like to know more about those strange people.'

'Mansur's entertainment tonight included the performance of an Arab dancer with Tanka blood,' Chiao Tai said eagerly. 'It seems that she lives on a flowerboat. I might pay her a visit tomorrow, and let her tell me about the waterfolk.'

The judge gave him a shrewd look.

'Do that,' he said evenly. 'A visit to this dancer seems more promising than your planned talk with the sea captain.'

'I'd better see him too, sir if you have no other work for me tomorrow morning, that is. I got the impression that Mansur hates Captain Nee. Therefore it might be worth while to hear what Nee has to say about Mansur!'

'All right. Report to me after you have made those two calls. You, Tao Gan, will come here directly after breakfast. We must draw up together a preliminary report to the Grand Council on the Censor's murder. We'll send that to the capital by special courier, for the Council must be informed of the Censor's death with the least possible delay. I shall advise them to keep this news secret for a day or two, so as not to prejudice the delicate balance of power at court, and give me a little time to discover what is behind this foul murder.'

'How did the Governor take the news about this second murder in his domain, sir?' Tao Gan asked.

'That I don't know,' Judge Dee answered with a faint smile. 'I told his physician that the Censor's body was that of one of my men, who had got into trouble with a Tanka woman. I had the corpse encoffined at once, to be sent to the capital at the first opportunity, together with Dr Soo's. When I see the Governor tomorrow, I shall tell him the same story as I told his physician after he had conducted the post mortem. We'll have to be careful with that doctor, by the way; he's a quick-witted fellow! He said that the Censor's face looked familiar to him, you know. Fortunately he had only seen the Censor all dressed up in his ceremonial dress when he paid his first visit to Canton six weeks ago. When we have finished the report to the Council, Tao Gan, we'll call together on Mr Liang Foo. He visits that confounded temple regularly to play chess with the abbot, and we could do with more information about that huge sanctuary. At the same time I shall consult Liang about the possibility of the Arabs making mischief here. They are only a handful compared to the total population of this vast city, but Chiao Tai just pointed out to me on the map the strategic points they control. They could easily create a disturbance, not important in itself, but dangerous in so far as it could be used as cover for some other devilry here or elsewhere. Can we trust that other expert on Arab affairs, Mr Yau Tai-kai?'

Chiao Tai frowned and replied slowly:

'Yau's jovial airs are not quite genuine, sir. He's not what I'd call a nice person to know. But as to engaging in murder, or in political plots . . . no, I don't think he is the type for that.'

'I see. Then there's still that enigmatic blind girl. She must be traced as quickly as possible, and without the local authorities getting wind of it. Tomorrow morning, Tao Gan, you will call at the tribunal on your way here. Give the headman of the constables a silver piece, and ask his men to look for her, as a personal favour. Tell him she's a niece of yours who misbehaved, and to report directly to you. In that way we won't endanger her safety.' He rose, straightened his robe, and added: 'Well, let's have a good night's rest now! I advise you two to keep your doors locked and barred, for it has now been proved that both of you are marked men. Oh yes, when you have had your talk with the headman, Tao Gan, visit the Prefect, and give him this scrap of paper. I have jotted down the name and address of the prostitute I talked with in the temple yard. Order Pao to summon her together with her owner, buy her out and have her conveyed back to her native place by the first military transport going north. Tell him to give her half a gold bar, so that she can get herself a husband when she's back in her village. All expenses are to be charged to my private account. The poor creature gave me valuable information, and she is entitled to a reward. Good night!'

## IX

The next morning Chiao Tai woke up before dawn. He washed quickly by the light of the single candle supplied by the inn, then dressed. About to slip his coat of mail over his head, he hesitated. He threw the heavy coat on the chair, and put on instead an iron-plated vest. 'My medicine against a sudden pain in the back!' he muttered, putting on his brown robe over the vest. After he had wound the long black sash round his waist and put on his black cap, he went downstairs and told the yawning innkeeper that when a litter came for him, the innkeeper should tell the bearers to wait for his return. Then he went outside,

In the semi-dark street he bought four oil-cakes, hot from the portable stove which the hawker was fanning vigorously. Munching them contentedly, he walked down to the Kuei-te Gate. On arrival at the quay, he saw that the red rays of dawn were colouring the masts of the craft moored alongside. Mansur's ship was gone.

A troup of vegetable dealers filed past him, each carrying on a pole across his shoulders two baskets loaded with cabbage. Chiao Tai accosted the last one, and after some complicated haggling in sign language bought the whole lot, including the carrying pole, for seventy coppers. The man trotted off singing a Cantonese ditty, happy that he had overcharged a northerner, and saved himself the long trip to the boats into the bargain.

Chiao Tai shouldered the carrying pole and stepped on to the stern of the first boat alongside the quay. From there he went over to the next, and on to the third. He had to tread warily, for the mist had made the narrow planks connecting the boats rather slippery, and the boat people apparently considered the gang-boards the proper place for cleaning fish. Chiao Tai cursed under his breath, for on many boats slatternly women were emptying buckets of night-soil into the muddy river, and the stench was overpowering. Here and there a cook hailed him, but he disregarded them. He wanted to find the dancer first, then have a closer look at the waterfolk. Thinking of Zumurrud gave him a queer tight feeling in his throat.

It was still fairly cool and his load was not too heavy, but being unaccustomed to this particular method of carrying things he was soon perspiring profusely. On the stem of a small boat he halted and had a look around. He couldn't see the city wall any more, for he was surrounded on all sides by a forest of masts and stakes, hung with fishing nets and wet laundry. The men and women moving about on the boats seemed a race apart. The men had short legs but long, muscular arms that accentuated their swift, loping walk. Their high cheekbones jutted out from their swarthy faces, and their flat noses had wide, flaring nostrils. Some of the young women were rather pretty in a coarse way; they had round faces and large, quick eyes. Squatting on the gangways of the Tanka boats and beating the laundry with heavy round sticks, they were busily chattering together in a guttural language that sounded completely unfamiliar.

Although men and women alike studiously ignored Chiao Tai, he had the uncomfortable feeling that he was being stealthily observed all the time. 'Must be because few Chinese come here!' he muttered. 'Those ugly dwarfs stare at me as soon as my back is turned!' He was glad when at last he saw a narrow strip of open water ahead. A bamboo bridge led to a long row of large, gaudily painted Chinese junks, anchored stem to stern. Alongside the first row was a second, then a third, connected by broad gangways provided with banisters. The fourth row was the last, close to midstream. Chiao Tai climbed onto the stern of the nearest junk and saw the broad expanse of the Pearl River. He could just discern the masts of the craft moored alongside the opposite bank. He counted and found he was on the third boat of the fourth row. The ship heading it was as large as a war junk. Its high masts were decorated with silk banners, and all along the eaves of the cabins hung limp garlands of coloured lampions, swaying to and fro in the faint morning breeze. He got on board by walking along the narrow side decks of the intervening junk, carefully balancing his baskets.

Three sleepy-eyed waiters were loitering near the hatch. They gave him a casual look and resumed their conversation as he brushed past them and entered the dark passage ahead. It was lined with shabby doors and a nauseating smell of cheap frying fat hung in the air. As there was no one about, he quickly put down his baskets and went on to the hind deck.

A plain girl wearing only a soiled skirt was sitting cross-legged on the wooden bench, paring her toenails. She gave him an indifferent glance and didn't even bother to pull her skirt down. Things looked rather dreary, but Chiao Tai's spirits rose when he arrived midships. On the other side of the neatly scrubbed deck he saw a high double door, lacquered a bright red. A fat man in a nightrobe of costly brocade was standing at the railing, gargling noisily. A sullen-looking young woman in a rumpled white gown held the tea-bowl for him. Suddenly the man retched and vomited, partly over the railing, partly over the girl's dress.

'Cheer up, dearie!' Chiao Tai told her in passing. 'Think of the fat commission you'll get on last night's wine bill!'

Ignoring her angry retort, he slipped inside. The passage was dimly lit by white silk lampions suspended from the curved rafters. Chiao Tai studied the names inscribed on the lacquered doors. 'Spring Dream', 'Willow Branch', 'Jade Flower'—all names of courtesans, but none that could be a Chinese rendering of the name Zumurrud. The last door, at the end of the passage, bore no name, but it was elaborately decorated with miniature paintings of birds and flowers. Trying the knob, he found the door was not locked. He pushed it open and quickly stepped inside.

The semi-dark room was much larger than an ordinary cabin,

77

and luxuriously appointed. A smell of musk hung heavily in the close air.

'Since you are here, why not come closer?' the dancer's voice spoke.

Now that his eyes had become adjusted to the light, he discerned in the rear of the room a high bedstead, with red curtains half-drawn. Zumurrud was there, reclining naked against a brocade pillow. She wore no make-up and her only jewelry was a necklace of blue beads set in gold filigree.

Chiao Tai went over to her. Confused by her breathtaking beauty, he was at a loss for words. At last he blurted out:

'Where's that emerald?'

'I only wear it when dancing, you silly fool! I just had my bath. You better have one too, you are covered with sweat. Behind the blue curtain there!'

He picked his way through the chairs and tables that stood about on the thick pile carpet. Behind the blue curtain was a small but elegant bathroom, decorated in plain, beautifully grained wood. He quickly stripped, squatted down by the tub of hot water and sluiced himself using the small wooden pail. While rubbing himself dry with the lining of his robe, he noticed a box containing sticks of liquorice lying ready on the dressing-table. He took one, chewed the end into the required shape and carefully brushed his teeth. Then he hung his robe and vest on the bamboo clothes rack and stepped back into the room, clad only in his baggy trousers, his muscular, scarred torso bare. Pulling up a chair to the bedstead, he said gruffly:

'I accepted last night's invitation, as you see.'

'You certainly lost no time getting here!' she remarked dryly. 'Anyway, you were wise in choosing the early morning, for that's the only time I can receive visitors.'

'Why?'

'Because I am not an ordinary courtesan, my friend. Whatever insulting remarks that rat Mansur may make. I am not for sale, for I have a permanent patron. A wealthy fellow, as you can see

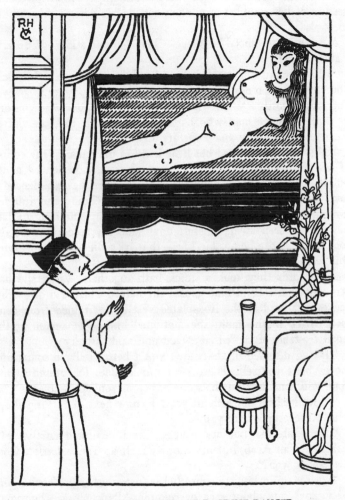

CHIAO TAI VISITS THE SMARAGDINE DANCER

from all this.' She indicated the surroundings with a sweeping gesture of her rounded arm, then added, 'He doesn't take kindly to rivals.'

'I am here on official business,' Chiao Tai said stiffly. 'Who says I am a rival?'

'I do.' She put her hands behind her head and stretched herself. She yawned, then darted a quick glance at him from her large eyes and asked crossly, 'Well, what are you waiting for? Are you one of those tiresome men who have to first consult the calendar to see whether the day and hour are auspicious?'

He got up and clasped her lithe body in his arms. In the course of his long and varied amorous career he had experienced many different types of love. Now for the first time, he experienced a love that was not only different, but final. Zumurrud fulfilled some indefinable need deep inside him, stirred something he had never even been aware of, but now suddenly recognized as the root of his entire being. He knew that he could not live without this woman—and wasn't even astonished at the discovery.

Afterwards they took a quick bath together. When she had put on a thin robe of blue gauze, she helped Chiao Tai dress. She cocked her head at the iron-plated vest but refrained from comment. Back in the cabin she motioned him to be seated at the small tea-table of carved rosewood and said casually:

'Having disposed of that now, you'd better tell me something more about yourself. There isn't much time, for presently my maid will come in, and she's one of my patron's paid spies.'

'I'd rather hear more about you! I know next to nothing about your Arab people. Are you ...'

'The Arabs are not my people,' she interrupted curtly. 'My father was an Arab, but my mother a cheap Tanka harlot. Does that shock you?'

'Not me! Working in a brothel is just another profession, and what do I care about race or colour? All people are bound to become Chinese anyway, sooner or later. Whether they are brown, blue or black! If a man is good at fighting, and a woman good

80

at making love, they are all right, as far as I am concerned!'

'Well, that's something, at least! My father was an Arab sailor. When he went back to his country, he left my mother with child. Me.' She poured a cup of tea for him and went on, 'I entered the trade at fifteen. I showed promise, so my mother was able to sell me to a larger flowerboat. I had to receive customers, and in my spare time serve the Chinese courtesans. Maltreating me was a favourite amusement of those nasty bitches!'

'They didn't treat you too badly though,' Chiao Tai remarked coarsely. 'There isn't a scar on your lovely body!'

'Nothing so crude as whipping or caning,' she said bitterly. 'The boss had forbidden them to mark me, because he saw big money in my future. So the bitches hung me by my hair from the rafters and stuck hot needles in me, just to while away a slack evening. And when they got really bored, they would tie me up with a large centipede in my trousers. Its bite doesn't show either, only you're kept guessing where exactly it'll bite! I've had it, all of it.' She shrugged. 'Never mind, that's all past and done with now. I got myself a patron who bought me out and rented these fine quarters for me. The only work I do is dancing at parties, and the money I earn he lets me keep. Mansur offered to take me back with him to his country and make me his first wife. But I don't like him, and I don't like my dear father's country, from what I have heard of it. See me sitting in a tent in the burning desert, with camels and asses for company? Thank you kindly!'

'Do you care a lot for your patron?'

'For him? Heavens no! But he's wealthy, and generous too. As nasty as they make 'em though.' She paused, pensively scratching the lobe of her ear. 'I cared for one man only, and he was head over ears in love with me too. But I acted like a damn fool, and spoiled everything.' Her wide eyes stared past him with a sombre glow.

Chiao Tai put his arm round her waist. 'You were very kind to me just now!' he said, hopefully.

She pushed him away and snapped impatiently, 'Leave me

81

alone! You just got all you wanted, didn't you? I groaned and panted at the right moments, and wriggled like an eel. You got it, complete with all the trimmings, so don't expect me to go on billing and cooing now! Besides, you aren't my type at all. I like refined gentlemen, not common bruisers like you.'

'Well,' Chiao Tai said uncertainly, 'I may seem just a bruiser, but I . . .'

'Save your trouble! I have learned to take men for what they seem to be. What do I care for what they think they are? If you want a real long and cosy talk about yourself, you'd better hire a nursemaid. So, let's get down to business. I went for you because you happen to be a colonel of the Imperial Guard, and according to Mansur the right-hand man of the President of the Metropolitan Court. That means that you could arrange that I get Chinese citizenship. You realize that I am legally a pariah, don't you? A Tanka woman, not allowed to marry a Chinese, not allowed even to dwell on Chinese soil?'

'So that's why your patron established you on this boat!'

'You certainly have an alert mind!' she scoffed. 'Of course he could not give me a house ashore. He is rolling in money, but he has no official position. But you are from the capital, and your boss is the highest judge in the land. Take me with you to the capital, see to it that I get Chinese citizenship, then introduce me to some really important men. The rest you can leave to me.' She half-closed her eyes and went on with a slow smile, 'To be a real Chinese lady, wear brocade dresses, have my own Chinese chambermaids, my own garden...' Suddenly she added in an impersonal voice, 'In the meantime, as a reward, I shall serve you as well as I can. And after our bout behind the curtains just now you'll agree that I know my job, I trust. Well, is it a deal?'

Her cold, frank words cut Chiao Tai to the quick. But he managed to answer in a steady voice:

'It's a deal!'

He told himself that he would succeed in making this woman fall in love with him. He must.

'Good. We'll have another meeting soon, to fix the details. My patron has a small house where he passes the afternoon with me when he's too busy to come here to the boat. It's to the south of the Kwang-siao Temple, in the west city. I'll send you a message as soon as the coast is clear. For you can't approach my patron, you see. Not yet. He wouldn't let me go, and he has an awful hold over me, could ruin me, if he chose to. Once you have spirited me away to the capital, however, I'll tell you who he is, so that you can let him have back the money he paid for me—in case your conscience should bother you!'

'You didn't commit a crime, did you?' Chiao Tai asked anxiously.

'I made an awful mistake, once.' She rose, pulled the thin robe close to her voluptuous body and said, 'Now you must really go, else there might be trouble. Where can I reach you?'

He told her the name of his inn, kissed her and left the cabin.

On deck he saw that the stern of the largest ship in the next row was within jumping reach. He sprang on board, then made the long journey back to the quay.

He re-entered the city by the Kuei-te Gate, and strolled to the Inn of the Five Immortals. In front of the gate stood a small litter. He asked the bearers whether it had been sent by Captain Nee. They came to their feet, shouting in unison that it had. He stepped inside and was swiftly carried away.

# X

Judge Dee had slept badly. He had dozed off, after having tossed about for a long time, and now that he had awakened after a fitful slumber, he found he had a dull headache. It was one hour before daybreak, but he knew he could not sleep any more, and stepped down from the broad bedstead. Clad only in his nightrobe, he stood for a while in front of the arched window, looking out over the palace roofs silhouetted against the grey morning sky. Inhaling the fresh air, he decided that a walk before breakfast would do him good.

He put on a gown of grey cotton, placed his skull-cap on his head and went downstairs. In the anteroom the majordomo was issuing the day's instructions to half a dozen heavy-eyed servants. Judge Dee told him to lead him to the park.

They walked through the dim corridors where the nightlamps had just been doused, on to the rear of the extensive palace compound. All along the back of the main building ran a broad marble terrace; below it was a beautifully laid out landscape garden, with paved pathways winding among the flowery shrubs.

'You need not wait,' he told the majordomo. 'I'll find my way back all right.'

He descended the dew-covered steps, and took a path leading to a large lotus pond. Through the thin morning haze that hung over the still water, he saw on the opposite bank a small pavilion and decided to stroll over there. He walked slowly round the pond, admiring the graceful lotus flowers that were just now opening their pink and red petals.

Approaching the pavilion, he saw through the window the back of a tall man, hunched over a table. He thought he recognized those round shoulders. As he climbed the steps, he noticed that the man was peering intently into a small pot of green porcelain which stood in front of him. Apparently he had heard Judge Dee's footsteps, for he said, still staring into the pot:

'So there you are, at last! Have a look at this tall fellow here!'

'Good morning,' Judge Dee said.

The Governor looked up with a startled frown. Seeing who his visitor was, he quickly rose and stammered:

'Excuse me, sir! I ... I really didn't ...'

'It's too early in the day for formalities!' the judge interrupted wearily. 'I didn't sleep too well, and came out for a morning stroll.' Taking the other chair, he added, 'Sit down, please! What have you got in that pot there?'

'My best fighter, sir! See those strong, sturdy legs! Isn't he a beauty?'

Judge Dee leaned forward. He thought the large cricket resembled a particularly nasty black spider.

'Fine specimen!' he commented, sitting back again. 'I must confess, however, that I am an outsider. The Imperial Censor who came to Canton a few weeks ago—there is a real enthusiast!'

'I had the honour to show him my collection,' the other said proudly. Then his face fell. He gave the judge a diffident look and resumed, 'He came back here, incognito, you know. I reported to the capital that he had been seen here, and I was ordered to establish contact with him. But shortly after I had sent out my men to make a search for him, the order was suddenly cancelled.' He hesitated for a while, nervously tugging at his moustache. 'Of course, I would never be so bold as to meddle with the affairs of the central government, but since Canton is my territory after all, I thought that a few words of explanation ...' He did not finish his sentence and gave the judge an expectant look.

'Yes!' Judge Dee said eagerly, 'that's true! The Censor wasn't present at the meeting of the Grand Council I attended just before I left. Well, since you have been ordered to cease your efforts, the

Censor has presumably gone back to the capital and resumed his duties.'

He leaned back in his chair, slowly stroking his beard. The Governor took a round cover of woven bamboo and carefully put it over the green pot. Then he said with a wan smile:

'My physician has informed me that you discovered a second murder yesterday. And the victim was one of your own men! I do hope that the Prefect isn't getting too old for his job. It's a large city, and...'

'It doesn't matter,' the judge said affably. 'Both affairs had their roots in the capital, and my men made awkward mistakes. It's I who should apologize!'

'Most considerate of you, sir. I hope you are satisfied with the progress of your investigation concerning the foreign trade here?'

'Oh yes. But it's a complicated subject. I think we must devise a better system for keeping all those various kinds of foreigners under control, you know. In due time I shall show you a draft-proposal to confine them severally to special quarters. I have just begun to look into Arab affairs. Then I shall go on to the others too, such as the Persians, and...'

'That's quite unnecessary!' the Governor interrupted suddenly. Then he bit his lips and added quickly, 'I mean to say, sir, those Persians are ... well, there can't be more than a few dozen. Nice, educated people, all of them.'

Judge Dee thought the Governor had grown very pale. But it might be the effect of the uncertain light. He said slowly:

'Well, I want to get the complete picture, you see.'

'Allow me to assist you, sir!' the Governor said eagerly. 'Ha, there's Pao!'

Prefect Pao Kwan made a low bow on the steps of the pavilion, followed by a second, even lower one when he got inside. With a worried face he said to the Governor:

'A thousand pardons, sir! Imagine the cheek of that woman! She hasn't turned up! I can't imagine why she...'

'And I can't imagine,' the Governor interrupted him coldly,

'why you don't make sure persons are dependable before you even think of introducing them to me. Well, since I am busy now with His Excellency, you...'

'I can't find words to say how sorry I am, sir,' the unhappy Prefect said, eager to excuse himself. 'But since I know of your interest in crickets, and since my wife said the woman had an uncanny knowledge of the subject...'

Before the Governor could dismiss the Prefect, Judge Dee said quickly:

'I didn't know there were also women-amateurs. She deals in those insects, I presume?'

'Yes, indeed, Excellency,' the Prefect said, grateful for the intervention. 'My wife told me that the girl has a remarkably fine eye for a good cricket. Well, the word "eye" is badly chosen, in this particular case, for she's blind, apparently.' He continued to the Governor, 'As I reported to you yesterday, sir, my wife ordered her to appear here at dawn, before your morning audience, so as to take as little as possible of your valuable time and...'

'I'd like to have her address, Mr Pao,' Judge Dee cut him short. 'It might be a good idea to take a few crickets back with me, as a souvenir of Canton.'

This request seemed to upset the Prefect even more. He stammered:

'I ... I asked my wife for her address, but the stupid woman said she didn't know.... She had met her only once, in the market. She had been so impressed by her sincere devotion to crickets that she...'

Seeing that the Governor was getting red in the face and was about to give the Prefect a severe dressing down, Judge Dee came to the rescue.

'It doesn't matter, really. Well, I'll go back to my own quarters now.' He rose and said quickly to the Governor, who had got up too, 'No, don't bother! Mr Pao will show me the way.'

He went down into the garden, followed by the flustered Prefect.

When they had come to the terrace, the judge said with a smile:

'Don't mind your chief's bad temper, Mr Pao! I myself am never at my best either, so early in the morning!' As the Prefect gave him a grateful smile, he continued, 'The Governor seems very diligent about his duties. He often makes the rounds of the city incognito, I suppose, in order to get a personal impression of the situation here.'

'Never, sir! He is a haughty man; he would consider that debasing himself! He is very hard to please indeed, Excellency. And since I am much older than him, and very experienced, I don't find my work here very ah ... agreeable. I have been serving here five years already, sir. My last post was magistrate of a district in Shantung, my native province. I did rather well there, hence my promotion to Canton. Here I took the trouble of learning Cantonese, and I have a thorough knowledge of local affairs, if I may be allowed to say so. The Governor ought to consult me before taking decisions, really. But he is a proper martinet, he...'

'Criticizing one's superiors behind their backs is considered unbecoming to an official,' Judge Dee interrupted him coldly. 'If you have complaints, you may communicate them to the Board of Personnel through the proper channels. I want you to accompany me when I call on Mr Liang Foo, presently. I want to have a further consultation with him. Be ready for me one hour after breakfast.'

The Prefect led the judge silently to his anteroom, and there took his leave with a bow.

Judge Dee ate a simple breakfast in his private dining-room, attended by the majordomo, then had a leisurely cup of tea. His headache was gone, but he still found it difficult to concentrate. Looking absent-mindedly at the red glow of dawn that was now colouring the paper windows, he wondered about the blind girl. Had the Governor really never met her before?

With a sigh he put his cup down and went up to his bedroom.

He changed into his official robe, put on high, winged cap, then went to the hall. As he seated himself behind his desk, his eye fell on a large, official-looking envelope. He slit it open and glanced through the brief message. Then he took a long roll of blank paper from the drawer, moistened his brush and began to write.

He was still thus engaged when Tao Gan came in and wished him a good morning. The lean man sat down and said:

'I just called at the tribunal, sir. The Prefect had not yet arrived, so I explained everything to the headman of the constables, a rather shrewd fellow. Too shrewd, I must say,' he added wryly. 'When I first ordered him to have that prostitute redeemed, then told him to make discreet inquiries about a blind girl, he gave me a knowing leer, and from then on addressed me in a tone which I found unduly familiar.'

'Excellent!' Judge Dee exclaimed. 'Since the rascal thinks you are just a common lecher, he won't blab to the Prefect. And it is essential that neither he nor the Governor gets to know about our interest in the blind girl.' He told Tao Gan about his conversation in the pavilion, then added, 'I got the impression that the Governor has met her before, but doesn't want the Prefect to know. We can only guess at the reason why she didn't keep the appointment. She can't have been kidnapped, for then she wouldn't have been able to take her crickets and her other belongings. I rather think she just wanted to disappear. Let's hope that the headman is as shrewd as you think, and finds a clue to her whereabouts. We must have a talk with her. Well, I am just finishing my preliminary report to the Grand Council. We'll go through it together presently.'

He went on covering the document roll with his strong calligraphy. After a while he sat back in his chair and read the report aloud. Tao Gan nodded. It was a concise statement of all the facts and he had nothing to add. The judge signed and sealed it; then he tapped the envelope lying on his desk and said:

'This letter just arrived from the capital by ordinary courier. It is an advance notice from the Chancery that a special messenger

TAO GAN AND JUDGE DEE

with a secret letter from the Grand Council is on his way, escorted by military police; he's due to arrive here tonight. Let us hope this means they have discovered the purpose of the Censor's clandestine visit here. For to tell you the truth, I can't make head or tail of what is going on !'

The majordomo came in and announced that Judge Dee's palankeen was standing ready in the front courtyard.

Prefect Pao was waiting for them there. He made his bow while a dozen mounted guards presented arms. Twenty uniformed bearers stood at attention by the magnificent palankeen. It had a high purple canopy, crowned by a three-tiered gilt spire.

'Can that cumbersome thing pass through Mr Liang's gate?' Judge Dee asked sourly.

'Easily, Excellency !' Pao replied with a smile. 'The late Admiral's residence is in fact a palace, built in the ancient style.'

The judge grunted. He ascended the palankeen, followed by the Prefect and Tao Gan. The cortège set into motion, preceded by the mounted guards.

## XI

Chiao Tai was roused from his confused thoughts by the litter being set down with a thud. He stepped out. It was a narrow, quiet street, apparently inhabited by retired shopkeepers. He gave the bearers a tip, and knocked on the plain wooden door.

An old bent woman opened it and welcomed him with a toothless grin. She led him through a small, well-kept flower garden to a two-storeyed, whitewashed building. Then she took him up a narrow wooden staircase, breathing noisily and muttering strange words to herself. She let him into a spacious, airy room of outlandish appearance.

All along the left side hung a curtain of embroidered silk that reached from the ceiling to the floor, of the same type as he had seen at Mansur's the night before. On either side of it stood two large flower vases of alabaster, on low ebony stands. On the right-hand wall hung a wooden rack bearing more than a dozen foreign swords. In the rear a row of four open arches afforded a fine view of a choice collection of potted orchids arranged on the broad sill. Beyond were the roofs of houses in the next street. The floor was covered by a spotless, thick reed mat. The furniture consisted of two armchairs of inlaid rosewood, and a low, round tea-table. There was no one about.

Just as Chiao Tai was going to examine the swords, the curtain parted and two young girls of about sixteen appeared. Chiao Tai gasped. They looked remarkably alike: both had round, rather pert faces set off by long golden earrings, and their wavy hair was done up in a curious foreign fashion. Their torsos were bare, showing their firm young breasts and smooth, light-brown skin. They wore pantaloons of flowered muslin, the ends wound tightly round their ankles, and identical necklaces of blue beads, with fringes of gold filigree.

One of them stepped forward, gave Chiao Tai a grave look, then spoke in excellent Chinese:

'Welcome to Captain Nee's house. The master will make his appearance presently.'

'Who might you two be?' Chiao Tai asked, hardly recovered from his astonishment.

'I am Dunyazad, and this is my twin-sister Dananir. We belong to the inner apartments of Captain Nee.'

'I see.'

'You think you do, but you don't,' Dunyazad remarked primly. 'We attend upon the captain, but he doesn't indulge in carnal relations with us.' She added decorously, 'We are virgins.'

'You don't say! And the captain a seafaring man!'

'The captain is committed to a third person,' Dananir said earnestly. 'Since he is a single-minded and extremely fastidious gentleman, his attitude to us is one of complete detachment. Which is a pity.'

'For the captain too,' Dunyazad observed. 'We possess a considerable capacity for passionate experience.'

'You two hussies don't know what you are talking about!' Chiao Tai said crossly.

Dunyazad raised her curved eyebrows.

'We are familiar with all the practical aspects,' she said coldly. 'When the captain purchased us from Merchant Fang four years ago, we were attached as chambermaids to his Third Lady, and regularly attended their amorous dalliance.'

'Admittedly, it was rather elementary,' Dananir added. 'Judging by the Third Lady's repeated complaints about the lack of variety.'

'Why do you two talk in that awful stilted book-language?' Chiao Tai asked horrified. 'And where in hell did you learn all those long difficult words?'

'From me.' Captain Nee's pleasant voice spoke up behind him.

'Sorry to have kept you waiting, but you are a bit late, you know.'
He wore a thin white woollen robe with red borders and a red
belt, and a kind of tiara, embroidered with coloured silk.

He took the smaller armchair and Dunyazad came to stand
by his side. Her sister knelt and looked up at Chiao Tai with a
provocative smile. Chiao Tai folded his arms and glared at
her.

'Sit down, sit down!' Captain Nee told Chiao Tai impatiently.
To the twins he said sternly, 'You are forgetting your manners.
Run along and make us some nice morning tea! Flavour it with
mint, will you.' When the two girls had gone, he went on, 'They
are rather clever: they know Chinese, Persian and Arabic. It
amuses me to read all kind of Chinese and foreign texts with them
at night, and they're always browsing in my library. Well, Mr
Chiao, I am relieved to see that you are all right. Evidently you
didn't get into trouble last night.'

'What made you think I might?' Chiao Tai asked cautiously.

'I have my eyes about me, my friend! I saw an Arab hooligan
and a Tanka strangler watching you from a strategic corner by
the door!'

'Yes, I noticed the pair too. They had nothing to do with us,
however. What was their quarrel with the waiter, by the way?'

'Oh, the fellow refused to serve the Tanka. Those outcasts are
supposed to taint everything they touch, you know. That's why
the waiter smashed the Tanka's beaker. Anyway, I saw that a
bearded scoundrel also kept an eye on you all the time. When he
followed you from the wine-house, I said to myself, Maybe the
colonel is in for a bit of trouble.'

'Why do you promote me suddenly to colonel?'

'Because I got a glimpse of your badge, colonel. Just as the
bearded man did. And I had heard that the famous Judge Dee had
arrived in Canton, accompanied by two lieutenants. If a person
then meets two ranking officials from up north who do their
damnedest to look like petty clerks, it sets him thinking, so to
speak.' When Chiao Tai made no comment, the captain went on,

CHIAO TAI CONVERSES WITH CAPTAIN NEE

'Last night it was being said in the tea-houses that Judge Dee had convened a conference in the palace, for a discussion of foreign trade here. That again set me thinking, for Judge Dee is famous as a detector of crimes, and you can't call foreign traders criminals, even though they charge atrocious prices. When I combined that with the fact that Judge Dee's two lieutenants were hanging about on the quay in disguise, I couldn't help asking myself: What mischief is brewing here in Canton?'

'You obviously know how to put two and two together!' Chiao Tai said with a grin. 'Well, we are indeed here to look into Arab trade. Where there are a lot of costly imports and high duties...' He let the sentence trail off.

'So it's smuggling you are after!' The captain stroked his moustache. 'Yes, I wouldn't put it beyond those Arab rascals.'

'What about the Chinese merchants who deal with them? Mr Yau Tai-kai, for instance. You know him, I suppose?'

'Slightly. Astute businessman, worked his way up from small beginnings to become one of the richest traders in the city. But he's a lecher, and lechery is an expensive hobby. He has a host of wives, concubines and stray mistresses whom he keeps in luxury —don't ask me what they have to put up with, that's neither here nor there. But he might be obliged to supplement his income by irregular means, perhaps. I must stress, however, that I have never heard any rumours of this. And I know practically everybody who counts in shipping circles.'

'What about that other expert on Arab affairs, Mr Liang Foo?'

'There you are wide of the mark, colonel!' Nee said with a smile. 'You can't mention him in one breath with Yau. Mr Liang is a born gentleman, of vast wealth and frugal habits. Mr Liang a smuggler? Out of the question!'

The twins came in with a brass platter. While they were serving tea, Captain Nee said with an apologetic smile:

'Sorry I can't entertain you more handsomely, colonel! I used to have a large residence, in the south city. But a couple of years ago I had to meet a heavy financial obligation, and sold it. I have come to like the quiet life ashore, and have decided to stay as long as my savings last me. At sea I had plenty of time to think about this and that, and I became interested in mysticism. Now I am passing the greater part of my time reading up on it. For exercise I go to the boxing and fencing club.' He rose and said, 'Well, let's have a look at my swords now.'

They walked over to the rack, and the captain pointed out to Chiao Tai the special merits of each sword, going into great detail about different methods of welding the blades. Then he told a few stories about the feats of famous Cantonese swordsmen. The twins listened avidly, their kohl-rimmed eyes very wide.

Suddenly the old crone came in and handed Nee a small envelope. 'Excuse me, will you?' he asked. He went to stand in front of the window arch and read the note. Then he stuffed it in his sleeve, sent the old woman away and said to Chiao Tai, 'Let's have another cup of tea !'

'I like this mint tea,' Chiao Tai remarked. 'Last night I had aniseed liquor in Mansur's place. Rather good too. Do you know the fellow?'

'You two go down and water the flowers,' Nee told the twins. 'It's getting quite hot already.' When they had left, looking highly indignant, the captain resumed, 'So you want to know about Mansur. Well, I'll tell you a little story about him. It goes back four years or so, when Mansur paid his first visit to our good city. There was a certain young lady here. Her parents were dead, and consequently her elder brother was the head of the house. A very wealthy and distinguished house, I should add. She was in love with a young man here, but they quarrelled, and he went away. Then her brother married her to an official, an awful dry stick nearly twice her age. Shortly after this ill-assorted marriage, she met Mansur and fell violently in love with him. One of those hectic, short-lived affairs, you know. She repented soon enough and told Mansur that it was all over. Know what Mansur said? That it was all right with him but that she'd have to pay him a round sum, for services rendered—as he chose to call it.'

'The dirty blackmailer! Know of any mischief he's engaged in now? I'd welcome a chance to collar the bastard!'

Captain Nee stroked his short beard. After a while he replied:

'No, I don't. I am sorry, for I am not very partial to Arabs. They trampled my mother's country underfoot. And I was very fond of my mother—Nizami was her Persian name. I changed my name to Nee, as a tribute to her memory.' He paused, then resumed, 'It's a large city, always buzzing with all kinds of rumours. But as a matter of principle I refuse to repeat vague rumours, which usually are just malicious gossip.'

'I see. By the way, at Mansur's party I met an Arab dancing girl called Zumurrud. Ever seen her?'

Captain Nee gave him a quick look.

'Zumurrud? No, I never met her. But I have heard her described as a beautiful and skilful dancer.'

'Do you happen to know who her patron is?'

'No. If she has one, he must be a wealthy man, for she's rather exacting, I've always heard.'

Chiao Tai nodded, and emptied his teacup.

'Talking about beautiful women,' he resumed, 'those twins you have around here don't look too bad either! They complained to me about your detached attitude, by the way!'

The captain smiled faintly.

'I've had them now for four years, have seen them change from children into young women. It has given me a kind of paternal feeling towards them.'

'They seem quite a handful! Where did you buy them?'

Nee did not reply at once. He gave Chiao Tai a searching look, then said:

'They are the illegitimate children of a very nice girl, a distant relative of my mother's, who was seduced by a Chinese official. She gave them away to a Chinese merchant of her acquaintance, for she feared that her lover would abandon her because of them. When he left her anyway, she killed herself. It created quite a stir

98

here, but her lover managed to keep his name out of it, so it didn't harm his career.'

'Pleasant fellow! Did you know him?'

'Of him. Didn't feel like meeting him. But I kept myself informed about the twins. They were treated well in the merchant's house, but he went bankrupt. I bought them when his possessions were auctioned off. I educated them as well as I could, and now I must look for a suitable husband for them.'

'I wouldn't put that off for too long,' Chiao Tai remarked judiciously. He got up adding, 'I'd better be off now.'

'You must come again for a boxing bout,' the captain said, as he took him downstairs. 'You are a bit heavier than me, but the years are on my side.'

'That's fine! I need practice. Used to exercise regularly with my blood-brother Ma. But the fellow's married now, and developed a paunch!'

In the small garden Dunyazad and Dananir were spraying the flowers with diminutive watering pots.

'Good-bye, children!' Chiao Tai called out.

They pointedly ignored him.

'They are cross that I sent them away,' the captain said with a smile. 'They are as inquisitive as a pair of monkeys. And they hate to be called children.'

'I am getting paternal too,' Chiao Tai said wryly. 'Many thanks for showing me your swords!'

When the captain closed the door behind him, Chiao Tai noticed that the street was crowded now; people were rushing back home after their early morning shopping. As he elbowed his way through them, he bumped into a young woman. He wanted to apologize but she had already brushed past him. He saw only her back as she disappeared in the throng.

# XII

Prefect Pao and Tao Gan helped Judge Dee descend from the palankeen in the front yard of Liang Foo's residence. The judge saw that the dimensions of the compound were indeed palatial. The court was paved with carved marble slabs, and the broad stairs that led up to the iron-bound double gate in the rear were of the same costly material. Mr Liang came hurrying down the steps, followed by an old man with a ragged grey beard, apparently the housemaster.

Liang Foo bowed deeply and bade the judge welcome. Then he started on a long speech explaining how unworthy he was to receive such an eminent official from the capital together with the Prefect of the city. Judge Dee let him go on for a while, then interrupted:

'I fully realize that my visit is against the rules of conduct for high officials, Mr Liang. I am keen, however, to see the house of such a great national hero as your late father. And I always like to see people in their own surroundings—a habit that has stayed with me from the days when I was still a district magistrate. Lead the way!'

Liang made another elaborate bow.

'Allow me to take Your Excellency to my late father's library. I have kept it exactly as it was.'

They ascended the marble stairs and walked through a dim hall lined on either side by enormous pillars. After they had crossed a flower garden, they entered a second two-storeyed building, even larger than the first. It was sparsely furnished with heavy antique pieces of carved ebony. Painted on the walls were pictures of naval battles, in full colour. Except for an old maidservant who scurried away as soon as she saw them, there was no one about.

'Don't you need a host of servants to keep up this palatial residence?' Judge Dee asked after they had crossed another courtyard.

'No, Excellency, for I use only one side wing. I come here really only at night; during the day I am always in my office downtown.' He paused and continued with a smile, 'Until now I have been kept so occupied by my business that I have always postponed getting married and founding a family. But next year, when I am thirty-five, I shall take that important step. Here we enter the section I actually live in. My father's library is at the rear.'

The old steward preceded them into the broad, covered corridor. Liang Foo followed behind him, together with Judge Dee and the Prefect. Tao Gan brought up the rear.

The corridor first led round a bamboo garden. Here the rustling leaves of tall trees afforded a cool shade. Then it brought them to another single-storeyed building. To the left of the corridor now broad windows gave on to a rock garden, while to the right was a row of closed rooms, with a black-lacquered balustrade all along their front. The sliding windows were pasted over with clean white paper.

Suddenly, Tao Gan tugged at Judge Dee's sleeve. He took him apart and whispered excitedly:

'I saw the blind girl! In the second room we passed. She's reading a book!'

'Go and get her!' the judge said tersely. As Tao Gan rushed back the way they had come, Judge Dee said to Mr Liang, 'My assistant reminded me that I had forgotten my fan. Let's wait here a while. What a beautiful rockery that is over there!'

An angry woman's voice resounded behind them.

'What's that?' Liang exclaimed. He hurried back, followed by Judge Dee and the Prefect.

Tao Gan stood gripping the balustrade in front of the second room. He was looking up in speechless astonishment at the beautiful young woman standing inside the small, elegantly furnished room. A screen decorated with a landscape was visible at the back. The woman angrily addressed Liang:

'Who is this impudent man? I had just slid the window open to get better light, when he suddenly appeared and began to shout that I had fooled him!'

'It was a mistake!' Tao Gan quickly told the judge, then added in an undertone, 'She resembles her, but it isn't she.'

'Who is this lady, Mr Liang?' the judge asked.

'My sister, Excellency. Our Prefect's wife.'

'When she heard that I was going to accompany Your Excellency here,' the Prefect explained, 'my wife decided to come too, and have a look at her old room here.'

'I see,' Judge Dee said. And to Mrs Pao, 'My apologies, Madam! My assistant mistook you for someone else.' Casting a cursory glance at the book lying open on the table, he added, 'I see that you are reading poetry. Excellent pastime. It improves the style.'

'Poetry?' Pao asked, giving his wife a curious look. She quickly closed the book and said curtly:

'Just a volume I picked up at random.'

The judge noticed that she was really very beautiful. She had an attractive, sensitive face, with the same long curved eyebrows that gave her brother a slightly feminine air. With a shy look she resumed:

'It's a great honour indeed to meet Your Excellency, I...'

'Your husband said that you know a girl who sells crickets,' Judge Dee interrupted. 'I would like to meet her.'

'I'll tell her so when I see her again, sir.' Then, with an annoyed glance at the Prefect, 'My husband scolded me just now for not having asked her address. But she told me she's about in the market practically every day, so...'

'Thank you, Madam! Good-bye.'

Walking on, Judge Dee asked Mr Liang:

'Have you other brothers and sisters, Mr Liang?'

TAO GAN DISTURBS A READING LADY

'No, Excellency, I am the only son. There were two daughters, but the elder one died a few years ago.'

'The accident happened shortly after our marriage,' Prefect Pao remarked in his dry, precise voice. 'It was a great shock for my young wife. And also for me, of course.'

'What kind of accident?' Judge Dee asked.

'When she was asleep,' Liang replied, 'the wind blew her curtain against an oil lamp and set the room afire. She must have become unconscious from the fumes. We only found the charred remains.'

The judge expressed his sympathy. Liang opened a heavy door and led them into a high-ceilinged, cool room. On a sign from Liang the steward shuffled to the windows and rolled up the bamboo sunshades. Judge Dee looked round with an appraising eye. The walls were covered with shelves loaded with books and rolls of papers. An enormous desk in the centre of a blue carpet was bare except for two silver candelabras and a set of writing implements. Mr Liang led them to the tea-table in the corner. He made Judge Dee sit down in the large armchair behind it, and offered the Prefect and Tao Gan the straight-backed chairs in front. He himself took a lower chair somewhat apart and ordered the steward to prepare the tea.

Stroking his long beard, the judge said with satisfaction:

'I perceive an atmosphere of subdued elegance—as one might expect in the studio of a man who excelled in the arts of both war and peace.'

Sipping tea, they spoke for some time about the naval campaigns of the Subduer of the South Seas, and Liang showed them some valuable old city maps from the admiral's collection. Examining one of the maps, the judge suddenly pointed with his forefinger and exclaimed:

'Here we have the temple of the Flowery Pagoda! I had occasion to visit it last night.'

'It's one of our historic sights, sir,' Liang said. 'I go there at least once a week, to have a game of chess with the abbot. He's a strong player! And a great scholar, too. He is now working on a new book, a historical account of the transmission of the scriptures.'

'Since he is of a studious disposition,' the judge observed, 'he leaves the administration of the temple to the prior, I suppose?'

'Oh no, sir! The abbot is most diligent about all his duties. Has to be, for such a large temple, open to the public, needs strict supervision. All kinds of shady characters go in there, wanting to fleece unwary visitors. I mean pickpockets, confidence tricksters, and so on.'

'You should have added murderers,' Judge Dee said dryly. 'I discovered the dead body of a government agent there yesterday.'

'So that's what those monks were talking about!' Liang exclaimed. 'The abbot was suddenly called away from our chess game. When he didn't come back, I asked the monks, who said something about a murder. Who did it, sir?'

The judge shrugged his shoulders.

'Hooligans,' he replied.

Liang shook his head. He took a sip of his tea, then remarked with a sigh:

'That's the other side of our prosperous city, Excellency. Where there is great wealth, there's bound to be dire poverty too. The casual observer sees only the glittering surface of city life. He doesn't know that underneath it there thrives a pitiless underworld where foreign criminals rub shoulders with Chinese hoodlums.'

'All kept under strict control,' Prefect Pao said coldly. 'Moreover, I wish to stress that their criminal activities remain confined to their own milieu, that of the scum one finds in every larger city.'

'I don't doubt it,' Judge Dee said. He emptied his teacup, then turned to Liang. 'You mentioned foreign criminals just now. I heard unfavourable rumours about Mansur. Would he employ Arab hooligans for some criminal purpose?'

Liang sat up straight. Pulling at his wispy goatee, he thought for a long while before he replied:

'I don't know Mansur personally, sir, but I have heard much about him, of course, mainly from my friend and colleague Mr Yau. On the one hand, Mansur is an experienced sea captain, resourceful and courageous, and also a shrewd trader. On the other, he is an ambitious Arab, with a fanatic devotion to his people and his religion. In his own country he is quite a prominent person, a distant nephew of the Khalif, under whom he fought many battles against other barbarians from the west. He ought to have been appointed military governor of one of the conquered regions, but he once offended the Khalif by some inadvertent remark, and was banished from court. So he embarked upon the adventurous career of sea captain. But he has never given up hope of regaining the Khalif's favour, and he'll shrink from nothing to attain that.'

Liang paused, considered for a while, and went on, choosing his words carefully:

'Thus far I have related facts which I have thoroughly checked. What I am going to say now is based on mere hearsay. Some people whisper that Mansur thinks if he could create a serious disturbance here in Canton, pillage the city and then sail home with rich booty, the Khalif would consider such a spectacular feat an addition to Arab prestige, and as a reward re-install Mansur in his former position at court. I repeat, however, that this is mere rumour. I may well be doing Mansur a grave injustice.'

Judge Dee raised his eyebrows. He asked:

'What could a handful of Arabs do against a garrison of over a thousand seasoned, well-armed soldiers? Not to speak of the guards, the harbour police, and so on?'

'Mansur took an active part in the siege of many a barbarian city, sir. So we may assume that he has much experience in these matters. He must be aware of the fact that Canton, unlike the cities up north, has a large number of two-storeyed houses built of wood. If on a dry, windy day fires were started in a few well-chosen places, there would be a disastrous conflagration. And in the general confusion small bands of determined men could achieve much.'

'By heaven, he is right!' the Prefect exclaimed.

'Further,' Liang continued, 'anyone who created a disturbance in the city would find eager allies as soon as the looting started. I mean the thousands of Tanka. They have been harbouring a deep resentment against us for hundreds of years.'

'Not entirely without reason,' Judge Dee remarked with a sigh. 'Anyway, what could those waterfolk do? They aren't organized, and they have got no arms.'

'Well,' Liang said slowly, 'they do have some kind of organization. It seems they rally around their chief sorcerers. And although they don't possess heavy weapons, in street fighting they are dangerous opponents. For they are quite handy with their long knives, and expert in strangling people with silk scarves. It's true that they mistrust all outsiders and keep very much to themselves, but since the custom of their women consists chiefly of Arab sailors, it would not be difficult for Mansur to get on a good footing with them.'

Judge Dee made no comment, he was pondering over Liang's remarks. Tao Gan addressed Liang:

'I noticed, sir, that the Tanka stranglers always leave behind the silver piece they weight their handkerchiefs with. They are quite valuable. Why don't they take them along after the deed, or use a piece of lead instead?'

'They are very superstitious,' Liang replied with a shrug. 'It's an offering to the spirit of their victim. They believe it prevents the ghost from haunting them afterwards.'

Judge Dee looked up.

'Show me that city map again!'

When Liang had rolled it out on the table, the judge made Prefect Pao point out to him those quarters where the houses were mostly of wood. They proved to include nearly all of the densely populated, middle-class and poor zones, crossed only by very narrow streets.

'Yes,' Judge Dee said gravely, 'a fire could easily destroy the greater part of this city. The loss of life and material damage would be so disastrous that we can not afford to ignore the rumours about Mansur. We must take adequate precautions, at once. I shall order the Governor to convene a secret meeting in the palace this afternoon, and to summon, besides you two, Mr Yau Tai-kai, the garrison commander and the chief of the harbour police. We shall then consider immediate preventive measures, and also discuss what to do about Mansur.'

'It is my duty to stress again, Excellency,' Mr Liang said worriedly, 'that Mansur may well be completely innocent. He drives a hard bargain, and there is keen competition among the big traders here. Some of them will stop at nothing to eliminate a successful rival. All this talk about Mansur may be nothing but malicious slander.'

'Let's hope you are right,' the judge said dryly. He emptied his teacup and rose.

Liang Foo conducted his distinguished guests ceremoniously through all the various courts and corridors to the front yard, where he took leave of them with many a deep bow.

## XIII

Chiao Tai had arrived at the palace two hours earlier, shortly after Judge Dee had left for the visit to Liang Foo. The majordomo ushered him into the hall of Judge Dee's wing.

Since that solemn palace employee had told Chiao Tai the judge was not expected back till noon, he went to the sandalwood couch, stepped out of his boots and threw himself down on the soft pillows. He intended to take a good nap.

But tired as he was, he could not get to sleep. He tossed about for a while, his spirits sinking lower and lower. Don't you get sentimental, at your age, you blasted fool! he told himself angrily. Didn't even pinch the behinds of those twin-hussies at Nee's, and they were practically asking for it! And what the hell is wrong with my left ear? He stuck his little finger into it and turned it round vigorously, but a ringing noise persisted. Then he located the sound. It came from his left sleeve.

He groped inside and brought out a small package about an inch square, wrapped up neatly in red paper. On it was written in a thin, spidery hand: To Mr Tao. Personal.

'So it's from her!' he muttered. 'Must have got a girl friend, the wench that bumped into me in front of the captain's house. The quick-fingered hussy slipped this into my sleeve. How did she know I would be visiting Nee, though?'

He got up and went to the entrance of the hall. He put the package on the side table there, as far as possible from Judge Dee's desk. Then he returned to the sandalwood couch and laid himself down again. This time he slept at once.

He woke up only towards noon. He had just stepped into his boots and was stretching his stiff limbs luxuriously when the door opened and the majordomo showed Judge Dee and Tao Gan inside.

Judge Dee walked straight to his desk in the rear of the hall. While Chiao Tai and Tao Gan sat down in their accustomed seats, the judge took a large city map from a drawer and spread it out in front of him. Then he said to Chiao Tai:

'We had a long talk with Liang Foo. Our first assumption seems to have been right, after all. The Censor must have come back to Canton because he had discovered that the Arabs here are planning to make trouble.'

Chiao Tai listened intently while Judge Dee gave him a summary of the conversation. The judge concluded:

'Liang confirmed what the prostitute in the temple told me, namely, that the Arabs frequent the Tanka brothels. So there is plenty of opportunity for those two groups to get together. That explains why the Censor was murdered with a poison peculiar to those sinister waterfolk. And the dwarf whom you two saw in the wine-house on the quay, together with the Arab assassin, was evidently a Tanka. Now the unknown person who strangled that assassin in the passage used the silk scarf of a Tanka murderer. So it would seem that the group opposing the Arab trouble-makers is employing Tanka also. It's all very puzzling. Anyway, I am not going to risk those Arabs starting anything here. I told the Governor to convene a meeting in the council hall at two o'clock to discuss precautionary measures. How did it fare with you, Chiao Tai?'

'I found the dancer, sir. And she has indeed Tanka blood, from her mother. Unfortunately her patron is a jealous fellow, so she didn't dare to have a longer talk with me on the boat where he has established her. She said, however, that sometimes he also meets her in a small house of his south of the Kwang-siao Temple, and she'll let me know when I can have a second meeting with her there. She only visits it occasionally, for being a pariah, she's not allowed to dwell ashore.'

'I know,' Judge Dee said peevishly. 'The pariah class must be abolished, it's a disgrace to a great nation like ours. It's our duty to educate those backward unfortunates, then grant them full citizenship. Did you also visit Captain Nee?'

'I did, sir. Found him a pleasant, well-informed fellow. He had quite a bit to say about Mansur—as I had expected.'

After he had been told the captain's story, Judge Dee remarked:

'You'd better be careful with that captain, Chiao Tai. I can't believe that tale. It doesn't tally with what I heard from Liang Foo. Mansur is a wealthy princeling; why should he stoop to blackmail? And where did Nee get that story, anyway? Let me see, he told you that he had decided to stay on shore for a few years, because he likes a quiet life, and wants to devote himself to the study of mysticism. That doesn't ring true at all! He is a sailor, and a sailor needs stronger reasons than that to keep away from the sea! I think Nee himself was in love with that woman, and her family married her off during one of his voyages. Nee is staying on here, hoping that sooner or later her elderly husband will die, thus enabling him to marry his old love. Of course Nee hates Mansur because of the Arab's affair with his lady-love, and therefore he concocted that blackmail story. How does that strike you?'

'Yes,' Chiao Tai said slowly, 'that could be quite true. It would fit nicely with what his two slave-girls told me, namely that the captain is deeply devoted to some woman.'

'Two slave-girls?' the judge asked. 'So that is why the Prefect said yesterday that Nee is leading a dissolute life.'

'No, sir. Those two girls—they are twins, by the way—said definitely that the captain never as much as makes a pass at them.'

'What is he keeping them for, then? As interior decoration?' Tao Gan asked.

'Out of piety to their mother, who was a distant relative of his. Rather a pathetic story.' He related in detail what Captain Nee had said, and added, 'The Chinese scoundrel who seduced that young lady must have been a mean bastard. I hate those fellows who think they can do what they like with a foreign girl, just because she isn't Chinese.'

The judge gave him a keen look. He remained silent for a long while, pensively playing with his sidewhiskers. At last he spoke:

'Well, we have more important things to worry about than a sea captain's private life. You two may go now and have your noon rice. But be back here before two o'clock, for the conference.'

When the two friends had greeted the judge and were about to leave the hall, Chiao Tai picked up the small package from the table. Handing it to Tao Gan, he said in an undertone:

'This was slipped into my sleeve by a girl in the street. She bumped into me expressly, when I was leaving Nee's house. Since it's marked personal, I didn't like to show it to our judge before you'd seen it.'

Tao Gan quickly opened it. Inside was an egg-shaped object, wrapped up in what seemed like an old blank envelope. It was a cricket-cage of beautiful carved ivory.

Tao Gan put it to his ear and listened a moment to the soft chirruping. 'It's from her all right,' he muttered. Then he suddenly exclaimed, 'Look here! What does this mean?'

He pointed at the square seal on the flap of the envelope. It read: 'Private seal of Lew, Imperial Censor.'

'We must show this to the judge at once!' he said excitedly.

They went back to the rear of the hall. When Judge Dee looked up astonished from the map he was studying, Tao Gan silently handed him the cage and the envelope. Chiao Tai told him quickly how he had got it. The judge put the cage aside, examined the seal, then slit the envelope open and took out a single sheet of thin notepaper. It was covered with small cursive writing. Smoothing the paper out on his desk, he scrutinized it carefully. At last he looked up and said gravely:

'These are a few notes the Censor jotted down for his own use. Concerning three Arabs who paid him sums of money, for goods received. He doesn't say clearly what goods. Besides Mansur, he mentions the names of two others, transcribed as Ah-me-te and Ah-si-se.'

'Holy heaven!' Chiao Tai exclaimed. 'Then the Censor was a traitor! Or is it a fake, perhaps?'

'It is perfectly genuine,' the judge said slowly. 'The seal is all right; I have seen it hundreds of times in the Chancery. As to the writing, I am familiar with the Censor's regular hand from the confidential reports to the Council he wrote out himself, but not with the shorthand that is used for such notes. But this memo is written in the highly cursive style that only great scholars achieve.'

He leaned back in his chair, and remained deep in thought for a considerable time. His two lieutenants watched him anxiously. Suddenly he looked up.

'I'll tell you what this means!' he said briskly. 'Someone is perfectly aware of our real purpose in visiting Canton! And since that is a closely guarded secret of state, the unknown person must be a ranking official in the capital who is in on all the secret deliberations of the Grand Council. He must belong to a political faction opposing the Censor. He and his accomplices lured the Censor to Canton, in order to involve him in Mansur's plot, accuse him of high treason and thus have him removed from the political scene. But the Censor saw through the clumsy scheme, of course. He feigned to be willing to collaborate with the Arabs, as proved by this note. He did that only in order to find out who exactly was behind the plot. However, the other party obviously discovered that the Censor had seen through the scheme. And had him poisoned.' Looking levelly at Tao Gan, he went on, 'The fact that the blind girl sent you the envelope proves that she means well, but at the same time that she was present when the Censor died. For blind persons can't pick up letters lying about on a table or in the street. She must have found it when she went through the dead man's sleeves with her sensitive fingers, and abstracted the envelope without the murderer noticing it. She took the Golden Bell also from the Censor's dead body. The story she told you about how she heard the cricket's sound while passing by the temple was so much eyewash.'

'Later she must have asked someone she trusted to have a look at the envelope,' Tao Gan remarked. 'When she was told that it bore the Censor's seal, she kept it. Then when she heard from the person or persons who visited her after I had left her room that I was investigating the Censor's disappearance, she sent the envelope to me—adding the cricket, to indicate that it came from her.'

The judge had hardly listened. He burst out angrily:

'Our opponents know exactly every move we make! It is an impossible situation! And that sea captain must be hand in glove with them, Chiao Tai! It can't be just a coincidence that the unknown girl put the package in your sleeve in front of his house. Go back to Captain Nee at once, and question him closely! Begin discreetly, but if he denies knowing the blind girl, you collar him and bring him here! You'll find me in my private dining-room.'

## XIV

Chiao Tai took the precaution of descending from the litter in the
street next to the one where Captain Nee lived, and then went on
afoot. Before knocking, he looked the street up and down. There
were only a couple of street vendors about; most people were
either eating their noon rice or preparing for their siesta.

The old crone opened the gate. She immediately started upon a
long story in what Chiao Tai presumed to be Persian. He listened
for a while to show his goodwill, then pushed her away and went
inside.

On the second floor a deep silence reigned. He opened the door
of the reception room. No one was there. He thought the captain
and his two charming slave-girls would have finished their noon
meal by now and would be taking their siesta. Severally—as
Dunyazad would doubtless have pointed out! he said to himself
peevishly. He would wait for a little while; perhaps the old
crone would have enough sense to rouse the captain. If no one
appeared, he would have to explore the rest of the house on his
own.

He stepped up to the sword rack and again admired the blades
displayed there. Absorbed in his study, he did not hear the two
turbaned men who climbed on to the flat roof outside. They came
noiselessly into the room, carefully stepping over the potted
orchids on the window sill. While the lean one drew a long thin
knife, the squat man took a firm hold of his club, stepped up
behind Chiao Tai and quickly brought the club down hard on the
back of his head. Chiao Tai stood stock-still for one brief moment,
then he fell to the floor with a heavy thud.

'There are plenty of good blades to choose from, Aziz,' the lean

Arab remarked as he turned to the sword rack. 'We'll finish Mansur's job quickly.'

'Allah be praised!' a silvery voice spoke in Arabic. 'I am rid of the lecherous unbeliever!'

The two ruffians whirled round and gaped at the girl who had come out from behind the curtain. She was stark naked, wearing only a blue necklace and white satin shoes.

'A houri descended straight from paradise!' the squat man said reverently. He stared with unbelieving delight at her perfect young figure.

'Call me a reward for all true believers,' Dananir said. Pointing at Chiao Tai, she added, 'The man wanted to assault me. He was just taking a sword to force me to submit to his odious embraces, so I fled behind the curtain. His mother was loved by an ass.'

'Just allow us a few moments to finish him off,' the lean fellow said with enthusiasm. 'Then we'll profit by your company! My name is Ahmed, by the way. My friend here is called Aziz.'

'Ahmed or Aziz, that's my problem,' Dananir said, looking them up and down with a provocative smile. 'Both of you are handsome young warriors. Let me see now!' She quickly came up to them, took each by the sleeve and made them stand side by side, with their backs against the curtain.

'By Allah!' the squat man exclaimed impatiently. 'Why worry your pretty head? First take...'

Suddenly his voice broke. He clasped his hands to his chest and sank to the floor, blood oozing from his distorted mouth.

Dananir put her arms round the other with a frightened cry.

'Allah preserve us!' she wailed. 'What is...'

A large alabaster vase crashed down on the man's head. Dananir let go of him, and he fell down on the reed mat.

Dunyazad came out from behind the curtain. She looked dazedly at the two prone Arabs.

'You did that very well,' Dananir remarked. 'But why didn't you stab the other too? The captain was rather fond of that vase, you know.'

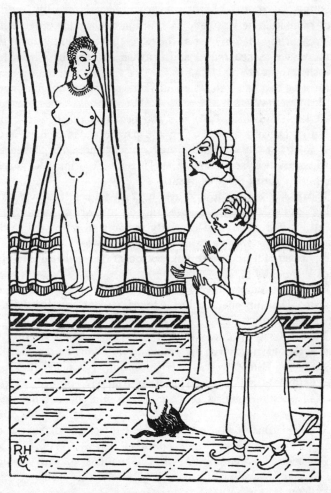

DANANIR WELCOMES UNEXPECTED GUESTS

'I noticed a bulge about his shoulders, and was afraid he was wearing a vest of mail.' Dunyazad tried to speak casually, but her voice trembled. She was very pale, a film of moisture covered her brow. Suddenly she ran over to the far corner and threw up on the floor. As she turned round and brushed the wet hair from her face, she muttered:

'Must be that fish I ate at noon. Come on, put your trousers on and help me revive him.'

She knelt by Chiao Tai's side and began to rub his neck and shoulders. Dananir fetched a jug and poured water over his head.

At long last Chiao Tai regained consciousness. He looked up dazed at the two faces above him. 'The awful twins!' he gasped and quickly closed his eyes again.

He lay still for a while. Then he raised himself slowly to a sitting position and felt the large lump on the back of his head. He did up his hair again, and carefully replaced his cap, well to the front. Giving the twins a baleful look, he growled:

'By heaven, I'll beat your little bottoms raw for that disgraceful prank!'

'Would you kindly have a look at the two men who attacked you, sir? The thin one is called Ahmed, the fat one Aziz,' Dunyazad said primly.

Chiao Tai sat up. He stared at the two Arabs sprawling in front of the curtain, and at the knife and club lying on the mat.

'While my sister diverted their attention, I stabbed the squat one,' Dunyazad explained. 'The other I merely stunned, so that you can question him, if so desired. He said Mansur had sent them.'

Chiao Tai came slowly to his feet. He felt sick and dizzy, but he managed to say with a grin, 'Good girls!'

'You ought to vomit now, really,' Dananir said, with a solicitous look at his chalk-white face. 'It's the normal reaction after a heavy blow on the head.'

'Do I look like a weakling?' Chiao Tai asked, indignant.

'It'll help if you imagine you are trying to swallow a large piece of lamb's fat, slightly rancid,' Dananir suggested. As he began to retch, she added quickly, 'Not on the mat! Over there in the corner, please!'

He stumbled to the place indicated and vomited. He had to admit that it relieved him considerably. He took a long draught from the water jug, spat through the window arch, then went over to the two prone men. He pulled Dunyazad's thin blade from the squat Arab's back. Wiping it off on the dead man's gown, he said with grudging admiration, 'You have a deft hand!' After he had examined the other's skull, he looked up. 'Too deft, as a matter of fact. This man is dead too.' As Dunyazad uttered a suppressed cry of horror, he said to her, 'The black stuff you smear on your eyes is running. You look awful.'

Dunyazad turned round and rushed behind the curtain.

'Don't mind her,' Dananir observed. 'She is hyper-sensitive.'

Chiao Tai went carefully through the clothes of the two dead men. But they had not carried one scrap of paper on them. He remained standing there, pensively fingering his moustache. When Dunyazad came back, her face newly made-up, he said:

'Wonder what those two were up to! Why didn't they stab me to death at once? That long knife looks very serviceable.'

'Didn't I tell you?' Dunyazad remarked to her sister. 'He is nice but dumb.'

'Hey! Why do you call me dumb, you impudent hussy?' Chiao Tai shouted.

'Because you are incapable of simple reasoning,' she replied composedly. 'Don't you see that it was their intention to kill you with one of the captain's swords? So as to make it appear that it was he who murdered you? If you can't follow me, I'll gladly explain it once more.'

'For heaven's sake!' Chiao Tai exclaimed. 'You must be right! Where is the captain?'

'He went out directly after his noon rice. We heard our old woman trying to explain that to you, but you didn't understand her and came up regardless. Fresh, we thought that.'

119

'Why in the name of heaven didn't you two show up when I came in?'

'All handbooks of love are agreed,' Dunyazad said earnestly, 'that the best method for judging a man's character is to observe him when he thinks he is alone. Since we are generally interested in you, we observed you. From behind that curtain.'

'Well I never! But thanks all the same!'

'Don't you think, mister colonel,' Dunyazad resumed in a businesslike voice, 'that this occurrence constitutes a compelling reason for buying and marrying the two of us?'

'Heavens no!' Chiao Tai cried out, horrified.

'Heavens yes!' she said firmly. Putting her hands on her hips, she asked: 'What do you think we saved your life for, eh?'

Dananir had been gazing steadily at Chiao Tai. Now she said slowly:

'Let's not be precipitate, sister. We are agreed that it must happen to us practically simultaneously, aren't we? Are you quite sure the man is sufficiently intense for accomplishing that?'

Dunyazad eyed him speculatively. 'I wonder. I see grey hairs in his moustache. He's forty if he's a day!'

'It'd be awful if one of us should be disappointed,' her sister continued. 'We always intended it to be a shared memory of ecstatic surrender, didn't we?'

'You lewd hussies!' Chiao Tai burst out angrily. 'Is that blind girl friend of yours of the same ilk?'

Dunyazad gave him a blank look. Then she told her sister disgustedly:

'He wants a blind girl! Well, that's probably the only kind he stands a fair chance of getting!'

Chiao Tai decided that he was no match for them. He said wearily to Dunyazad:

'Tell the old crone to call two litters, so that I can take the dead bodies to the office of my boss. Pending their arrival, I'll help you clear away the mess here. On one condition, namely that you two keep your rosy little mouths shut!'

## XV

In the meantime Judge Dee had eaten his noon rice in his private dining-room, together with Tao Gan. They had lingered over their tea, waiting for Chiao Tai. When it was getting on for two o'clock, and Chiao Tai had not yet made his appearance, the judge rose and told the majordomo to take them to the Council Hall.

The Governor and Prefect Pao stood waiting just inside the entrance, and by their side a bearded man in shining armour. The Governor introduced him as the garrison commander, and the other, slightly younger officer standing behind him as the harbour master. After Mr Liang Foo and Yau Tai-kai had also greeted the judge, the Governor led him to the head of the large conference table that had been prepared in the centre of the hall.

It took some time before all these distinguished persons had been seated in the proper order. At last, after the scribes had taken their places at two lower tables somewhat apart, and moistened their writing-brushes to take down the proceedings, Judge Dee opened the conference. After he had outlined briefly the problem confronting them, he called upon the garrison commander to give them an outline of the strategic situation.

The commander did so in a commendably succinct manner. Within half an hour he had completed his description of the lay-out of the city, and the distribution of the garrison forces. He was interrupted only once, when a clerk came in and handed a letter to Prefect Pao. The Prefect glanced through it, then asked the judge to excuse him for a while.

Judge Dee was just going to ask the commander what safety measures he would recommend, when the Governor rose and began a speech, intended, as he was careful to point out, to present the city's main features from a broader, administrative angle. While he was talking, Prefect Pao came back and resumed his seat. The Governor spoke for more than half an hour, going into much irrelevant detail. Judge Dee was just beginning to shift impatiently in his chair, when an adjutant came in. He asked Judge Dee in a whisper whether he might show in Colonel Chiao, who wanted to speak to him urgently. Judge Dee, welcoming this opportunity to stretch his legs, decided to disregard official protocol by going outside to see him. He rose and asked the company to excuse him for a few moments.

In the anteroom Chiao Tai quickly told him what had happened in Captain Nee's house.

'Go to the Arab quarter and arrest Mansur at once!' Judge Dee said angrily. 'This is the first direct proof we have against the scoundrel! And Ahmed and Aziz were the two the Censor mentioned in his note. Take my four agents with you.' As Chiao Tai turned to leave with a happy grin, the judge added, 'Try also to get Captain Nee. If he is not yet back, tell the tribunal to issue a warrant for his arrest to all the city wardens. I want to have a talk with that sea captain! A mystic forsooth!'

After Judge Dee had resumed his seat at the head of the conference table, he said gravely:

'One of the items on our agenda is what measures to take concerning Mansur, the leader of the Arab community here. I have just received certain information that has obliged me to issue orders for his immediate arrest.' As he said this, he quickly surveyed the faces of the persons round the table.

All nodded in approval except Mr Yau, who looked very doubtful.

'I too have heard rumours about an impending Arab revolt,' he said. 'But I dismissed them at once as based on irresponsible gossip. As to Mansur, I think I may say that I know him well. He is a quick-tempered, haughty man, but I am certain he would never even dream of engaging upon such a treacherous undertaking.'

The judge threw him a cold glance.

'I admit,' he said evenly, 'that I have no concrete evidence against Mansur—as yet. But since he is the head of the Arab community, he is personally responsible to us for everything happening among his compatriots. He will now have every opportunity to prove himself innocent. Of course, since we must reckon with the possibility that Mansur is not the ringleader after all, his impending arrest does not make precautionary measures superfluous. I request the garrison commander now to formulate those measures.'

When the commander had done so, in his customary crisp manner, the harbour master added a few suggestions regarding a restriction of the movement of Arab vessels in port. After agreement had been reached on these proposals, Judge Dee ordered Prefect Pao to draw up the texts of the necessary orders and proclamations. It took considerable time for all the texts to be completed and approved, but at long last Judge Dee could sign and seal the papers. Just as he was about to close the conference, the Governor took a bulky package of notes from his bosom and put it on the table. He cleared his throat importantly, then spoke:

'I deeply regret that the sudden cropping up of this Arab affair has taken so much of Your Excellency's valuable time. Since I am not oblivious of the fact that the purpose of Your Excellency's visit here is to review the foreign trade situation, I have had the port authorities draw up a report, which quotes in detail the import and export figures of all more important commodities. If Your Excellency will allow me, I shall now, on the basis of these documents, briefly describe the general position.'

Judge Dee was about to remark sharply that he had better things to do, but checked himself in time. After all, he had to keep up appearances. And the Governor had shown commendable zeal. Thus he nodded and resignedly leaned back in his chair.

While the Governor's voice droned on, he thought over what Chiao Tai had told him about Captain Nee. The fact that Mansur had intended Nee to be accused of Chiao Tai's murder seemed to prove that the captain was not involved in the nefarious scheme.

Was he perhaps working together with the blind girl? When Chiao Tai was visiting him, the captain had received a written message, and when Chiao Tai had left the blind girl's package had been put into his sleeve. The judge wanted to whisper something to Tao Gan, but saw that his lieutenant was listening in rapt attention to the Governor's speech. He sighed. He knew that Tao Gan was always keenly interested in financial matters.

The Governor's speech lasted more than an hour. When he was through at last, the servants came in to light the silver candlesticks. Now Liang Foo rose and began to discuss the figures quoted by the Governor. Judge Dee was glad when he saw the adjutant come in again. With a worried face he said quickly to the judge:

'The warden of the north-west quarter is here, Excellency, with an important message for the Prefect.'

Pao looked questioningly at the judge. When he nodded his assent, the Prefect hastily got up and followed the adjutant outside.

Judge Dee had just began to compliment the Governor and Mr Liang on their masterly speeches, when suddenly Prefect Pao came rushing inside, his face a deadly pale.

'My wife has been murdered!' he brought out in a choking voice. 'I must...'

He broke off as he saw Chiao Tai come in. Chiao Tai quickly stepped up to the judge and said contritely:

'Mansur has completely disappeared, sir. And so has Captain Nee. I can't understand what...'

Judge Dee cut him short with his raised hand. He quickly ordered the Governor, 'Send out your men to arrest Mansur. And also the sea captain Nee. At once!' Then he told Chiao Tai that Mrs Pao had been found murdered. He turned to the Prefect. 'Accept my sincere sympathy, Mr Pao. I shall accompany you to your house now together with my two lieutenants. This new outrage...'

'It didn't happen in my house, sir!' the Prefect cried out. 'She was murdered in a house south of the Kwang-siao Temple, an

124

address I have never even heard of! On the south corner of the second street!'

Mr Yau uttered a suppressed cry. He stared at the Prefect with his mouth open, his bovine eyes enlarged by fright.

'Do you know that place, Mr Yau?' Judge Dee asked sharply.

'Yes, indeed. I ... it belongs to me, as a matter of fact. I use it for entertaining business associates.'

'I order you to explain how ...' the Prefect began, but Judge Dee cut him short.

'Mr Yau shall accompany us to the scene of the crime. He shall give further explanations there.'

He rose briskly, told the Governor to execute at once the measures agreed upon, then left the Council Hall followed by his two lieutenants, Prefect Pao and Yau Tai-kai. In the front courtyard the guards were lighting the lanterns already. While the judge stood waiting there for his palankeen, he asked Pao:

'How was it done?'

'She was strangled from behind with a silk scarf, sir,' Pao answered in a toneless voice.

Judge Dee gave his two assistants a meaningful look, but he refrained from comment. As the stepladder of the palankeen was being lowered, he told the Prefect:

'You'll ride together with me, Mr Pao, there's plenty of space inside. Warden, you'll take Mr Yau in your litter.'

He made Prefect Pao sit next to him, and Chiao Tai and Tao Gan took the seat opposite. As the bearers hoisted the long shafts on their calloused shoulders, Chiao Tai said eagerly:

'Yau mentioned that address to me last night, sir! It seems he keeps a couple of nice girls there. He put a woman in charge and ...'

'Now I know why that worthless wife of mine went there!' the Prefect burst out. 'She went there to meet that lecher, Captain Nee! They were lovers before I—old fool that I was—married her. I often suspected they had been continuing their sordid affair behind my back. Cheap adultery! And Yau connived at it.

125                                                    E*

I demand that Yau and Nee are placed under arrest, sir, and I...'

Judge Dee raised his hand.

'Calm yourself, Mr Pao! Even if your wife went there to meet the captain, that does not prove that it was he who murdered her.'

'I shall tell you exactly what happened, sir! My wife knew that I would be in the palace the whole afternoon, for the conference, and therefore she made the appointment with her paramour. But although she is flighty, and often rather foolish, she is fundamentally a decent woman ... I am to blame, sir, I neglected her. Had to, the Governor always kept me so busy, I had no time...' His voice trailed off. He shook his head and passed his hand over his face. Then he took hold of himself and resumed in a soft voice, as if to himself, 'This time my wife must have told Nee that she wanted to put an end to the sordid affair, once and for all. Nee flew into a rage, and killed her. That must have been how it happened.'

'The fact that Nee seems to have gone into hiding may indeed point to his guilt,' Judge Dee remarked. 'But let's not indulge in premature deductions, Mr Pao.'

## XVI

Four constables stood in front of the two-storeyed house, two of them waving paper lanterns on which four red letters signified 'The Tribunal of Canton'. They stood at attention when the bearers set the large palankeen down. Judge Dee descended, followed by Prefect Pao and his two lieutenants. He waited till the warden and Mr Yau had stepped from their litter, then asked the former:

'In what room was the murder committed?'

'The tea-room just to the left of the hall, Excellency,' the warden replied. 'Allow me to show the way.'

He conducted them into a fairly large hall, lit by lampions of white silk, hanging from two beautifully carved stands. A constable stood at the door on the left; on the right there was a sidetable and a big armchair. In the rear of the hall was a moondoor, a round door-opening with a half-drawn curtain of blue beads. They made a rattling sound as a white hand quickly pulled the curtain close.

'You sit down there and wait!' Judge Dee told Mr Yau, pointing at the armchair on the right. Then he asked the warden, 'You didn't touch anything on the scene of the crime, did you?'

'No sir. I went inside only once, put two lighted candles on the table, and verified that she was indeed dead. The woman in charge here knew her as Miss Wang. But I found in her sleeve a brocade folder with visiting cards, which said clearly that she was our Prefect's wife. I left everything exactly as it was, sir.'

The constable had opened the door. They saw a small tea-room. In the centre stood a table of rosewood and three chairs; on the left a wall-table, bearing a vase filled with wilting flowers. The walls were plastered a spotless white, and decorated by a few choice scroll paintings of birds and flowers. In front of the single window lay a woman, dressed in a simple brown gown, her face to the floor. By her side was the fourth chair, overturned. Evidently it had been standing by the side of the table nearest to the window.

Judge Dee took one of the candles from the table, and gave a sign to Tao Gan. His lieutenant knelt and turned the dead woman over on her back. The Prefect quickly averted his face. Chiao Tai went to stand between him and the dead body. Her features were horribly distorted, her swollen tongue protruding from her blood-stained mouth. With some difficulty Tao Gan loosened the silk scarf that had been tightened round her neck with savage force. He silently showed the judge the silver coin tied in the corner of it.

Judge Dee motioned Chiao Tai to cover the dead face, then he turned round and asked the warden, who had remained standing just outside the door:

'How was the murder discovered?'

'About half an hour after she had arrived here, sir, the youngest maid went in to serve tea, assuming that the man she was wont to meet here would have arrived too. When she saw the dead body, she began to shriek at the top of her voice. People passing in the street heard her. The window there was open, you see, just as it is now. It gives on to a narrow alley between this house and the next. Well, two men who were passing the entrance of the alley heard the maid shout and at once ran to my office to warn me. So I hurried here to see what was wrong.'

'Quite,' Judge Dee said. He ordered Chiao Tai and Tao Gan to search the room for possible clues, then to arrange the removal of the dead body to the tribunal. To Prefect Pao he said, 'I shall now interrogate the woman in charge here, together with you, Mr Pao. Warden, where did you put the inmates?'

'The woman in charge, a kind of housekeeper, I put in the reception room back of the hall, sir. The four young girls who are living here I ordered to keep to their own rooms, on the second floor. The maidservants I told to stay in the kitchen.'

'Good work! Come along, Mr Pao!'

As he went across the hall to the moon-door, Mr Yau jumped up from the armchair, but Judge Dee pointedly ignored him. The Prefect glared at him in passing and the harassed Mr Yau quickly resumed his seat.

The small reception room contained only a tea-table of carved blackwood, two chairs of the same material, and a high cupboard. The quietly dressed, middle-aged woman who was standing at the cupboard quickly made a low bow. Judge Dee sat down at the tea-table and motioned the Prefect to take the other chair. The warden pressed the woman down on her knees, then remained standing behind her, his arms crossed on his breast.

Judge Dee began to question her, starting with her name and age. She spoke the northern tongue haltingly, but by skilful questions the judge elicited that Mr Yau had bought the house five years ago, and put her in charge of four girls. Two were ex-courtesans bought out by Mr Yau, the others former actresses. All of them were being paid a generous salary. Mr Yau used to come there about twice a week, either alone or with two or three friends.

'How did you come to know Mrs Pao?' Judge Dee asked her.

'I swear I never knew she was the wife of His Excellency the Prefect!' the woman wailed. 'Else I'd of course never have agreed to Captain Nee bringing her here. He ...'

'Didn't I tell you so?' Prefect Pao shouted. 'The lecher has ...'

'Leave this to me, Mr Pao,' the judge interrupted. He glanced at the housekeeper. 'Proceed!'

'Well, the captain came here a couple of years ago, as I said, and he introduced her as a Miss Wang. Could he use a room now and then in the afternoon, to have a talk with her? he asked. Now the captain is a well-known man, sir, and since he offered to pay well for the tea and cakes, I ...'

'Did Mr Yau know of the arrangement?' the judge asked.

The woman went red in the face. She stammered:

'Since the captain always came in the afternoon, sir ... and only for a cup of tea, I ... I didn't think it necessary, really, to consult Mr Yau and...'

'And you pocketed the captain's money.' Judge Dee completed her sentence in a cold voice. 'You know, of course, full well that the captain slept with the woman. This means that you'll be flogged, for having kept a bawdy house without a proper licence.'

The woman knocked her forehead on the floor several times, then she cried out:

'I swear that the captain never as much as touched her hand, sir! And there isn't even a couch or bench in that room, anyway! Ask the maids, please, sir! They went in and out there all the time, bringing tea and sweets, and so on. They'll tell you how they just sat there talking. Sometimes they played a game of chess —that was all!' She burst into tears.

'Stop your sniffling and rise! Warden, verify her statement with the maids!' Then he asked the woman again, 'Did the captain always warn you beforehand when he came here with Mrs Pao?'

'No sir, he didn't.' She wiped her face with the tip of her sleeve. 'Why should he? He knew that Mr Yau never came in the afternoon. The captain and she always came separately, sometimes the captain was first, other times she was. Today she arrived first. The maid let her into the room they always used, thinking that the captain would turn up too, before long. But he didn't come this time.'

'Of course he came!' the Prefect shouted angrily. 'But you did not see him, you fool! He came through the window, and...'

Judge Dee raised his hand. He addressed the woman:

'So you did not see the captain. Did other visitors come, directly before or after Mrs Pao's arrival?'

'No sir. That is to say, yes ... there was of course that poor girl; she came just before Madame Pao. Since she was blind, I...'

'A blind girl, you say?' the judge asked sharply.

'Yes sir. She wore a plain brown dress, rather old, but she spoke civilly enough. Said she came to apologize for not having kept her appointment with Mr Yau the other night. I asked her whether she was the girl that used to sell crickets to Mr Yau and she said yes.'

The housekeeper stopped abruptly and cast a frightened look over her shoulder at the moon-door.

'Come on, tell me all you know about the girl!' the judge ordered.

'Well, then I remembered that Mr Yau had indeed been waiting for her, sir. He had told me that she used to come to his residence whenever she had a good cricket to sell, but that from now on she would be coming here. Mr Yau also ordered me to prepare a room, upstairs. Although she's blind, she is quite good-looking, sir, and very well-educated. And since Mr Yau likes variety...' She shrugged. 'Anyway, she did not turn up that night, and Mr Yau spent the night with one of the other girls here.'

'I see. Did that blind girl go away at once when you told her that Mr Yau was not at home?'

'No sir. We stood talking there for a while, at the door. She told me that besides seeing Mr Yau, she had wanted to look in this neighbourhood for a girl friend of hers who had entered a kind of private establishment recently. Somewhere near here, behind the Flowery Pagoda, she thought it was. I told her that she must be mistaken, because I knew of no such house in this neighbourhood. "Try the brothel behind us here, dearie," I said. For when girls enter the profession, they often tell their friends that they are joining a private establishment; that sounds better, you see. Well, I took her straight to our back door, and explained to her how she could get to the brothel.'

Suddenly the bead curtain was pulled aside and the warden came in, followed by Captain Nee between two constables. Prefect Pao wanted to rise but the judge laid his hand on his arm.

'Where was the captain arrested, warden?' he asked.

'He came here in a litter, sir, with two friends! Walked inside as cool as a cucumber! And there's a warrant out for his arrest!'

'Why did you come here, Mr Nee?' the judge asked evenly.

'I had an appointment with an acquaintance, sir. I should have been here earlier, but on the way I dropped in on a friend of mine, and found there a sea captain I used to know. We had a few rounds, talked about old times, and it grew late before I knew it. Therefore I took a litter, and my two friends accompanied me here, hoping that the trip would cool their heads. Then I saw constables at the door. Has there been an accident, sir?'

Before answering Nee, the judge told the warden, 'Verify that statement with the two other gentlemen!' Then he asked Nee, 'Who was the acquaintance you were going to meet here?'

'Well, sir, I'd rather not say. It's one of Yau's girls, really, you see. I used to know her rather well before Yau had ...'

'Those lies are quite unnecessary, captain,' the judge cut his explanations short. 'She was murdered. In the tea-room where you always used to meet.'

Nee grew pale. He wanted to ask something, then glanced at the Prefect and checked himself. There was a long, awkward silence. The Prefect had been fixing Nee with a furious glare. Now he wanted to speak up, but then the warden came in and said to Judge Dee:

'Those two gentlemen confirmed the captain's statement, sir. And the maids told me that what this woman here said about those meetings was perfectly correct.'

'All right, warden. Take the captain to Colonel Chiao; he can explain it all to him. You may return to your guard-duty outside, constables!'

As they went outside, Prefect Pao hit his fist on the table and burst out in incoherent protests. But Judge Dee cut him short:

'Your wife was murdered by mistake, Mr Pao.'

'By mistake?' Pao asked, perplexed.

'Yes. Just before her arrival, the blind girl came. She had been followed here by one or more persons who wanted to kill her. As soon as they had seen her enter this house, they started to reconnoitre a way to get inside unseen. In the meantime the blind girl had been shown out by the back door, and your wife had been admitted by the maid. Your wife was dressed in approximately the same manner as the blind girl. When the assassins looked through the window of the tea-room from outside, and saw your wife sitting there with her back towards them, they mistook her for the blind girl, stepped inside and strangled her from behind.'

The Prefect had been listening with a bewildered look. Now he nodded slowly.

'My wife had met that cricket seller!' he suddenly spoke up. 'That blind girl must have been in league with the murderers! She came here to divert the attention of the housekeeper so as to give those unspeakable scoundrels a free hand!'

'That's an alternative theory I shall keep in mind,' the judge said. 'You'd better go home, Mr Pao. You will have understood by now that your wife never deceived you. Her continued association with Captain Nee, the friend of her youth, was unwise. But it did not tarnish your house. Good-bye!'

'She is dead. Gone,' the Prefect said stonily. 'And she was still so young, she . . .' His voice choked. He quickly rose and went outside.

Looking after his bent figure, Judge Dee decided that he would see to it that Pao never came to know about his wife's brief Arab interlude. He vaguely wondered how a well-born Chinese lady could ever fall in love with an Arab, then took hold of himself and turned to the woman who was still standing there. He addressed her harshly:

'Speak up! What other outside women used to come here? Including Arab ones!'

'None, Excellency, I swear it! Mr Yau made some changes in the fixed personnel, from time to time, but . . .'

'All right, I'll check that with him. Now as regards the men he took here, did you ever see among them a tall, good-looking northerner?' He added a description of the Censor. But she shook her head and said that all of Mr Yau's friends were Cantonese.

The judge rose. When Mr Yau saw him coming through the moon-door he again jumped up from the armchair.

'Wait for me outside, in my palankeen,' the judge told him curtly, then went on to the tea-room.

Captain Nee was talking there with Chiao Tai and Tao Gan. The dead body had been removed. Tao Gan said eagerly:

'The murderer came from the roof, sir! Next to this window stands a tall tree that reaches up to the eaves of the second floor. I saw several branches had been broken quite recently.'

'That clinches it!' Judge Dee said. And to Nee, 'Mrs Pao was murdered by robbers. Your association with Mrs Pao has come to a tragic end—as it was bound to, sooner or later. There is no advantage in trying to keep alive a friendship with a married woman, captain.'

'This was different, sir,' the captain said quietly. 'Her husband neglected her, and they had no children. She had no one she could really talk to.'

'Except her blind girl friend,' the judge remarked dryly.

Captain Nee gave him a blank look. Then he shook his head.

'No, she never mentioned a blind girl, sir. But you are right in so far as I am responsible for all this. For I ran out on her after a silly quarrel, some years ago. I went on a voyage, expecting to be back in a couple of months. But we ran into bad weather, I was shipwrecked on an island in the South Seas and it took me over a year to get back here. She had given me up, and married Pao. Then her sister died, and that together with her unhappy marriage made her an easy prey for Mansur. She wanted to consult me, and I thought that Yau's private house was the safest meeting-place. Mansur blackmailed her, and...'

'Why should a wealthy man like Mansur practise blackmail?' Judge Dee interrupted.

'Because at that time he was pressed for funds, sir. The Khalif had confiscated all his possessions. When Mansur discovered I was the one who was paying, he asked more, because he knows I have Persian blood, and he hates all Persians.'

'Talking of Persians, who was the father of those two slave-girls of yours?'

Nee darted a quick appraising glance at the judge. Then he shrugged.

'That I don't know, sir. I could have found out, formerly, but that wouldn't have brought their mother back to life, neither would it have given the twins a real father.' He stared for a while at the empty place on the floor in front of the window, and resumed pensively, 'She was a strange woman. Highly-strung, and very sensitive. I felt our talks meant so much to her, she...' He broke off, desperately trying to control his twitching lips.

Judge Dee turned to his two lieutenants.

'I am going back to the palace now,' he told them. 'I'll have a talk with Mr Yau there, then eat my dinner. After you two have taken your evening rice, come straight to the palace. There is much to discuss.'

When Chiao Tai and Tao Gan had seen the judge to his palankeen, they went back inside.

'I breakfasted at dawn, on a pair of oil-cakes,' Chiao Tai told the captain gruffly. 'Then, instead of my noon rice, I got a wallop on the head. I am in urgent need of a good square meal and a large jug of the best. I invite you to join us, captain, on condition that you lead us to the nearest restaurant, by the shortest route!'

The captain nodded gratefully.

## XVII

Judge Dee remained deep in thought throughout the journey to the palace. His silence seemed to perturb Mr Yau still further. He shot the judge an uneasy glance now and then, but could not summon sufficient courage to address him.

Arriving at the palace, the judge took him straight to the hall he used as his private study. Yau was visibly impressed by its grand dimensions. Judge Dee sat down behind his large desk, and motioned Yau to take the chair opposite him. After the major-domo had served tea and disappeared again, the judge slowly emptied his cup, fixing Yau with a sombre stare all the while. As he put down his teacup, he asked suddenly:

'How did you come to know the blind cricket seller?'

Yau gave him a startled glance.

'Well, in the ordinary way, sir! Met her in the market. Cricket-fighting is rather a hobby of mine, you see. I noticed at once that she knew a tremendous lot about the subject. She used to come to my residence every time she had found a particularly good fighter. But recently I decided that it was more er ... expedient to have her come to my er ... private address.'

'I see. Where does she live?'

'I never asked her, sir! Didn't need to, either. As I just said, she would come when...'

'I know. What is her name?'

'Her personal name is Lan-lee, so she said, sir. I don't know her family name.'

'Do you mean to tell me,' Judge Dee asked coldly, 'that you know nothing about your mistresses beyond their personal name?'

'She isn't my mistress, sir!' Yau cried out, indignant. He

thought for a few moments, then went on in an apologetic tone, 'I admit that I have toyed with the idea, once or twice. She's a remarkably cultured girl, sir. She's good-looking too, and since her blindness makes her different, I ... er ...'

'Quite,' Judge Dee said dryly. 'It so happens that she is connected with a crime that was recently committed here.' He cut short Yau's excited questions with a raised hand. 'I am having her traced, for she is also involved in Mrs Pao's murder. As soon as she has been arrested, I shall check your statement, Mr Yau. Now you'll write down the names and full particulars of the girls in your private establishment. In this case you know a little more than just their personal names, I suppose?'

'Certainly, sir!' Yau answered obsequiously. He selected a writing-brush.

'Good. I'll be back presently.'

Judge Dee rose and went outside. In the anteroom he ordered the majordomo:

'Tell my four agents to follow Mr Yau when he leaves the palace. If he should go to a private house of assignment near the Flowery Pagoda, they must come and warn me at once. If he goes and meets a blind girl, they must arrest the two of them and bring them here. Wherever he goes, he is to be watched. The men must come and report to me as soon as they have any news.'

He went back inside, glanced through what Yau had written, then told him he could go. The portly merchant left, looking greatly relieved.

Judge Dee sighed. He called the majordomo, and told him to serve the evening rice.

When Chiao Tai and Tao Gan entered the hall, they found the judge standing in front of the window where there was a slight breeze. After his two assistants had greeted him, he sat down behind his desk and said in a matter of fact voice:

'As I explained already to Prefect Pao, his wife was murdered by mistake. The intended victim was the blind girl.' Ignoring Tao Gan's astonished exclamation, he quickly told them what he had

137

learned in Yau's love-nest. 'The blind girl,' he went on, 'is apparently conducting an investigation all on her own. As I said before, she must have been present when the Censor died. But she does not know where exactly it happened. She suspects that it was in a house of assignment in the neighbourhood of the Flowery Pagoda, hence her questioning of Yau's procuress. Her associates discovered that she was on their trail, and decided to silence her. The assassin they employed must have been a Tanka, for again a scarf was used, weighted with a silver coin. As to Mr Yau Tai-kai, we shall soon know whether he spoke the truth about his relations with the blind girl, for I had him followed when he left here before dinner. He is an uncommonly shrewd customer, but I believe I frightened him sufficiently to try to contact some accomplice of his at once. Yau knows that we want to trace the blind girl, so if he is guilty he may make a second attempt on her life. I realize that she is trying to help us, but the issues at stake are too grave to let our concern for the girl—about whom we know next to nothing—interfere with our investigation.' He paused and pulled pensively at his moustache. 'As regards the murderous attack on you, Chiao Tai, I can't understand how Mansur could have known that you would be going back to Nee's house. I ordered you to do so on the spur of the moment. Even if those two Arabs had followed when you left here, how could they have had time to report to Mansur, receive his instructions, then go back to Captain Nee's house? And what was the motive? We know that Mansur hates Nee, but the attack was evidently aimed in the first place at you. And murder seems a rather drastic method of settling one's private feuds. I fear that there's much more behind it than meets the eye.' He gave Chiao Tai a searching look. 'I must say that those twins are plucky girls. Since you owe them your life, Chiao Tai, you'd better pay them a visit to thank them, and give them a suitable present.'

Chiao Tai looked embarrassed. He muttered something about consulting Captain Nee first, then went on hastily:

'If you have no other work for us tonight, sir, Tao Gan and I might have a look around for Mansur. I have a lump on my head as big as an egg; I'd love to get my hands on that sneaky bastard! At the same time we might try to locate the blind girl. It's true that the constables are looking for them too, but I have a very personal reason for getting Mansur, and brother Tao knows exactly what the girl looks like.'

'All right. But whether you achieve anything or not, both of you come back here before turning in. I am still hoping that the secret letter from the Grand Council will arrive tonight, and its contents may necessitate immediate action.'

The two friends bowed and took their leave.

When they were standing outside in the street waiting for an empty litter, Chiao Tai said:

'We'll just have to trust to luck in our search for Mansur. It's no use having a second look in the Arab quarter: they know me there by now, we don't speak their blasted language, and anyway I don't think he would hide there. We might board the Arab ships in port, and make a search for him there. Got any ideas about where to look for the girl?'

'Well, she's got to hide not only from the constables, but also from her own people, who are out to kill her. That means inns or lodging-houses are out. I think she'd hide in a deserted house. Since she told me that she's thoroughly familiar with the market quarter, we might start there. We could narrow that down further by finding out which spots in that neighbourhood are known to be frequented by crickets, for those are the places she knows best, of course.'

'Good,' Chiao Tai said. 'Let's go to the market first.' He hailed a passing litter, but it was occupied. Fingering his small moustache, he went on, 'You had a long talk with that wench, brother Tao. You don't know a thing about women, but you can give me at least a general idea of what kind of girl she is, I suppose.'

'The kind that makes trouble,' Tao Gan replied crossly, 'for everybody including herself. The silly kind—too silly to be allowed to walk around on two legs! Believes everybody is just

139

too kind, everybody means well, really—so help me! Heaven preserve me from that goody-goody type! Look what she's doing now, getting herself in heaven knows what trouble by hobnobbing with the Censor's murderers! Probably believes they poisoned the Censor as a kind afterthought, as the only permanent cure for his hangover. For heaven's sake! Sends me a croaking little cricket instead of coming to me herself and telling me what it's all about. If we find her,' he added venomously, 'I'll have her clapped in jail at once, just to keep her from getting herself into more trouble!'

'Quite some speech, brother Tao!' Chiao Tai said dryly. 'Ha, here comes a litter!'

# XVIII

They stepped down in front of the ornamental gate that marked the west entrance of the market. Inside, the crowd had not yet thinned, and all the passages were brightly lit by oil lamps and coloured lampions.

Peering over the heads of the crowd, Chiao Tai noticed a pole from which hung a number of small cages. He halted and said:

'There's a cricket dealer ahead. Let's ask him for a good place hereabouts to catch crickets.'

'You don't expect him to tell us the tricks of his trade, do you? He'll say he catches them in the mountains thirty miles up river, and then only on the third day of the waning moon! We'd better cross the market, leave by the south gate, and have a look at that deserted place where they are pulling down old houses. It's there that I met her.'

When they were passing the cricket stall, they heard violent curses followed by agonized screams. They elbowed the onlookers aside and saw that the dealer was pulling a boy of about fifteen hard by his ears. Then he slapped him soundly and shouted, 'Now you go and get those cages you forgot, you lazybones!' He sent the boy outside with a well-aimed kick.

'After him!' Tao Gan hissed.

In the next passage Tao Gan overtook the boy who was stumbling along holding his hands over his ears. He put his hand on his shoulder and said:

'Your boss is a first-class bastard; last week he cheated me out of a silver piece.' As the boy wiped his tear-stained face, Tao Gan went on, 'My friend and I were thinking of catching a few good fighting-crickets tonight. What place would you suggest, as an expert?'

'Catching a good fighter is no work for amateurs,' the boy declared importantly. 'They change their places ever so often, you see. Until a couple of days ago, you had a good chance near the Temple of the War God. Lots of people still go there. Nothing doing! We insiders know. It's the Examination Hall you have to go to now!'

'Thanks very much! Put a centipede in your boss's boot tomorrow morning. That's always a nice surprise.'

As he was guiding Chiao Tai to the east gate of the market, Tao Gan resumed contritely:

'I ought to have thought of that! The Examination Hall is two streets to the east and takes up an entire block. There are several hundred cells there, since candidates for the Autumnal Literary Examinations gather here in Canton from all over the province. This time of the year the Hall is empty—an ideal place to hide! And for catching a few good crickets into the bargain!'

'But isn't the compound guarded?'

'There'll be a caretaker, but he won't take much care! No vagabonds or beggars would dare to take shelter there. Don't you know that Examination Halls are always haunted?'

'Good heavens, that's true!' Chiao Tai exclaimed. He remembered that every year, during the public literary examinations held all over the Empire, many poor students committed suicide. They had to toil at the Classics day and night, often pawning their belongings or contracting debts at atrocious interest, in order to be able to continue their studies. If they passed, they got an official post at once, and their troubles were over. Failure, however, meant at best another year of gruelling work, often financial ruin, and sometimes utter disgrace. Therefore, when a student had been locked into his cell for the day and saw that the examination papers were too difficult for him, he often ended his life then and there, in despair. Chiao Tai unconsciously slackened his pace. He halted at a stall and bought a small lantern. 'It'll be pitch-dark inside!' he muttered to Tao Gan.

They left the market by the east gate. A brief walk brought them to the Examination Hall.

The blind wall of the compound ran the entire length of the dark, deserted street. Round the corner a high red gatehouse marked the one and only entrance. The double doors were closed, but the narrow side gate stood ajar. When Chiao Tai and Tao Gan had gone inside, they saw a light behind the window of the caretaker's lodge. They slipped past it, and hurriedly entered the paved road that crossed the compound from north to south.

Lit only by the uncertain moonlight, the road ran straight as a die as far as they could see. On either side was an interminable row of identical doors. Each cell contained only a small desk and a chair. On the morning of the examination each student was put in one with his food-box. After he had been expertly searched for miniature dictionaries or other cribs, the examination papers were handed to him and the door was sealed. It was opened again only at dusk, when the completed papers were collected. In the autumn, when the examinations were in progress the place was a beehive of activity. But now it was as quiet as the grave.

'How many of those damned cells do we have to search?' Chiao Tai asked peevishly. He didn't like the eerie atmosphere.

'Couple of hundred!' Tao Gan replied cheerfully. 'But let's first reconnoitre a bit and get the layout.'

Walking along the desolate passages and studying the numbers marking the cell doors, they soon found that the rows of cells were built in quadrangles around a paved yard. There stood an imposing, two-storeyed building, the Examination Hall, where the examiners gathered to study and mark the papers handed in.

Tao Gan halted in his steps. Pointing at the building, he said:

'That's an even better place for hiding than those cramped cells! Inside you have any amount of tables, couches, chairs, and what not!'

Chiao Tai did not answer. He had been staring up at the balcony that jutted out from the east corner of the second floor. Now he whispered:

'Hush! I saw something move up there!'

The two men looked intently at the balcony for a while. It was screened by intricate latticework, that showed but one small window. The curved end of the roof was outlined clearly against the starry sky. But nothing was stirring.

They quickly crossed the yard, went up the marble steps, and stood close to the door, so that the eaves overhead made them invisible from above. When Tao Gan found the door was not locked, he carefully pushed it open, and they went into the pitch-dark hall.

'I'll light the lantern,' Chiao Tai whispered. 'Light won't make any difference; it's her acute hearing we must reckon with!'

The light of the lantern showed that the spacious hall was octagonal. Against the back wall was the high, throne-like platform from which the Chief Examiner proclaimed the results. Over it hung an enormous red-lacquered board, bearing the engraved inscription: 'Braving the current, the Jade Gate is reached'—meaning a student would be successful if he emulated the force and perseverance of the carp swimming upstream every year. On either side of the hall were two flights of stairs. They went up the staircase on the right, calculating that that must bring them to the east corner of the second floor.

However, the circular hall upstairs did not match the symmetrical pattern of the ground floor. They saw no less than eight narrow door-openings. Tao Gan orientated himself, then entered the second on their right, drawing Chiao Tai with him. But at the end they only found two empty, dusty office rooms. They ran noiselessly out again and into the next passage. When Tao Gan had slowly pushed open the door at the end of it, he found himself on a small balcony, open on all three sides. On his right was the screened balcony they had seen from below. Across the inter-

144

vening space of about fifteen feet, he vaguely saw a seated girl, bent over a table. She seemed to be reading.

'It's her!' Tao Gan whispered close to Chiao Tai's ear. 'I recognize her profile!'

Chiao Tai muttered something. He pointed at the long rows of cells down below, crossed by the white pavement of the passages dividing them.

'Something small and black just crept along the cells to the left there,' he whispered hoarsely. 'Then another. They have no legs, only long, spidery arms!' Gripping Tao Gan's arm tightly, he added: 'They suddenly disappeared into the shadows. They aren't human, I tell you!'

'Must be a trick of the moonlight,' Tao Gan whispered back. 'Let's go get the girl, she's human all right!'

He turned round. At the same time there was a loud crash. The slip of his robe had caught on the thorny branch of a potted rose, standing on a slender base in the corner of the balcony.

They ran inside again and paused for a moment in the circular hall. Hearing and seeing nothing, they rushed into the next passage. It ended in a small reading-room. Cursing roundly, they ran back and entered the third passage. This one brought them at last to the screened balcony. But she was not there anymore.

Chiao Tai ran back to the hall and down the stairs, hoping to overtake the fugitive. Tao Gan quickly surveyed the small room. There was a narrow bamboo couch, its padded cover neatly folded up. On the table stood a diminutive cage of silver filigree. As soon as Tao Gan lifted it up, the cricket inside began to chirrup. He put it down again and picked up two folded pieces of paper. Taking them to the window, he saw they were maps. One represented the estuary of the Pearl River, the other the Arab quarter round the mosque. Chiao Tai's Inn of the Five Immortals had been marked with a red dot.

He put the maps and the cage in his sleeve and walked back to the hall. Chiao Tai came upstairs, panting.

'She fooled us all right, brother!' he said disgustedly. 'The back

145

door's standing ajar. How could a blind person make such a quick getaway?'

Tao Gan silently showed him the maps.

'How could a blind person study maps?' he asked crossly. 'Well, let's quickly have a look around down in the compound, anyway.'

'All right. We won't get the girl, but I'd like a second look at those weird dark things I saw creeping along. Just to make sure I'm not the one who's getting eye trouble!'

They went downstairs and out into the paved yard. Then they walked along the rows of cells in the east section of the compound, occasionally opening a door at random. But there was nothing in the small dark rooms besides the standard equipment of desk and chair. Suddenly, they heard a muffled cry.

'In the next row!' Chiao Tai hissed.

They ran down the passage as fast as they could. Chiao Tai reached the corner well ahead of Tao Gan and was round it like a flash. About half-way down, a cell door was standing ajar. He heard the sound of a chair, crashing to the floor, then the piercing shriek of a woman. When Chiao Tai reached the door, the shrieking stopped abruptly. Just as he was about to push it open, he felt a length of smooth silk close round his throat.

His fighter's instinct made him press his chin to his breast and strain his heavy neck muscles. At the same time he threw himself with his hands on the ground and turned a quick somersault, his assailant still clinging to his back. This is the deadly countermove against a stranglehold from behind. While his full body weight crashed down on the man under him he felt a searing pain in his throat. But at that moment there was a sickening sound of snapping bones, and the silk round his neck grew slack.

He was on his feet in a trice and tore the silk scarf from his neck. Another small, squat man burst from the cell opposite. Chiao Tai tried to grab him but missed. As he went after him, he was suddenly stopped by a fearful jerk on his right arm. It was caught in a wax-thread noose. While he was trying desperately to

146

loosen it, the small dark shape disappeared at the far end of the passage.

'Sorry!' Tao Gan panted behind him. 'I aimed my noose at the man's head!'

'You are out of practice, brother, Tao!' Chiao Tai snapped. 'The dog escaped.' He looked sourly at the scarf and felt the silver coin tied to its corner. Then he put the scarf in his sleeve.

A slender figure came from the cell and Chiao Tai felt two soft bare arms round his neck, and a small curly head pressing against his breast. Then a second girl came out of the cell door behind him, clutching her torn trousers.

'Almighty heaven!' Chiao Tai exclaimed. 'The awful twins!'

Dunyazad let go of him. Tao Gan raised the lantern. The light shone on the twins' pale faces and on their bare torsos, disfigured by ugly bruises and bleeding scratches.

'The devils tried to rape us!' Dunyazad sobbed.

'And severally, too!' Chiao Tai remarked with a grin. 'It wouldn't even have been a shared experience! Speak up, how did you two get here?'

Dananir wiped her face.

'It's all her fault!' she cried out. 'She dared me!' She gave her crying sister a venomous look and went on hurriedly: 'The captain didn't turn up for dinner, so we decided to have a bowl of noodles in the market. Then she said that there were ghosts in this compound and I said no there weren't and she said yes there were and I'd never dare go inside. So we came here, slipped by the caretaker's lodge and had a quick look at the first passage. Just when we wanted to run out of this creepy place again, those two awful small men came out of nowhere and chased us. We ran like hares, into this cell, but they forced the door open. One dragged my sister to the cell opposite, the other held me with my back down on the table and began to tear at my trousers.' Holding the torn garment close to her, she added with satisfaction, 'When he tried to kiss me, I poked my thumb in his left eye.'

'They were growling and muttering in some horrible language all the time!' Dunyazad wailed. 'They can't be human!'

'This one was human enough to have his back broken,' Tao Gan remarked. He had been examining the figure sprawling on the pavement. Chiao Tai recognized the wizened face: the high cheekbones, flat nose and low corrugated forehead.

'One of the waterfolk,' he told Tao Gan. 'They were after the blind girl again. Would have finished her off too, up there on the balcony. But their little lecherous interlude spoiled everything. Well, let's see these two enterprising wenches home!'

The two girls went inside the cell. When they came out they looked fairly presentable in their flowered jackets and trousers. They meekly followed Chiao Tai and Tao Gan to the caretaker's lodge.

After repeated knocking the man thrust his sleep-heavy face through the door. Chiao Tai told them who they were, and ordered him to lock the gate behind them, then wait till the constables came to fetch a dead body. 'And I don't mean you!' he added unkindly.

They took the street leading south. A short walk brought them to Captain Nee's house.

The captain himself opened the gate. Seeing the twins, he said with relief:

'Heaven be praised! What have you been up to again?'

The twins rushed into his arms and began to babble excitedly in what Chiao Tai assumed to be Persian.

'Put them to bed, captain!' he cut them short. 'They came very near to losing what they presumably refer to as the flower of their maidenhood. You better see to it personally that tonight that danger is eliminated once and for all!'

'That might be a good idea!' Nee said, giving the two girls a fond smile.

'Good luck! But for heaven's sake don't let them abuse their new status, captain! My oldest friend, my blood-brother, in fact, married twins. Before his marriage he was a fine boxer, and a splendid wencher and winebibber. And what has become of him now, eh, Tao Gan?'

Tao Gan pursed his lips and sadly shook his head.

'What happened to him?' the captain asked, curious.

'He went into decline,' Chiao Tai replied darkly. 'Good-bye!'

## XIX

They found Judge Dee sitting behind his desk, making notes by the light from two enormous silver candelabras. Laying his writing-brush down and staring at their dishevelled clothes, he asked astonished:

'What have you two been at?'

Chiao Tai and Tao Gan sat down, and gave an account of what had happened in the compound of the Examination Hall. When they had finished, the judge smote his fist on the desk.

'Tanka stranglers, Arab hooligans, all these sinister killers seem to be roaming about at will in this city! What in the name of heaven are the Governor's men doing?' Mastering himself, he added, calmer, 'Show me those maps, Tao Gan!'

Tao Gan took the cricket cage from his sleeve and put it carefully at the end of the table. Then he got the maps out and folded them open. The cricket began to make a penetrating, whirring sound.

Judge Dee gave the cage a sour look, then settled down to a study of the maps, slowly tugging at his sidewhiskers. He looked up and said:

'These maps are old; this one of the Arab quarter is dated thirty years back, when the Arab ships began to arrive regularly here. But it is fairly accurate, as far as I can see. That red spot marking Chiao Tai's inn has been put in quite recently. The girl is no more blind than you or I, my friends! Can't you make that noisy insect shut up, Tao Gan?'

Tao Gan put the small case back into his sleeve. Then he asked:

'Have the men who followed Yau Tai-kai come back yet, sir?'

'No,' Judge Dee replied curtly. 'The letter from the capital hasn't arrived either. And it's getting on for midnight!'

He fell into a morose silence. Tao Gan got up and poured fresh tea. When they had drunk a cup, the majordomo came in with a thin man in a plain blue gown who was wearing a small skull-cap. His moustache was grey but he carried his broad shoulders in a soldier-like fashion. After the majordomo had left, he reported in a dry voice:

'Mr Yau went straight home, and had his evening rice alone, in his garden-pavilion. Then he retired to his inner apartments. Our subsequent interrogation of the maidservants revealed that he then summoned his four wives and scolded them for being lazy good-for-nothings. Accusing his first lady of being responsible, he had the maids pull her trousers down and hold her while he personally gave her a caning. Then he called his six concubines and informed them that their allowances would be halved. Finally he went to his library and got himself thoroughly drunk. When the house steward said that Mr Yau was sound asleep, I came here to report to Your Excellency.'

'Is there any news of Mansur?' the judge asked.

'No sir. He must have hidden somewhere outside the city walls, for we combed the Arab quarter, and the constables checked all the low-class inns.'

'All right, you may go.'

When the agent had left, Chiao Tai burst out:

'What a mean bastard that Yau is!'

'Not a very pleasant person,' Judge Dee agreed. 'And shrewd enough to have foreseen that I was going to have him followed, apparently. He tugged at his moustache, then suddenly asked Chiao Tai, 'Are Nee's two slave-girls all right?'

'Oh yes, they escaped with a shaking!' He added with a grin, 'However, by now they are no longer slaves, nor are they girls—if I appraised the situation correctly. I had the distinct impression, sir, that the captain, after he had recovered somewhat from the shock of his old love's murder, suddenly realized that their pure, detached relationship had worn a bit thin in the course of the years—even for a mystic like him! And that now that he had become a free man again, so to speak, he had better reconsider his paternal attitude towards his two young wards. Especially since those two saucy bits of skirt would like nothing better !'

Tao Gan had given the judge a curious look when he heard his question about the twins. Now he asked :

'Are those twins connected with the Censor's case, sir?'

'Not directly,' Judge Dee replied.

'What could those two, even indirectly...' Chiao Tai began, astonished. But Judge Dee raised his hand and pointed to the entrance. The majordomo was ushering in two officers in full battle-array. They wore peaked helmets and brass-bordered coats of mail, marking them as captains of the mounted military police. After they had stiffly saluted the judge, the elder took a large, heavily sealed letter from his boot. Laying it on the desk, he said respectfully :

'This letter we brought here on the orders of the Grand Council, in a special mounted convoy.'

Judge Dee signed and sealed the receipt, thanked the captains and ordered the majordomo to see to it that all the members of the convoy got food and suitable lodgings.

He slit the envelope open, and slowly read the long letter. His two assistants anxiously watched his worried face. At last he looked up and said slowly :

'Bad news. Very bad. His Majesty's illness has taken a turn for the worse. The physicians in attendance fear that the Great Demise is imminent. The Empress is forming a powerful political alliance that will advocate a Regency, with all executive power vested in her as Empress-Dowager. The Council insists that the Censor's disappearance must now be officially announced, and someone appointed to replace him at once, else the loyal group will have no one to rally to. Since any further delay would have disastrous consequences, the Council orders me to abandon my search for the missing Censor, and return to the capital at my earliest convenience.'

The judge threw the letter on the desk, sprang up and began to pace the floor, angrily shaking his long sleeves.

Chiao Tai and Tao Gan exchanged an unhappy look. They did not know what to say.

Suddenly Judge Dee halted in front of them.

'There's only one thing we can do,' he said firmly. 'A desperate measure, but justified by our woeful lack of time.' He resumed his seat. Leaning forward on his elbows, he went on, 'Go to the atelier of a Buddhist sculptor, Tao Gan, and buy a wooden model of a man's severed head. It must be nailed tonight to the gate of the tribunal, up high, so that from below you can't see it is a fake. Underneath it, on a placard, will be posted an official announcement, which I shall draw up now.'

Ignoring the astonished questions of his two lieutenants, he moistened his writing-brush and quickly jotted down a brief text. Then he sat back in his chair and read it aloud:

President Dee of the Metropolitan Court, now on a tour of inspection in Canton, has discovered here the corpse of a prominent official who, guilty of high treason, had fled from the capital with a price on his head. After the autopsy proved that the said criminal had been poisoned, the corpse was posthumously quartered, and the head is now displayed for three days in succession, as prescribed by the law. Whosoever brought about the death of this despicable traitor is ordered to present himself before the aforesaid President, so that he may receive a reward of five hundred gold pieces. All crimes or offences he may have committed previously, with the exception of capital crimes, shall be pardoned.

As he threw the paper on the desk, Judge Dee resumed:

'The main criminal won't be taken in by this ruse, of course. I am counting on his Chinese henchmen; for instance, the two men disguised as constables who brought the Censor's dead body to the Temple of the Flowery Pagoda. If the head is displayed and the same notice put up all over the city this very night, there's a good chance that someone seeing them early tomorrow morning will come rushing here before his principal has had time to warn him that it is nothing but a hoax.'

Chiao Tai looked dubious, but Tao Gan nodded eagerly and said:

'It's the only way to get quick results! The main criminal must have at least a dozen or so accomplices, and five hundred gold pieces they wouldn't get in five hundred years! They'll come rushing here, trying to beat each other to the reward!'

'Let's hope so,' Judge Dee said wearily. 'It's the best I can think of, anyway. Set to work!'

# XX

Chiao Tai was awakened at dawn by the booming voice of the Moslem priest. From the top of the minaret he was calling upon the faithful for the morning prayer. Chiao Tai rubbed his eyes. He had slept badly, and his back was aching. Passing his finger carefully along his swollen throat, he muttered to himself, 'One late night and a scuffle shouldn't count for a hefty fellow of forty-five, brother!' He got up naked as he was and threw the shutters open.

He took a long draught from the spout of the teapot in the padded basket, gargled and spat lukewarm tea into the porcelain spittoon. With a grunt he lay down on the plank bed again. He thought he would grant himself a little nap before getting up and preparing himself for going to the palace.

Just as he was dozing off, he was roused by a knock on the door.

'Go away!' he shouted, annoyed.

'It is I! Open up, quick!'

Chiao Tai recognized Zumurrud's voice. With a delighted grin he sprang up and stepped into his trousers. He pulled the bolt back.

She hastily came inside and bolted the door behind her. She was all wrapped up in a long, hooded cloak of blue cotton. Her eyes were shining; he thought she was looking even more beautiful than before. He pushed the only chair towards her and sat down on the edge of the bed.

'Want a cup of tea?' he asked awkwardly.

She shook her head, kicked the chair away and said impatiently:

'Listen, all my troubles are over! You needn't take me to the capital any more. Only take me to your boss. Now!'

'To my boss? Why?'

'Your boss promised a reward, big money, that's why! I heard the fishermen shouting the news to the people of my boat. They had seen the placard put up on the gate of the custom-house. I didn't know that the Censor had been mixed up in political trouble, thought he had come to Canton only for me. But that doesn't matter any more. What matters is that I can claim the reward. For I am the one who poisoned him.'

'You?' Chiao Tai exclaimed, aghast. 'How could you...'

'I'll explain!' she interrupted him curtly. 'Just to show you why you must take me to your boss at once. And put in a good word for me, too.' She took off the blue cloak, and carelessly threw it on the floor. Underneath she wore only a single robe of transparent silk that showed every detail of her perfect body. 'About six weeks ago,' she resumed, 'I passed the night with my patron in the house near the temple. When I was leaving in the morning, he said that there was a festival in the Flowery Pagoda, and that I'd better call there on my way to the quay to pray for him—the bastard! Well, I went anyway and burned incense before the large statue of Our Lady of Mercy there. Suddenly I noticed that a man standing close by was eyeing me. He was tall and handsome, and although he was plainly dressed, he had a marked air of authority. He asked me why I, an Arab, prayed to a Chinese goddess. I said a girl can't have too many goddesses looking after her. He laughed, and thus began a long conversation. I knew at once that this was the man I had been hoping to meet all my life. Treated me like I was a real lady, too! I fell in love with him, at first sight, like a snotty chit of sixteen! Since I felt that he liked me, too, I asked him to have a cup of tea with me in the house. It's quite near the back entrance of the temple, you see, and I knew that my patron had left. You can imagine for yourself what followed. Afterwards he told me he wasn't married and that he had never slept with a woman before. That didn't matter, he said, because now he had met me. He said many other such nice things, then added that he was an Imperial Censor! When I had explained my troubles to him, he promised he would get me Chinese citizenship, and pay my patron all my expenses. He would have to leave Canton in a few days, but he would come back to fetch me and take me to the capital with him.'

Patting her hair, she continued with a reminiscent smile:

'The days and nights we passed together were the happiest in my life, I tell you! Imagine me, who has slept with heaven knows how many hundreds of men, feeling like a young girl in the throes of her first love! I was so silly about him that I got into a bad fit of jealousy when he was about to return to the capital. And then I acted like a blooming fool, messed up everything with my own hands!' She paused and wiped her perspiring brow with the tip of her sleeve. Grabbing the teapot, she drank from the spout, then resumed listlessly, 'You must know that we waterfolk prepare all kinds of weird drugs, love philtres, some good medicines, but also some poisons. The recipes have been handed down among us Tanka women for generations. We have one particular poison which our women give to their lovers when they suspect they intend to leave them for good, under the pretext of going on a journey. If the chap returns, they give him an antidote, and he never knows what has been done to him. I asked the Censor when he would come back to Canton to fetch me, and he said in two weeks, without fail. At our last meeting I put the poison in his tea, a dose that would be harmless if he took the antidote in three weeks' time. But if he deceived me and never came back, I wanted him to pay for it with his life.

'Two weeks went by, then another one. That third week was terrible.... I could hardly eat, and those nights ... After the three weeks had passed, I lived in a trance, mechanically counting the days.... On the fifth day he came. Came to see me on my boat, early in the morning. Said he had been detained in the capital by an urgent affair. He had arrived in Canton two days before, strictly incognito, accompanied only by his friend Dr Soo. He had put off calling on me because he had to see some Arab acquaintances, and also because he hadn't been feeling well, and wanted to have a brief rest. But he had become worse, therefore he had come now, ill as he was, hoping that my company would cure him. I was frantic, for I hadn't got the antidote with me, I had hidden it in the house near the temple. I talked him into going there with me at once. He fainted as soon as we were inside. I poured the antidote down his throat, but it was too late. Half an hour later he was dead.'

She bit her lips and stared for a while at the roofs of the houses outside. Chiao Tai looked up at her, dumbfounded. His face had turned deadly pale. She went on slowly:

'There was no one in the house I could turn to, for my patron didn't even keep a maidservant there. I rushed to him and told him what had happened. He only smiled and said he would take care of everything. The bastard knew that I was now completely at his mercy, for I, wretched pariah, had murdered an Imperial Censor. If he denounced me, I'd be quartered alive! I told him that Dr Soo would start to worry if the Censor didn't return to their inn that night. My patron asked whether Dr Soo knew about me and the Censor. When I said no, he said he'd see to it that Soo made no trouble.'

She took a deep breath. Giving Chiao Tai a sidelong glance, she continued:

'If you had taken me to the capital, I would have taken a chance on my patron keeping his mouth shut. He counts for nothing in the capital, and you are a colonel of the guard. And if he had blabbed, you could have hidden me where they couldn't get at me. But now everything has turned out for the best. Your boss announced that the Censor was a traitor, which means that instead of committing a crime, I did the state a great service. I'll tell him that he can keep half of the gold, if he gets me citizenship, and a nice little house in the capital. Get dressed and take me to him!'

Chiao Tai looked up in utter horror at the woman who had just pronounced her own death sentence. Staring at her as she stood there with her back to the window, her magnificent body outlined against the red morning sky, he suddenly saw in his mind's eye, with horrifying clarity, the scene of the scaffold at dawn—this lithe, perfect body mutilated by the executioner's knife, then the limbs torn asunder.... A long shudder shook his powerful frame. He rose slowly. Standing in front of the exultant woman, he groped frantically for some way to save her, some way to . . .

Suddenly she cried out and fell into his arms, so vehemently that he nearly lost his balance. Clasping her supple waist, he bent his head to kiss her full, red mouth. But then he saw that her large eyes were getting glazed; her mouth twitched, blood stained her chin. At the same time he felt warm drops trickling down his hands, pressed in the small of her back. In utter confusion he felt her shoulders. His fingers closed round a wooden shaft.

He stood there motionless, the dying woman's round bosom against his breast, her warm thighs against his. He felt her heart flutter, as it had once before when he had held her in his arms on the boat. Then it stopped beating.

He laid her down on the couch and drew the javelin from her back. Then he softly closed her eyes, and wiped her face. His mind was frozen. Dazedly he stared at the flat roofs of the Arab houses outside. Where she had stood at the window she had been an easy target for an expert javelin thrower.

Suddenly he realized that he was standing there by the dead body of the only woman he had ever loved, loved with his entire being. He fell on his knees in front of the couch, buried his face in her long, curling locks and burst into strange, soundless sobs.

After a long time he rose. He took her blue cloak and covered her.

'For the two of us, love meant death,' he whispered. 'I knew it, as soon as I had seen you, that first time. I then saw a battlefield, smelled the heady smell of fresh blood, saw its red flow. . . .'

He cast one long look at the still figure, then locked the room and went downstairs. He walked all the way to the palace, through the grey streets where only few people were about at this early hour.

The majordomo told him that Judge Dee was still in his bedroom. Chiao Tai went upstairs and sat down on one of the couches in the anteroom. The judge had heard him. Bare-headed and still wearing his nightrobe, he pulled the door-curtain aside. He had a comb in his hand; he had just been doing his beard and whiskers. Seeing Chiao Tai's haggard face, he quickly stepped up to him and asked, astonished:

'What in heaven's name has happened, Chiao Tai? No, don't get up, man! You look ill!' He sat down on the other couch and gave his lieutenant a worried look.

Staring straight ahead, Chiao Tai told him the whole story of Zumurrud. When he had finished, he added in a toneless voice, looking the judge full in the face, 'I thought it all out on my way here, sir. She and I were lost, either way. If the assassin hadn't murdered her, I would have killed her myself, then and there. Her life for that of the Censor, a life for a life, she would have understood that. It's in her blood, as it is in mine. Then I would have killed myself. As it is, I am still alive. But as soon as this case has been disposed of, I beg you to release me from my oath to serve you, sir. I want to go and join our northern army, now fighting the Tartars beyond the border.'

There was a long silence. At last Judge Dee spoke quietly:

'I never met her, but I understand. She died a happy woman, happy because she thought her one and only dream would now come true. But she had died already before she was killed, Chiao Tai. For she had only that one dream left, and one needs many dreams to stay alive.' He straightened his robe, then looked up and said pensively, 'I know exactly how you feel, Chiao Tai. Four years ago, in Peichow, when I was solving the nail murders, the same thing happened to me. And I had to make the decision which Zumurrud's murderer took out of your hands. Moreover, she had saved my life and my career.'

'Was she executed, sir?' Chiao Tai asked tensely.

160

'No. She wanted to spare me that. She committed suicide.' Slowly stroking his long beard, he went on, 'I was going to give up everything. I wanted to retire from a world that suddenly seemed grey and lifeless, dead.' He paused, then he suddenly laid his hand on Chiao Tai's arm. 'No one can give you any help or advice. You must decide yourself what course to follow. But whatever your decision may be, Chiao Tai, it will never change my friendship and my high regard for you.' Rising, he added with a wan smile, 'I must finish my toilet now; I probably look like a scarecrow! And you had better order my four agents at once to go to her boat, apprehend the maid who was her patron's spy, and question the crew. For we must learn the identity of her patron. Then you go back to your inn with a dozen constables, fetch the body, and take the routine measures for tracing the murderer.'

He turned round and disappeared behind the door-curtain.

Chiao Tai rose and went downstairs.

## XXI

Shortly after Judge Dee had sat down to his breakfast, Tao Gan came in. After he had wished the judge a good morning, he eagerly asked whether someone had turned up to claim the reward. The judge shook his head and motioned him to be seated. He finished his rice gruel in silence. After he had laid down his chopsticks, he leaned back in his chair and folded his arms in his wide sleeves. Then he told Tao Gan everything about the unexpected result of the faked proclamation.

'So it was a love affair that brought the Censor back to Canton!' Tao Gan exclaimed.

'Partly. At the same time he wanted to investigate Mansur's seditious plot. For he told Zumurrud clearly that he had to see some Arabs here.'

'But why did he keep everything to himself, sir? Why didn't he take up the matter with the Grand Council on his return to the capital, after his first visit here, and...'

'He knew little about women, Tao Gan, but he was indeed well versed in all affairs of state. He suspected that it was his enemies at court who were behind the plot. Therefore he could take no one into his confidence until he had concrete proof; his enemies are highly placed officials, they may well have their spies in the Chancery who keep them informed about the secret deliberations in the Council. In order to obtain that concrete proof, the Censor came back to Canton. And was killed here by the misguided woman he loved.'

'How could a refined gentleman like the Censor lose his head over a vulgar Arab dancer, sir?'

'Well, for one thing she was quite different from the elegant, cultured Chinese ladies the Censor used to meet in the capital. And she must have been the first Arab woman he ever saw. For unlike Canton, in the capital one hardly sees any Arabs, and certainly no Arab girls. I imagine that it was the novelty of the experience that first appealed to him. Thereafter her strong sexual attraction must have roused his long-suppressed desire. Such burning passion would have bridged any gap in race, social status and education. Chiao Tai was also extremely fond of her, Tao Gan. You had better not mention her to him; the tragedy shocked him deeply.'

Tao Gan nodded sagely.

'Brother Chiao always has bad luck with his women,' he remarked. 'Who could have murdered her, sir?'

'Chiao Tai thinks it was Mansur. He says that Mansur was in love with her too, and that when she was introduced to Chiao Tai at Mansur's party, the Arab took her interest in Chiao Tai very badly. Mansur may have followed her when she went to Chiao Tai's inn, and climbed on the roof of the house behind it to watch them. When he saw them together, scantily dressed, he thought it was an amorous meeting, and killed her in an excess of jealousy. Plausible, but not convincing.'

Judge Dee took a sip of his tea, and resumed:

'However that may be, this tragedy has now been reduced to a side issue. The main issue is to discover who her patron was. The man who tried to involve the Censor in the Arab plot, who wanted to conceal the Censor's death, and who is responsible for the murder of Dr Soo and Mrs Pao. We must finish the task the Censor had to leave unaccomplished, namely to obtain the concrete proof needed to unmask his enemies, the cowardly traitors at court. Since it was they who took Zumurrud's patron into their employ, it is he who must reveal to us their identity. We could not have prevented the Censor from being murdered, but it is our duty to prevent his enemies from reaping the results of their infamous crimes. And they have already begun to do just that, as evidenced by the bad news contained in the secret letter from the

Grand Council. I must therefore locate this man, before I return to the capital today. My agents are questioning her maid and the crew of her boat, but I don't expect much from that routine measure. The fellow will have seen to it that no one knew his true identity.'

'What are we to do then, sir?' Tao Gan asked worriedly.

'After Chiao Tai had left,' Judge Dee replied, 'I surveyed again all that has happened here these last two days. I have tried to arrange the known facts into a more or less logical pattern, and have formed a theory. On the basis of this theory I shall take action, this very morning.' He emptied his teacup and continued, slowly tugging at his sidewhiskers:

'We do have some clues to the identity of the dancer's patron. They open up some quite interesting possibilities.' He pushed a sheet of notepaper over to Tao Gan. 'You'd better note down my list of clues, for I shall refer to them when I explain my theory.

'Now then. First, our man must occupy a fairly important position here in Canton, else the Censor's enemies at court would never have chosen him as their agent here. Those traitors are no fools; they would never select a common crook who would sell them out to the highest bidder. Second, it follows that the man's motive must be a compelling ambition. For he is risking his position and his life. They must have promised him, as a reward, a high official position, perhaps even a post in the central government. Third, he must have friends or relations in the capital, for the court hardly bothers with this region in the far south, and someone in the capital must have recommended him. Fourth, he must live in the palace or be closely connected with affairs here, for he knows every move we make. The implication of this point is that we may confine our suspicions to those people we are in regular contact with here. Fifth, he must have good connections with the underworld, as proved by his employing both Arab hooligans and Tanka stranglers. Note, Tao Gan, that these contacts are maintained through henchmen; Mansur, for instance. I shall come back to that later. Sixth, he must have a special reason for wanting to eliminate Chiao Tai; and he must hate Captain Nee, because he wanted Nee to be accused of Chiao Tai's murder. *Seventh*, he is interested in crickets. *Eighth*, he must have close relations with the blind girl. Yet that does not prevent him from making two determined efforts to kill her, as soon as he knows that she is turning against him. She, on her part, tries to help us in an indirect way. She can't bring herself to denounce him openly to us. Jot down as a query: Is she his daughter, or his mistress, perhaps? *Ninth*, he must, of course, qualify as lover and protector of Zumurrud. Have you got all that?'

'Yes sir.' Tao Gan perused his notes, then resumed, 'Shouldn't we add, sir, that he hasn't got an official position? For Zumurrud told Chiao Tai clearly that her patron, though very wealthy, had no official status, and could not, therefore, procure Chinese citizenship for her.'

'No, Tao Gan, not necessarily. For my first point, namely that he must be a man of some prominence here, implies that he must have met her incognito. Arab dancers are never invited to Chinese parties, of course. He must have made her acquaintance while visiting the flowerboat where she was employed, and kept his real identity hidden from her ever since. There was no risk of her finding that out, for she would never meet him in company.' As Tao Gan nodded, Judge Dee went on, 'The Governor heads our list. To all appearances he is a loyal, industrious, slightly fussy official; but perhaps he is at the same time a consummate actor. He has, of course, many friends in the capital who could have recommended him to the Censor's enemies, when they were casting about for a possibility of compromising the Censor in some out of the way place. That he answers my fourth point goes without saying. As to his motive, he is devoured by ambition, and they may well have promised him the post of Metropolitan Governor he is hankering after. The intermediary for his Arab contacts is Mansur, whom he employs as a kind of sub-agent.'

Tao Gan looked up and exclaimed:

'How could the Governor ever condone Mansur's scheme for

sacking Canton, sir? Such a major disturbance here would break his career, no matter who supported him at court!'

'Of course he does not intend that scheme ever to be executed. He needed it only for bringing about the Censor's ruin. That aim achieved, he will doubtless eliminate Mansur. The simplest way would be to accuse Mansur, and have him executed as a rebel. Who would believe a wretched Arab criminal if he stated in court that a man like the Governor had abetted a plan to burn and plunder his own city? If the Governor is our man, it was he who had the rumours about the Arab scheme spread, probably by a second sub-agent of his, a Chinese, who maintains contact with the Chinese underworld on his behalf. As to the Governor's attempt at eliminating Chiao Tai, that is easily explained by Chiao Tai's rendezvous with Zumurrud; Chiao Tai crossed the Tanka boats on his way to her junk, and Tanka spies must have reported that visit. The Governor hates Chiao Tai as a rival in love, and at the same time he is afraid that Zumurrud may disobey the iron rule of the "world of flowers and willows", which forbids a girl ever to talk about her clients, and tell Chiao Tai something about him that would give us a clue to his identity. As to the Governor's hatred for Captain Nee, I have a certain theory that would offer a plausible explanation; I can easily verify it, but I prefer not to go further into this now. As regards point seven, we know that the Governor is interested in crickets, and concerning point eight, I told you already that I have reason to believe he knows the blind girl. Add a query there, Tao Gan: Is she perhaps the Governor's illegitimate daughter? All right, now we come to the last point: Does he qualify as the lover of Zumurrud? Well, reputedly he has a happy family life, but the novelty of the experience may have attracted him—as it did in the case of the Censor—and I have reason to believe that he is not averse to foreign women. Further, he wouldn't mind her being a pariah, for he is a northerner. One has to be born and bred in Canton to develop that abhorrence for the pariah class. Finally, it appears that the Censor distrusted him.'

Tao Gan put his writing-brush down.

'Yes,' he said pensively, 'we have quite a substantial case against the Governor. But how are we going to prove it?'

'Not so fast! There are others on our list besides the Governor. What about Prefect Pao? The man is emotionally perturbed, for the Governor is a hard taskmaster, and he thought that his beautiful young wife was deceiving him with Captain Nee. Frustrated, he may have taken up with Zumurrud; her sneering references to her patron suggest an elderly man. Being a native of Shantung, he would have no prejudice against her race and status. And he may have fallen for the proposals of the Censor's enemies at court when they promised him a high position in the capital as reward. That would give Pao an opportunity for getting even with the Governor, and at the same time for gratifying Zumurrud's wish to obtain citizenship. As a career civil servant, the Prefect has of course plenty of acquaintances in the capital who could have recommended him to the court clique. Further, he maintains a close and continuous contact with us. He is no amateur of crickets, but his wife knew the blind girl—probably better than she made it appear. The blind girl suspects Pao, but in deference to Mrs Pao she does not want to come out into the open and say so. The Prefect hates Nee, of course, and Chiao Tai too, for the same reasons as stated in our hypothetical case against the Governor.'

The judge paused and emptied his cup. As Tao Gan refilled it for him, he resumed:

'If Prefect Pao is indeed our man, then I have to abandon of course my theory that Mrs Pao was killed by mistake. Disgusted by the failure of the two Arab assassins to murder Chiao Tai in Nee's house, the Prefect sends that same afternoon Tanka stranglers to Yau Tai-kai's establishment, to kill there his adulterous wife together with Captain Nee. Mrs Pao is indeed strangled, but the captain fails to turn up. Didn't you notice that Pao received a written message during the conference yesterday? That may have been the news that the attack in Nee's house had miscarried.'

Tao Gan looked dubious. After a while he said:

'In that case, sir, Pao must indeed have a remarkably large and efficient secret organization.'

'Why shouldn't he? He is the head of the city administration, which gives him facilities for secretly maintaining contact with Mansur as well as Chinese hooligans. Finally, both he and the Governor have the education, experience and mental capacity to organize a complicated plot, and supervise its execution by underlings such as Mansur, while they remain in the background and pull the strings.

'Education, experience and mental capacity are there also in the case of our third suspect, namely Liang Foo. Liang, by the way, answers exactly Zumurrud's description of her patron: a wealthy man without official position. And his frequenting the Flowery Pagoda to play chess with the abbot could be a cover for visiting Zumurrud in the house behind the temple. These points, however, are not important—as I shall explain presently. As to Liang's motive, it is true that he occupies already a prominent position in this city and possesses vast wealth, but he may well be chafing under his status as a merchant, and yearn for an influential official post in the capital, as occupied by the late Admiral, his illustrious father. Being born and bred in this city, and being well versed in Arab affairs, it would be an easy matter for him to establish secret contact with Mansur. The fact that he went out of his way to draw our attention to Mansur's seditious plans would indicate that he is preparing to make Mansur the scapegoat, as I explained when reviewing the case against the Governor. He is not interested in crickets, and he has no relations with the blind girl, but to those two objections I shall come anon. For there is a third, and much more serious snag. Namely, that it is utterly unthinkable that Liang Foo, a well-born Cantonese gentleman, since his youth steeped in local prejudice, would ever stoop to associate with an Arab dancer of pariah blood. In order to solve this problem, we must assume just as in the case against the Governor, that Liang has two henchmen. One is Mansur, the other a Chinese. This second sub-agent must be the other Arab expert, Mr Yau Tai-kai. All clues that don't apply to Liang, apply to him.

'Yau cannot be the main criminal. He is a self-made man, well-known locally, but without the connections in the capital to recommend him to the traitors at court. Moreover, he is a shrewd businessman, but utterly incapable of evolving a complicated political plot. However, he is a vulgar lecher, and his depraved appetite for variety in his amorous exploits may well have made him overcome his prejudice against a pariah. Yau, too, answers exactly Zumurrud's description of her patron. He hates Chiao Tai because of his rendezvous with Zumurrud, and Nee because the captain meets in Yau's own house Mrs Pao, an attractive, well-born lady whom Yau could never hope to make his mistress. He also covets the blind girl, but when he discovers that she is getting on his trail and may denounce him and his boss Liang Foo, he decides to have her murdered. When the attempt in his own house fails, he sends his Tanka stranglers after her in the Examination Hall. Only a man who knew her well could be aware of the fact that she used to hide herself there.'

Tao Gan slowly wound the three long hairs that sprouted from his left cheek round his long bony forefinger.

'Yau would indeed do nicely as patron of Zumurrud,' he said.

Judge Dee nodded and resumed :

'Finally, I come back to this morning's outrage. Mansur has gone into hiding; he wouldn't dare to follow and spy on Zumurrud. I think it was either her patron or his henchman who sent the javelin-thrower, to kill her. For he was afraid that she would reveal his identity, and he had to sacrifice her to his own safety.

'Now I shall tell you the practical consequences of all this theorizing. On the basis of the facts at our disposal now, we can't take any steps against the Governor, the Prefect or Mr Liang, for to all appearances none of them is in any way connected with the crimes perpetrated here. We must, therefore, attack the criminal, whoever he is, through his henchmen. Mansur has disappeared, but we still have Yau. I shall have him arrested at once, on the charge of being implicated in Mrs Pao's murder. The arrest will be made in complete secrecy, by my four agents. I shall send you two away on some faked mission, to divert the attention of the criminal who is watching our every move. Once Yau is under lock and key, I shall search his house, and...'

The door burst open and Chiao Tai came rushing in, breathing heavily.

'Her body is gone!' he shouted.

Judge Dee sat up in his chair.

'Gone?' he asked perplexed.

'Yes, sir. When I unlocked the door, we saw only the empty bed. There were a few drops of blood on the floor between the bed and the window, and a large smear on the sill. Someone must have entered by the window. He took the body away, over the roofs into the Arab quarter. We made house to house inquiries there, but nobody had heard or seen anything. It is...'

'What about her maid, and the people on her boat?' Judge Dee interrupted. 'Did they know who her patron was?'

'The body of the maidservant was found floating in the river, sir. Strangled. And the crew had hardly ever seen her patron; he used to come and go in the night, and always kept his face covered with his neckcloth. The swine, they...' He choked on the words.

The judge leaned back in his chair. 'Utterly preposterous!' he muttered.

Chiao Tai sat down heavily, and vigorously rubbed his moist face with the tip of his sleeve. Tao Gan bestowed a thoughtful glance upon him. He started to say something, then changed his mind and looked at Judge Dee. When the judge made no comment, Tao Gan poured a cup of tea for Chiao Tai. His friend gulped it down, then sat there staring straight ahead with unseeing eyes. There was an uneasy silence.

At last the judge got up, came round from behind his desk, and began to pace the floor, his bushy eyebrows creased in a deep frown.

Tao Gan anxiously watched Judge Dee's face every time he

walked past, but he seemed completely oblivious of his two lieutenants. Finally he halted in front of the nearest window, and
remained standing there, his hands behind his back, looking out
over the palace yard, which was sweltering in the strong morning
sun. Tao Gan pulled Chiao Tai's sleeve. He told him in a whisper
about the impending arrest of Yau Tai-kai. Chiao Tao nodded
absent-mindedly.

Suddenly Judge Dee turned round. Stepping up to them, he said
in brief, hurried phrases:

'The stealing of the body is the criminal's first mistake. But a
fatal one. I now understand his warped personality. I was partly
right, but the main point escaped me. Now I see all that has
happened here in its true light. I shall confront that man at once
with his dastardly crimes, and make him tell me who his sponsors
are!' He paused, then added with a frown, 'I can't arrest him
outright, for he is a resourceful and determined man, and he
might kill himself rather than give me the information I so desperately need. On the other hand he may have his henchmen
about him, and I must take certain precautions. You will accompany me, Tao Gan. Chiao Tai, you call my four agents, and the
captain of the palace guards!'

## XXII

The headman of Judge Dee's palankeen bearers had to knock for a long time before the high double gate opened. The bent figure of the old house steward appeared. With bleary eyes he looked astonished at the two visitors.

'Please announce us to your master,' the judge told him affably. 'Tell him that this is quite an informal visit; I want to see him for a few moments only.'

The steward led the judge and Tao Gan to the second hall and asked them to sit down on one of the enormous benches of carved ebony. Then he shuffled away.

Judge Dee silently stared at the huge coloured murals and slowly stroked his long beard. Tao Gan darted uneasy glances now at the judge, now at the door.

Sooner than Judge Dee had expected, the steward came back. 'This way, please!' he wheezed.

He took them through a corridor in the west section of the compound to a wing that seemed completely deserted. They met no one in the series of empty courtyards, whose white flagstones lay blazing in the sun. At the rear of the third, the old man entered a cool, semi-dark corridor. It led to a flight of broad wooden stairs, blackened by age.

At the top the steward halted for a moment to regain his breath, then took them up two other staircases, each narrower than the one before. They came upon a spacious landing. A faint breeze blew through the latticework of the high windows. Apparently they were on the top floor of a kind of tower. No carpet covered the floorboards, there was only a tea-table and two high-backed chairs. Above the double door in the back wall hung a huge wooden board bearing four engraved characters: 'Ancestral Hall of the Liang Family', in the impressive calligraphy of the former Emperor.

'The master is waiting for Your Excellency inside,' the steward said, as he pushed the door open.

Judge Dee gave a sign to Tao Gan who took one of the chairs at the tea-table. Then the judge entered.

He was met by the heavy smell of Indian incense. It came from the large bronze burner on the high altar in the rear of the hall, dimly lit by two candelabras. Below the altar stood a magnificent antique sacrificial table, laid out for a memorial service. Liang Foo was sitting at a lower table in front of it, wearing a ceremonial robe of dark-green brocade and the high cap indicating his literary degree.

He rose quickly and came to meet the judge.

'I do hope you did not mind all those steps, sir!' he said with a courteous smile.

'Not at all!' Judge Dee assured him quickly. After a glance at the life-size picture of Admiral Liang in full armour hanging on the wall opposite, he added, 'I deeply regret that I have to interrupt memorial rites for your late father.'

'Your Excellency is welcome at any time,' Liang said calmly. 'And my late father won't mind interruption; he was always wont to put official matters before his family interests—as his children knew only too well! Be seated, please!'

He led his guest to a chair on the right of the table. On it lay a large chess-board, a few black and white pieces distributed over it in a pattern suggesting the final phase of a game. By its side stood two brass bowls, one containing the discarded white pieces, the other the black. Liang had apparently been studying a chess problem. Sitting down and straightening his robe, Judge Dee said:

'I wanted to discuss with you a few new facts that have come to light, Mr Liang.' He waited till his host had seated himself on the other side of the table, then added, 'More in particular about the theft of a woman's dead body.'

JUDGE DEE DISCUSSES A CHESS PROBLEM

Liang raised his curved eyebrows.

'What a curious object to steal! You must tell me more about it! But let's first have a cup of tea!'

He rose and went to the tea-table in the corner.

The judge quickly looked round him. The flickering light of the candles shone on the offerings on the sacrificial table, covered with a piece of embroidered brocade. On it stood golden vessels heaped with rice cakes and fruit, between two fine antique vases filled with fresh flowers. The broad niche above the sacrificial table, where the soul-tablets of the ancestors are always displayed, was hidden by a scarlet curtain. The heavy fragrance of the incense could not conceal the curious smell of foreign spices, which seemed to come from behind the scarlet curtain. Raising his head, the judge saw that the room was very high, and the grey incense clouds clustered about the blackened rafters. The bare floor consisted of broad wooden boards, polished to a dark, glossy finish. He rose abruptly. Pulling his chair round to the left side of the table, he remarked casually to Liang, who was coming up to him:

'I'll sit here, if I may. The light of the candles is bothering me.'

'Certainly!' Liang turned his own chair round so as to face the judge. Sitting down, he resumed: 'From here we have a better view of the ancestral portrait.'

The judge watched him as he poured the tea in two small cups of blue porcelain. He placed one in front of Judge Dee, then cupped the other in his hands. The judge noticed through the thin, long fingers a crack in the delicate glaze. Liang pensively looked at the picture.

'It is an excellent likeness,' he said, 'done by a great artist. Do you notice how carefully he painted every small detail?' Putting down his cup, he rose and walked over to the picture. Standing with his back to the judge, he pointed out the details of the broad-sword lying across the Admiral's knees.

Judge Dee shifted their tea cups. He quickly emptied that of

Liang in the bowl of chess-pieces nearest to him, then got up and stepped up to his host, the empty cup in his hand.

'I hope you still have that sword?' he asked. As Liang nodded, he went on, 'I too possess a famous sword, inherited from my ancestors. Its name is "Rain Dragon".'

'Rain Dragon? What a curious name!'

'I'll tell you its story, some other time. Could I have another cup of tea, Mr Liang?'

'By all means!'

After they had sat down again, Liang refilled Judge Dee's cup, then emptied his own. Folding his thin hands in his sleeves, he said with a smile:

'Let's now have the story of the stolen body!'

'Before I come to that,' Judge Dee said briskly, 'I would like to give you a brief sketch of the background, so to speak.' As Liang nodded eagerly, the judge took his fan from his sleeve, and leaned back in his chair. Slowly fanning himself, he began:

'When I arrived in Canton the day before yesterday to trace the missing Censor, I only knew that his business was in some way or another connected with the Arabs here. In the course of my inquiries I found that I had an opponent who knew perfectly well the real object of my visit, and who was watching every move we made. When I had discovered the Censor, murdered by a Tanka poison, I assumed that one of the Censor's enemies at court had engaged a local agent to lure the Censor to Canton, and have him killed here by Arab conspirators. But I perceived also other forces that seemed intent on thwarting the evil scheme. As my investigation went on, things became ever more complicated. Arab hooligans and Tanka stranglers were roaming about, and a mysterious blind girl kept flitting in and out of the picture. It was only this very morning that I at last obtained a definite clue. Namely when the dancer Zumurrud told Colonel Chiao that it was she who had poisoned the Censor, and that her patron knew all about it. She kept to the rule of the "world of flowers and willows" that a girl should never divulge the name of a customer. I suspected the

Governor, the Prefect and thought in passing of you. It led me nowhere.'

He snapped his fan close and put it back into his sleeve. Liang had been listening with a bland air of polite interest. Judge Dee sat up straight and resumed:

'So I tried another approach, namely to piece together a mental picture of my opponent. Then I realized that he had the typical mind of a chess-player. A man who always stays in the background and makes others act for him, moving them about like chess-men on the board. I and my assistants were also his chessmen, we were an integral part of his game. This realization was an important step forward. For a crime is half-solved already when one has understood the criminal's mind.

'How very true!'

'I then reconsidered you, the expert chess-player,' the judge resumed. 'You certainly had the subtle intellect required for evolving a difficult scheme, and for supervising its execution. I also could imagine a good motive, namely your frustration at not being able to follow in the footsteps of your illustrious father. On the other hand, however, you were definitely not the type of person to fall in love with an Arab dancer tainted by pariah blood. I decided that if you should be our man, then one of your henchmen would be the dancer's lover. Since Mr Yau Tai-kai would eminently fit that role, I resolved to have him arrested. Just then, however, the theft of the dancer's body was reported to me. And that made me come straight to you.'

'Why to me?' Liang asked calmly.

'Because when I then began to think about the dead dancer and about the Tanka and their savage passions, I suddenly remembered the chance remark of a poor Chinese prostitute who had been a slave of the Tanka. At their drunken orgies the Tanka used to boast to her that about eighty years ago an important Chinese had secretly married one of their girls, and that their son had become a famous warrior. Then I thought of the peculiar features of the Subduer of the South Seas.' He pointed at the picture on the wall. 'Look at the high cheekbones, flat nose and low forehead. "Old Monkey-face", as his sailors affectionately nicknamed the Admiral.'

Liang nodded slowly.

'So you have unearthed our jealously guarded family secret! Yes, my grandmother was indeed a Tanka. My grandfather committed a crime in marrying her!' He grinned. There was a malignant glint in his eyes when he resumed, 'Imagine, the famous Admiral tainted by the blood of an outcast! He was not as fine a gentleman as people always thought him to be, eh?'

Ignoring the sneering remark, Judge Dee continued:

'Then I realized that I had been thinking of the wrong game of chess. Namely of our Chinese literary chess played with pieces all of equal value; or the military one, representing a battle between two opposing generals. I suddenly understood that I ought to have referred to the game as people say it is played in India. There the king and the queen are the two most important pieces. And in the particular game of chess you were playing it was not primarily a high position in the capital that was the gage, but the possession of the queen.'

'How cleverly put!' Liang said with a thin smile. 'May I ask in what stage the game is now?'

'The last. The king is lost, for the queen is dead.'

'Yes, she is dead,' Liang said quietly. 'But she is lying is state, as befits a queen. The queen of the game of life. Her spirit now presides over these solemn death rites, rejoices in rich offerings, in fresh flowers. Look, she smiles her beautiful smile....' He rose and quickly pulled the curtain above the altar aside.

Judge Dee gasped at this shocking, unspeakable outrage. Here in the sacred ancestral hall of the Liang family, facing the dead Admiral's portrait, and in the niche destined for the soul-tablets of the departed, Zumurrud's naked body lay stretched out on the gold-lacquered altar top. She was lying on her back, her hands folded behind her head, her full lips curved in a mocking smile.

'She has only received preliminary treatment,' Liang remarked

178

casually, as he drew the curtain shut again. 'Tonight the work will be continued. Has to be, in this hot weather.'

He resumed his seat. The judge had now mastered himself. He asked coldly:

'Shall we reconstruct the game together, move by move?'

'I'd like that very much,' Liang replied gravely. 'An analysis of the game always affords me the keenest pleasure.'

'Now then, the gage was Zumurrud. You had bought her, so you possessed her body. That was all. You thought you would win her love if only you could gratify the one desire that dominated her, namely to be raised from her pariah status to that of a great Chinese lady. Since that could be done only by one of the highest metropolitan officials, you decided you would become one of those. You had to act upon that decision quickly, for you were obsessed by the fear of losing her, either to a man she would fall in love with, or to one who could make her realize her ambitions. Mansur fell in love with her. Apparently she did not care for him, but you feared nonetheless that sooner or later her Arab blood would speak, and therefore you wanted to eliminate Mansur. Then you heard from one of your friends in the capital that a powerful person at court, close to the Empress and her clique, was looking for a means to ruin the Imperial Censor Lew, and was willing to reward handsomely anyone who could help to achieve that aim. That was your chance! You began at once to work out a scheme, carefully planning the moves that would win you the queen. You put an ingenious proposal before that person at court. You...'

'Let's have everything neat and orderly!' Liang interrupted testily. 'That person is Wang, the Chief Eunuch of the Imperial Seraglio. Our contact was a mutual friend, the wealthy wine-merchant who is purveyor to the court.'

Judge Dee grew pale. The Emperor mortally ill; the Empress tormented by her perverse passions; the sinister, hybrid figure of the Chief Eunuch ... he suddenly saw the hideous pattern.

'Now guess what position he promised me! Yours! And with the backing of the Empress I shall rise higher still! My father was the Subduer of the South Seas. I shall be the Subduer of the Empire!'

'Quite,' Judge Dee said wearily. 'Well, you proposed to lure the Censor to Canton by giving him to understand that the Arabs were planning a revolt, with the connivance of an unnamed person at Court. You would fan Mansur's foolish ambitions, so that when the Censor came to investigate he would indeed find something brewing here. Then you would have him murdered, and accuse Mansur. When questioned under severe torture, Mansur would be made to confess that the Censor had backed his plot. Neat solution! Mansur out of the way, the Censor dead and his reputation smeared, and you going to the capital, together with Zumurrud.

'The game opened exactly as you had planned. The Censor came here incognito, to check the rumours about unrest among the Arabs. He did not dare to inform the authorities of his visit, because it had been suggested to him that a person at court was involved in the scheme, and he wanted to discover who that was, of course. However, he came also for another reason, then unknown to you. On his first visit to Canton the Censor had met Zumurrud, and they had fallen in love with each other.'

'How could I have foreseen that she would meet him in that confounded temple?' Liang muttered. 'She...'

'That is where life differs from chess, Mr Liang,' Judge Dee cut him short. 'In real life you have to reckon with unknown factors. Well, after the Censor had studied the situation here together with Dr Soo, he suspected that a trap was being laid for him. He approached Mansur and feigned to sympathize with his seditious plans. He probably even helped Mansur and two of his accomplices to smuggle arms into the city. When Mansur reported this to you, you knew that your scheme was succeeding even better than you had expected: if Mansur was brought to justice, he would have to confess only the truth! But since you realized that the Censor was fooling Mansur, you decided to speed up his murder.

'Then Zumurrud poisoned the Censor. She had to tell you everything, and ...'

'*Had* to tell me, you say?' Liang shouted suddenly. 'She always insisted on telling me! Every time, directly after she had slept with one of her vulgar, stray lovers! Tormented me by telling all the sordid, unspeakable details, then laughed at me!' Burying his face in his hands, he sobbed. 'That was her revenge, and I ... I could do nothing. She was stronger than me. The fiery blood pulsated in her veins, while mine was thin, thinned by two generations....' He looked up, his face haggard. Taking hold of himself, he said harshly, 'All right, she had not told me about the Censor before, because he was going to take her away. Proceed! Time is getting short.'

'Just at that time,' Judge Dee continued calmly, 'I and my two assistants arrived. Ostensibly to inspect foreign trade. You suspected that I had come to investigate the Censor's disappearance. You had my two lieutenants closely watched, and found your suspicions confirmed by the interest they displayed in the Arabs here. You decided that we fitted nicely into your game. For who could better denounce Mansur's treacherous scheme than the President of the Metropolitan Court? Your only problem was Dr Soo. Zumurrud had said that Dr Soo was ignorant of her affair with the Censor, but you had to make sure. Now Dr Soo must have become worried when the Censor did not return to their inn that night, and the next morning, that is the day before yesterday, he roamed along the waterfront looking for him. You had him followed by one of Mansur's Arab assassins, and one of your own Tanka stranglers. They reported in the afternoon that Dr Soo apparently knew Colonel Chiao, and that he followed my lieutenant when he left the wine-house. You ordered the Tanka to assist the Arab in killing Dr Soo, but to strangle him before he could kill Chiao Tai. For you wanted to spare Colonel Chiao so that he could follow up Dr Soo's murder, which would, in due course, further strengthen the case against Mansur.

'Then, however, you had a stroke of bad luck. My man Tao Gan happened to meet the blind girl. She must be your sister, the one you said had died in an accident. For Tao Gan mistook Mrs Pao for her, and so did your Tanka killers whom you had sent to Yau's house. She evidently wanted to prevent you from ruining yourself, and...'

'The sanctimonious little fool!' Liang interrupted angrily. 'She is the cause of all my troubles, for she wilfully threw away a splendid future, by my side. She and I inherited my father's talents; our younger sister was nothing but a stupid woman, swayed by her ludicrous petty passions! But Lan-lee! When the old houseteacher was reading the classics with us, she would understand at once the most difficult passages! And she was beautiful! My boyhood ideal of the perfect woman! I often spied on her when she was bathing, her...' Suddenly he fell silent. He swallowed a few times before he went on, 'After we had grown up and our parents died, I spoke to her about our ancient myths, of the Founding Saints of our Empire, who took their sisters as spouse. But she, she refused, said awful, terrible things to me, said she would leave me, and never come back. So I put boiling oil into her eyes while she was asleep. For how could I allow a woman who had dared to scorn me ever to look upon another man? Instead of cursing me, she pitied me, the little hypocrite! In a rage I set fire to her room, I wanted to ... to...' He choked, his face distorted in impotent anger. After a while he resumed, calmer, 'She had said she would never come back, but recently she would come to snoop here in my house, the slick bitch. I heard that she had met my two men who brought the Censor's body here before taking it to the temple, and had stolen that damned cricket. Although she knew nothing of my scheme, she was clever enough to put two and two together. Fortunately my men spotted her when that assistant of yours took her home, and they eaves dropped on their conversation. The nasty bitch was setting you on my trail by saying that she had caught the cricket near the temple where the Censor's body was. So I brought her here and locked her up. But she escaped the next morning, just after breakfast. How she managed to do that, I still...'

'It was indeed the clue of the cricket that led me to the temple,' Judge Dee said. 'My discovery of the Censor's dead body was an unexpected setback for you; you had wanted the body to disappear, so that the Tanka poison would not be identified. Later you would make Mansur confess that he had thrown it into the sea, I presume. However, you succeeded in turning this setback into your favour. During my visit here you cleverly suggested that the Arabs had close contacts with the Tanka, implying that Mansur had ample opportunity for obtaining the poison. So everything was going very well indeed. Then, for the second time, the human element cut across your beautiful game. Colonel Chiao met Zumurrud and fell in love with her. Your spies reported that he visited her on the boat yesterday morning, evidently slept with her. What if she had persuaded him to spirit her away to the capital? What if she had inadvertently given him a clue to your identity? Chiao Tai had to go. He was to be killed in Nee's house.' The judge looked thoughtfully at his host and asked, 'By the way, how did you know that Chiao Tai would call there a second time?'

Liang Foo shrugged his narrow shoulders.

'Two of my men had established a regular watchpost in the house at the back of Nee's, directly after your man Chiao's first visit to Nee. Mansur was hiding there too. When he saw your lieutenant going there, he sent his two men over the roofs at once to kill him with one of the captain's swords. I thought that quite a good idea of Mansur, for Nee deserved to die on the scaffold, as a murderer. The lecher debauched my sister.'

'He did not. But let's not digress; let's return to the game of chess; its last, concluding phase. Your chess-men had got completely out of hand. My scheme of exposing the faked head of the Censor worked. Early this morning Zumurrud went to Colonel Chiao's inn, and asked him to take her to me so that she could claim her reward. There she was killed. Now the queen has been taken and you have lost the game.'

'I had to have her killed,' Liang muttered. 'She was going to leave me, to betray me. I used the best javelin-thrower I knew. She did not suffer.' He stared into space, absent-mindedly stroking his long moustache. Suddenly he looked up. 'Never measure a man's wealth by what he possesses, Dee. Measure it by what he failed to acquire. She despised me, because she knew me for what I really am, a coward, afraid of others, and of myself. And so she wanted to leave me. But now, embalmed, her beauty will be with me forever. I shall talk to her, talk to her every night, of my love. No one will come between us anymore.' Righting himself, he added fiercely; 'And least of all you, Dee! For you are on the verge of dying!'

'As if your murdering me would help you!' the judge said with scorn. 'Do you think I am such a fool as to come here and confront you with your crimes, without having acquainted the Governor and my lieutenants with all the facts I have discovered against you?'

'Yes, I certainly do think so!' Liang answered smugly. 'As soon as I knew that you were going to be my opponent, I made a careful analysis of your personality, you see. You are a famous man, Dee. The many astounding criminal cases you have solved during the last twenty years have become public property, they are told and re-told in the tea-houses and wine-shops all over the Empire. I know exactly how you work! You have a logical mind, rare intuitive power, and an uncanny knack of connecting seemingly unconnected facts. You pick your suspect, mostly through your shrewd insight into human nature, and relying heavily on your intuition. Then you pounce on him, bringing to bear on him the full force of your personality—which is rather overwhelming, I admit. You get your man to confess in one brilliant, spectacular move—and you explain afterwards. That is your typical method. You never bother about building up a complete case, patiently plodding along till you have collected conclusive evidence, and sharing your discoveries with your assistants, as other criminal investigators do. For that would run counter to your character.

Therefore I know most assuredly that you did not tell the Governor a thing. And your two lieutenants only very little. And therefore, my dear Counsellor, you are going to die here.' He bestowed upon the judge a patronizing look, then went on placidly, 'My dear sister shall die here too. My Tanka stranglers failed to kill her twice, first in Yau's house and then again in the Examination Hall, but I know she is here in this house now, and I shall catch her at last. With her goes the only witness that could testify against me. For the stupid Tanka I employ know nothing, and they live in a world apart where they can never be traced. Mansur has his suspicions, but that clever scoundrel is on the high seas by now, in an Arab ship bound for his own country. The Censor's case will be recorded for what it essentially was: a murder of passion, committed by a misguided pariah woman, killed in her turn by a jealous Arab lover who stole her dead body. Neat case!'
After a sigh he continued: 'It will be universally regretted that in your zeal to solve the case you over-exerted yourself, and died from a heart attack while visiting me for a consultation. Everybody knows that you have been working too hard for many years, and human strength has its natural limits. The poison I used produces exactly the same symptoms as heart failure, and it can't be traced. Got the recipe from Zumurrud, as a matter of fact. Well, that such a famous man breathes his last in my humble house I consider a signal honour! I shall call your man Tao Gan inside, later, and he shall help me with the preparations for conveying your body to the palace. The Governor shall take all the other routine measures, I trust. Your two lieutenants are competent and intelligent—I never underestimate my enemies—and they'll doubtless have their suspicions. But by the time they have convinced the Governor to take a closer look at my affairs, all traces of what really happened here will have been effaced. And don't forget that I shall be appointed as your successor soon! As to the men you so thoughtfully posted in my front courtyard, and the guards who surround my house, I shall explain that you expected a murderous attack on me by Arab scoundrels. I shall let your men discover

one Arab hooligan here, and he shall be duly executed. Well, that is all.'

'I see,' Judge Dee said. 'And so it was the tea. I must confess that I had expected a more ingenious manner of attack. A secret trap door, or something coming down from the ceiling, for instance. You'll have noticed that I took precautions against that by shifting my chair.'

'But you hadn't forgotten that old trick of the poisoned tea either,' Liang said with an indulgent smile. 'You shifted our cups, as I had expected you would while I had turned my back on you; mere routine on the part of an experienced investigator like you, of course. The poison was smeared on the inside of my cup, you know. Your own cup contained only harmless tea. So you drank the poison, and it should start to work by now, the dose was carefully graded. No, don't move! If you rise the poison will work at once. Don't you feel a dull pain in your heart region?'

'I don't,' Judge Dee said dryly. 'And I shan't either. Didn't I tell you I knew you have the chess-player's mind? He thinks in sequences of connected moves. I knew that if you chose poison as your weapon, you'd never adopt the crude method of putting it in my cup. That was confirmed when I noticed that your cup was cracked, which meant that you wanted to be able to make sure that I had indeed made the anticipated move of shifting our cups. Well, I made a second move. I not only shifted the cups, but also their content. I poured the poisoned tea in this bowl of chees-pieces here, you know, and the harmless tea into the cracked cup. Then I poured the poisoned tea from the chess-bowl into my cup, now yours. You can see it for yourself.' He took the chess bowl and let Liang look at the wet chess-men inside.

Liang sprang up. He went to the sacrificial table, but half-way he halted. Swaying on his feet, he clasped his hands to his breast.

'The queen! I want to see her. I...' he brought out in a choking voice.

Stumbling ahead, he succeeded in grasping the edge of the sacrificial table. Then he gasped for air; a convulsive movement shook his thin frame. He fell, dragging the table cover down with him. The sacrificial vessels dropped on to the floor with a loud crash.

## XXIII

The door burst open and Tao Gan came rushing in. He halted abruptly when he saw Judge Dee bent over Liang's prone figure. The judge felt Liang's heart. He was dead. As the judge began to search the corpse, Tao Gan asked in a whisper:

'How did he die, sir?'

'He believed me when I told him he had drunk the poison he had intended for me, and the shock brought about a heart attack. That is as it should be, for he knew secrets of state that should never be divulged.' He briefly told Tao Gan about the shifting of the cups. 'The poison I poured into that chess-bowl; it is half full of chess-pieces. Liang saw that they were wet, but could not see that the bowl contained in fact the entire content of the cracked cup. Take this bowl with you.' Pulling a long, razor-sharp blade from the leather sheath he had found in Liang's sleeve, he added, 'Take this too. Be very careful, there is some brown substance on its tip.'

Tao Gan took a piece of oiled paper from his sleeve. While he was wrapping the bowl and the dagger, he said:

'You should have actually let him drink his own infernal poison, sir! Suppose he hadn't believed you? Then he'd have killed you with that poisoned knife. One scratch would have sufficed!'

Judge Dee shrugged.

'Until he thought that I had drunk the tea, I took care to stay out of his reach.' Then he added, 'Getting on in years, one isn't so sure of oneself any more, Tao Gan. One tends more and more to shift decisions on matters of life and death to a Higher Tribunal.' He turned round and left the hall, followed by his lieutenant.

On the landing stood a slender young woman, quietly dressed

in a dark-brown robe. Her opaque eyes were staring straight ahead.

'She came just now, sir,' Tao Gan explained hurriedly. 'To warn us about Liang.'

'Your brother is dead, Miss Liang,' Judge Dee told her soberly. 'He had a heart attack.'

The blind girl nodded slowly.

'He had been suffering from heart trouble, these last years,' she said. After a pause she asked suddenly, 'Did he kill the Censor?'

'No. Zumurrud did.'

'She was a dangerous woman,' she said pensively. 'I always feared that my brother's devotion to her would be his undoing. When I heard that his men had brought here the dead body of a high official who had been Zumurrud's lover, I thought my brother must have murdered him. I found the room where the corpse was, and while the two men were busy disguising themselves as constables, I quickly went through its sleeves and delivered the Golden Bell from its crushed cage. I also took what felt like an envelope, because it was the only paper the dead man carried, and therefore had to be important.'

'I presume it was your sister, Mrs Pao, who slipped that envelope into Colonel Chiao's sleeve yesterday morning, very early?'

'Yes, sir. She was an old friend of Captain Nee and had just delivered a note asking him to meet her that afternoon in Mr Yau's house. She had planned to leave my package addressed to Mr Tao in the tribunal, but when she saw Mr Tao's friend, she thought it safer to let him have it.' She paused and pushed her hair back from her smooth forehead. She went on, 'We saw each other regularly, in secret of course. For both my brother and I wanted it to be believed that I was dead. But I could not bear my own sister sorrowing over me, and after a year I went to see her and told her I was still alive. She was always worrying about me, although I kept assuring her I had all I needed. Yet she insisted on introducing me to all kinds of people who might buy crickets from me. Yesterday morning, after I had fled from here, I told her that I

189                                                             G*

feared our brother was getting into trouble. It was at my request that she went through the desk in his bedroom when you were visiting him with her husband, sir. She took two maps, and later explained to me that on one Mr Chiao's inn had been marked. I had hoped to meet her again in Mr Yau's house that same afternoon, but I just missed her. Who murdered her, sir? She had no enemies, and although my brother despised her, he did not hate her, as he did me.'

'She was killed through a misunderstanding,' Judge Dee answered, then added quickly, 'I am most grateful for the help you gave us, Miss Liang!'

She raised her thin hands in a futile gesture.

'I hoped you would find the Censor's murderer, sir, before my brother became too deeply involved.'

'How did you manage to conceal yourself so effectively?' the judge asked, curious.

'By keeping to those places I knew well,' she replied with a faint smile. 'This old house I know, of course, like the palm of my hand! All the hidden rooms, as well as many secret passages and emergency exits my brother did not know of. And I am also thoroughly familiar with the Examination Hall, which was my favourite hideout. When Mr Tao and his friend had seen me, I slipped out by the back entrance and hid in the godown where the palankeens are stored. Later I heard a woman scream. What happened there, sir?'

'My two lieutenants ran into a vagabond who was molesting a woman,' Judge Dee replied. 'Well, your brother had Zumurrud's body brought here to the house, Miss Liang. I shall have it removed to the tribunal at once. Is there anything I can do for you? Now you'll have to take charge of this house and all your brother's affairs, you know.'

'I shall call on an old uncle of my mother. He shall see to my brother's burial, and...' She shook her head disconsolately. After a while she went on in a barely audible voice, 'It's all my fault. I shouldn't have left him, left him alone with all the terrible thoughts that were tormenting him. And he was only a boy then! Used to play every day in a corner of the garden with his toy soldiers, imagining the great battles he would fight, later ... But then he learned he was unfit for a military career. And after I had left him, he realized that he was incapable of possessing a woman. The second blow broke him; he wanted to kill himself. But he met Zumurrud, and she ... she proved to be the first and only woman he could embrace. He lived only for her; but she didn't care for him, told him so in cruel, humiliating words.... It's all my fault—I should have refused him more gently, I should have tried to interest him in another woman, a kind woman, who would ... But I was too young, I didn't understand. I didn't understand....'

She buried her face in her hands. Judge Dee gave a sign to Tao Gan. They went downstairs.

Chiao Tai was waiting in the large hall, with four agents and a dozen constables. Judge Dee told them that robbers had concealed themselves in the house, and that Mr Liang had died from a heart attack when he had suddenly come upon one of them. They were to make a thorough search under the direction of Chiao Tai and arrest any persons found there. Thereupon he took the eldest agent apart, and told him that Mansur had gone aboard one of the Arab ships anchored in the estuary of the Pearl River. The agent was to go at once to the harbour-master, and have him send four fast military junks to overtake and arrest Mansur. As the agent hurried away, Judge Dee ordered the old steward to take him and Tao Gan to Mr Liang's bedroom.

Tao Gan discovered a secret wall safe behind the bedstead. He picked the lock, but the safe proved to contain only contracts and other important papers relating to the routine of Liang's business. The judge had not expected to find any incriminating documents, for Liang was much too clever to keep any. He trusted he would find all the written proof he wanted in the capital, when the residence of the Chief Eunuch was raided by his men. He ordered Tao Gan to take the necessary measures for removing Zumurrud's body secretly to the tribunal, then he ascended his palankeen and was carried back to the palace.

He had an adjutant take him straight to the Governor's private study on the second floor of the main building.

It was a small but elegantly furnished room. The arched windows looked out over the palace garden and the lotus lake. A teaset of eggshell porcelain and a jade bowl filled with white roses stood on the tea-table to the left, the right wall being taken up entirely by a heavy ebony bookcase. The Governor was sitting behind a high desk that stood in the rear. He was giving instructions to an old clerk standing by the side of his chair.

When the Governor saw Judge Dee, he hurriedly rose and came round from behind his desk to greet him. He invited the judge to be seated in the comfortable armchair next to the tea-table, and himself took the chair opposite. After the old clerk had served tea, the Governor dismissed him. Leaning forward with his hands on his knees, he asked tensely:

'What's afoot, Excellency? I saw the proclamation you issued. Who is that high official?'

Judge Dee eagerly emptied his teacup. He suddenly noticed how tired he was. He put his cup down, loosened the collar of his robe and then said placidly:

'It was a most unfortunate tragedy. The Censor Lew was murdered here, you know. The dead body I found in the Temple of the Flowery Pagoda was his, in fact. I shall now give you the official version of what happened. The Censor came to Canton because of a love affair with a local girl. She had a lover already, and that scoundrel poisoned him. My proclamation was a ruse. It made a friend of the murderer come forward and denounce him. He has been arrested, and even now is being conveyed to the capital, for a secret trial. You will understand that even this official version, concise as it is, must not be divulged. The central government does not like the indiscretions of high officials to be bruited about.'

'I see,' the Governor said slowly.

'I fully realize how awkward your position is,' Judge Dee said gently. 'I remember vividly the occasions when a ranking official from the capital visited my territory, when I was still a district magistrate. But such things can't be helped; they are inherent in our administrative system.'

The Governor gave the judge a grateful glance. Then he asked:

'Would it be possible to tell me why the residence of Mr Liang has been surrounded by military guards?'

'I received information that Tanka robbers had entered his house. I went there to warn him, but found that he had met one, and had died from a heart attack. My lieutenants are now rounding up the robbers. This affair too must be treated with the utmost discretion. For Mr Liang was a distinguished citizen, and if it became known among the people of Canton that it was Tanka who had caused his death, there might be communal trouble. You shall leave this matter entirely in the hands of my two lieutenants.' He took a sip from his tea. 'As to the Arab question, I have taken measures for the arrest of Mansur, the ringleader. After he has been put behind lock and key, the emergency measures for the maintenance of the public peace can be cancelled. I shall lay before the Grand Council the proposal I outlined to you yesterday relating to the segregation of barbarians. So there need be no fear of future trouble from them.'

'I see,' the Governor said again. After a while he resumed, rather diffidently, 'I hope that all the ah ... irregularities that occurred here will not be ascribed to an inefficient administration, sir. If the authorities in the capital received the impression that I had been er ... remiss in my duties, I...' He darted a worried glance at his guest.

But Judge Dee did not take the hint. Instead he said quietly:

'In the course of my investigation there have come to light a few facts not germane to the main issue, yet not without importance. In the first place the circumstances of the death of Mrs Pao. The Prefect is looking into those, and I prefer that you leave it to him to wind up that tragic case. Second, I learned about another tragedy that occurred here, many years ago. Regarding a

Persian lady who committed suicide.' He cast a quick glance at his host. The Governor's face had suddenly paled. The judge went on, 'When we met in the garden pavilion yesterday morning, you were most eager to take the investigation of the Persian community out of my hands. Since apparently you have made a special study of their affairs, you can supply me with more details about this tragedy, I suppose.'

The Governor averted his face. He stared out through the window at the green palace roofs. Judge Dee took a large white rose from the bowl, and inhaled its delicate fragrance. The Governor began in a strained voice:

'It happened many years ago, when I had been sent out to serve as a junior assistant in the tribunal here. My first post, as a matter of fact. I was young and impressionable, and the exotic features of the foreign communities captured my fancy. I frequented the house of a Persian merchant, and met his daughter. We fell in love with each other. She was a refined, beautiful girl. I failed to notice that she was highly-strung, of an extremely nervous disposition.' He turned round and looking the judge full in the face, went on, 'I loved her so much I decided to give up my career and marry her. One day she let me know that she could not see me any more. Like the foolish youngster I was, I suspected nothing, I thought she wanted to end our relationship. In despair I began to frequent a Chinese courtesan. Then, after some months, she sent a message. It said that I was to meet her that day at dusk, in the Temple of the Flowery Pagoda. I found her sitting in the tea-pavilion, all alone.' He lowered his eyes and fixed them on his tightly clasped hands. 'She was wearing a long saffron robe; a thin silk shawl was draped round her small head. I wanted to speak, but she cut me short and told me to take her up the pagoda. In silence we climbed the steep stairs, higher and higher, till we were on the narrow platform of the highest storey, the ninth. She went to stand by the balustrade. The rays of the setting sun threw a reddish glow over the sea of roofs, far below. Without looking at me, she told me in a strange, impersonal voice that she had twin girls by me.

Since I had deserted her, she had drowned them. While I stood there petrified, she suddenly stepped over the balustrade. I ... I ...'

He had been controlling his voice with a great effort, but now he broke down completely and buried his face in his hands. Judge Dee caught a little of what he was muttering: 'I meant well, heaven is my witness! And she ... It was just that ... that we were too young. Too young. ...'

The judge waited for the Governor to regain his self-control. He slowly turned the rose round in his hand, watching the white petals as they dropped on to the shining black table top, one by one. When the Governor at last raised his head, the judge put the flower back into the bowl and said:

'She must have loved you very dearly, else she would not have become possessed by such a fierce desire to hurt you. And so she killed herself, and told you the lie about killing your two daughters.' As the Governor was about to jump up, Judge Dee raised his hand. 'Yes, that was a lie. She gave the twins to a Chinese friend. When he went bankrupt, a Chinese with Persian blood, who had known her mother, took them and looked after them well. They have grown up into charming young girls, I am told.'

'Where are they? Who is the man?' the Governor burst out.

'His name is Nee, the sea captain I mentioned to you once. He is a mystic, a somewhat peculiar man, but a man of principles, I must admit. Although he had been told that you had basely deceived the young Persian lady, he preferred to remain silent, because he thought that no one would be served by stirring up this old affair, least of all the two girls. You might go to see him some day; incognito, perhaps. The captain has technically become your son-in-law by now, if my information is correct.' The judge rose. Straightening his robe, he added, 'I shall forget everything you have told me here and now.'

While the Governor, too deeply moved to speak, was conducting him to the door, Judge Dee remarked:

'Before I broached the subject of the Persian lady, you gave me to understand that you are worrying about your reputation in the capital. Now I want to tell you that I shall deem it my duty to report to the Grand Council that I found you an excellent administrator of exemplary zeal.' Cutting short the Governor's confused protestations of gratitude, he concluded, 'I have been ordered to return to the capital without delay, and I shall leave Canton this afternoon. Kindly see to it that a mounted convoy is put in readiness for me. Many thanks for your hospitality! Goodbye!'

## XXIV

Judge Dee ate a late noon meal in his private dining-room, together with Chiao Tai and Tao Gan. His two lieutenants had arrested in the Liang mansion two Tanka and three Chinese hooligans, and also an Arab assassin. The six men had been put in the tribunal jail.

During the meal Judge Dee gave his two assistants a full account of all that had happened. He only omitted his last conversation with the Governor. After he had also outlined his official version of the Censor's case, he pursued:

'Thus the task the Censor set himself, which cost him his life, has now been accomplished. The Chief Eunuch will get his deserts, and his political party will collapse. The Crown Prince will not be ousted from his rightful position, and the clique of the Empress will retreat into the background—for the time being.' The judge fell silent. He was thinking of the Empress, handsome, energetic, extremely capable, but completely ruthless, swayed by strange passions and devoured by ambition for herself and her kin. In this first, indirect clash he had got the better of her. But suddenly he had a dark premonition of other, more direct clashes to come, and of bloodshed, much wanton bloodshed. He felt the chilling presence of the Spirit of Death.

Chiao Tai worriedly looked at Judge Dee's drawn face. There were heavy black pouches under his eyes, deep lines marked his hollow cheeks. With an effort the judge collected himself. He said slowly:

'The Censor's murder may be my last criminal case. From now on I shall probably devote myself entirely and exclusively to political problems. If some of these, like the Censor's case, should have criminal aspects, I shall order others to deal with them. Liang

Foo's remarks about my methods of criminal detection were very much to the point. They made me realize that the time is coming for me to close my career as a criminal investigator. My methods have become too widely known, and clever criminals can use this knowledge to their advantage. My methods are part of my personality, and I am too old now to change that. Younger and more competent men will continue where I left off. A special convoy will take me back to the capital later this afternoon, when the worst heat is over. You two will follow as soon as you have wound up the Censor's case. You will keep strictly to the official version, and see to it that nothing transpires of what really happened here in Canton. You need not worry about Mansur; he has fled to an Arab ship, but fast military junks have been sent to the estuary to overtake him. He will be executed in secret, for he knows affairs of state that must on no account reach the ears of the Khalif.' He rose and added, 'We all need an hour or so of good rest! You two need not return to your dismal lodgings downtown. Take your siesta in my dressing-room; there are two spare couches there. After the siesta you may see me off, then set to work. I trust you'll be able to leave Canton tomorrow.'

As the three men were walking to the door, Tao Gan said bleakly:

'We've been here only two days, but I have seen all I want of Canton!'

'Me too!' Chiao Tai said curtly. Then he added in a matter-of-fact voice, 'I am looking forward to resuming my work in the capital, sir.'

Judge Dee cast a quick glance at his lieutenant's pale, haggard face. He reflected sadly that one lives and learns—at a price. He gave his lieutenants a warm smile and said:

'I am glad to hear that, Chiao Tai.'

They ascended the broad staircase that led to Judge Dee's living quarters on the second floor. When Chiao Tai had surveyed the two luxurious, curtained bedsteads in the anteroom, he said with a wry grin to Tao Gan:

'You take the one you like, or both!' And to the judge: 'I prefer to have my nap on that reed mat in front of the door of your bedroom, sir! Especially in this heat!'

The judge nodded. He pulled the door-curtain aside and entered his bedroom. It was hot and sultry there. He walked to the broad, arched window to pull up the bamboo roll curtain. But he quickly let it drop again, for the glare of the midday sun, reflected by the glazed rooftiles of the adjoining palace buildings, shone right into his eyes.

He went to the rear of the room and laid his cap on the small table beside his couch. His dagger was lying there behind the teapot. While he felt if the pot was still warm, his eye fell on his sword Rain Dragon hanging on the wall. The sight of his cherished sword reminded him suddenly of the one of the Subduer of the South Seas, in the painting in Liang's ancestral hall. Yes, the Admiral had had Tanka blood. But in him its primitive savagery had been checked by a noble mind, its elemental passions had been sublimated into a nearly superhuman courage. Stifling a sigh, he took off his heavy brocade robe. Clad only in his white silk under-robe, he stretched himself out on the couch.

Staring up at the high ceiling, he thought of his lieutenants. He was partially responsible for Chiao Tai's tragic experience, really. He should have seen to it long before that Chiao Tai settled down to family life—that was one of the duties one had towards one's retainers. Ma Joong had married those two nice daughters of the puppeteer. He ought to have arranged a suitable marriage for Chiao Tai too. He would do something about that when he was back in the capital. It wouldn't be easy, though. Chiao Tai belonged to a distinguished family of warriors that had settled down in the north-west centuries ago. They were hardy men of a simple, staunch character, who lived for fighting, hunting and hard drinking, and who liked women of the same strong and independent type. In this respect Tao Gan presented no problem, fortunately, for he was an inveterate women-hater.

Then he thought of the weighty decisions he would have to

take in the capital. He knew that the loyal party would approach him with a request to take over the political activities of the dead Censor. But was it not better to wait till the Great Demise before taking such a step? He tried to survey all possible developments, but found it difficult to think coherently. The muted voices of Chiao Tai and Tao Gan, which he could hear vaguely through the door-curtain, made him drowsy. When the murmuring ceased, the judge dozed off.

It was very quiet in this secluded wing of the palace. Except for the guards at the outer gates, everybody was taking his siesta.

The bamboo curtain was pushed aside with a faint rustling sound. Mansur stepped noiselessly over the window sill. He wore only a white loincloth, a curved dagger stuck in its folds. Instead of his large turban, he had wound a piece of cloth tightly round his head. His dark, muscular body glistened with perspiration, for he had climbed across the roofs to reach his goal. Standing in front of the window, he waited for a while to regain his breath. He noticed with satisfaction that Judge Dee was fast asleep. His silk underrobe had come apart in front, baring his broad chest.

Mansur walked up to the couch with the lithe grace of a panther stalking its prey. He laid his hand on the hilt of his dagger, then checked himself as his eye fell on the sword hanging on the wall. It would be nice to report to the Khalif that he had killed the infidel with the dog's own sword.

He took the sword down and drew it in one quick movement. But he was unfamiliar with Chinese swords. The loose guard clattered on to the stone flags.

Judge Dee stirred uneasily, then opened his eyes. Mansur uttered an oath. He raised the sword to plant it in Judge Dee's breast, but whirled round as he heard a loud shout behind him. Chiao Tai came rushing in, wearing only his baggy trousers. He sprang at Mansur, but the Arab lunged with the sword and drove it into Chiao Tai's breast. As Chiao Tai staggered backwards, dragging Mansur with him, the judge jumped from the couch and grabbed his dagger from the tea-table. Mansur cast a quick glance at him over his shoulder, uncertain whether to defend himself with the sword, or leave it and fight with his own, more familiar curved dagger. That moment's hesitation sealed his doom. The judge leapt on him and thrust the dagger into his neck with such savage force that the blood spurted high in the air. The judge threw the dead Arab aside, and knelt down by Chiao Tai.

The razor sharp Rain Dragon had penetrated deeply into Chiao Tai's breast. His face had turned white, his eyes were closed. A thin stream of blood trickled from the corner of his mouth.

Tao Gan came rushing inside.

'Get the Governor's doctor, and alarm the guards!' Judge Dee barked.

He put his arm under Chiao Tai's head. He did not dare to remove the sword. A stream of confused memories passed before his mind's eye: their first meeting in the woods, when he had fought against Chiao Tai with this same sword; the many dangers they had faced shoulder to shoulder; the many times they had saved each other's lives.

He never knew how long he knelt there, looking at the still face. Suddenly he found many people crowding around him. The Governor's physician examined the wounded man. As he carefully pulled out the sword and staunched the bleeding, Judge Dee asked him hoarsely:

'Can we move him to the couch?'

The physician nodded. Giving the judge a grave look, he whispered:

'It's only his remarkable vitality that keeps him alive.'

Together with Tao Gan and the captain of the guard they lifted Chiao Tai up and softly laid him down on Judge Dee's couch. As the judge took the sword, he ordered the captain:

'Tell your men to take this dead Arab away.'

Chiao Tai opened his eyes. Seeing the sword in Judge Dee's hands, he said with a faint smile:

'It's by that sword we met, and by that sword we part.'

The judge quickly sheathed it. Laying it on Chiao Tai's tanned, scar-covered breast, he said softly:

'The Rain Dragon shall stay with you, Chiao Tai. I shall never carry a sword stained by the blood of my best friend.'

With a happy smile Chiao Tai folded his large hands over the sword. He gave Judge Dee a long look. Then a film seemed to spread over his eyes.

Tao Gan cradled Chiao Tai's head in his left arm. Tears trickled slowly down his long lean face.

'Shall I order the watch to start beating the Dead March, sir?' the captain of the guard asked in a whisper.

Judge Dee shook his head.

'No. Let them beat the Triumphant Return. At once!'

He motioned the physician and the guards to leave them alone. Bending close over the couch, he and Tao Gan looked at their friend's face, very still now. His eyes were closed. After they had been watching him for a long time, they noticed that his cheeks reddened. Soon his face was glowing with fever; perspiration streamed from the dying man's forehead. His breathing came in gasps, and more blood oozed from his distorted mouth.

'Left column ... forward!' Chiao Tai brought out.

Suddenly the quiet outside was shattered by the heavy rumble of the large leather drums on the watchtowers of the palace. Their rhythm quickened, then came the piercing blast of the long trumpets, announcing the return of the victorious warriors.

Chiao Tai opened his eyes, now partially glazed. He listened intently, then his bloodstained lips curved in a happy smile.

'The battle is won!' he suddenly said, very clearly.

There was a rattling sound in his throat; a long shudder shook his tall frame. The smile became fixed.

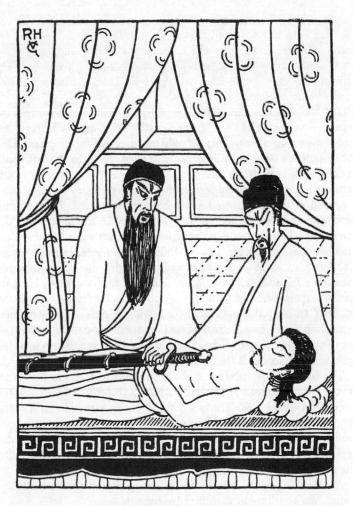

A WARRIOR'S DEATH

## XXV

Night had fallen when Tao Gan, working with the four agents, wound up the case of the Censor's death. With quiet efficiency he had covered up all evidence of what had really taken place. The Arab dancer's dead body had been secretly taken to the tribunal, then openly brought to the Temple of the Flowery Pagoda to be cremated. Liang's accomplices had been taken away by the military police, without even having been interrogated. They would be disposed of as soon as the convoy arrived in the mountains up river. Tao Gan was dead tired when at last he signed and sealed all the necessary documents, in Judge Dee's name. For the judge had left Canton as soon as he had personally made the arrangements for Chiao Tai's body to be removed to the capital. He had left in a special mounted convoy. A platoon of military police rode in front to clear the road. They carried the red-bordered banner signifying that they were entitled to requisition new horses at every post they passed. It would be a gruelling ride, but it was the quickest way to reach the capital.

Tao Gan left the tribunal and told the litter bearers to take him to the Liang mansion. The main hall was brilliantly lit by oil lamps and torches. Mr Liang's body was lying in state on a magnificent canopied bier. A steady stream of people was passing in front. They burned incense and paid their last respects to the deceased. A dignified elderly gentleman whom Tao Gan took to be the uncle received the visitors, assisted by the old housekeeper.

As Tao Gan sourly watched the solemn ceremony, he suddenly found Mr Yau Tai-kai standing by his side.

'A sad, sad day for Canton!' Mr Yau said. But his melancholy voice was belied by the crafty look on his face. Evidently he was gleefully calculating already which of the dead man's interests he could now take over. 'I hear that your boss has left,' Yau resumed. 'He seemed to suspect me of something, you know, for he questioned me closely, once. But now that he has gone back to the capital without summoning me, that means that I am in the clear, I suppose.'

Tao Gan gave him a baleful look.

'Well,' he said slowly, 'I am not allowed to discuss official business with outsiders, really. But since I like you, I'll give you a piece of inside information that might come in useful. When a person is put on to the rack, he shouldn't forget to ask the executioner's assistant to place a wooden gag between his teeth. It happens not infrequently, you see, that people in their agony bite their tongue off. But I wouldn't worry too much, Mr Yau, if I were you! Worrying has never yet saved a man. Good luck!'

He turned round and walked off, leaving Mr Yau standing there, a look of stark terror in his bovine eyes.

Somewhat cheered by this encounter, Tao Gan dismissed his litter and went on to the market place on foot. His back was aching and his feet were sore, but he felt he needed time to sort out his thoughts. The market was teeming with noisy humanity, and the dark back street he entered seemed by contrast even more dismal than before.

When he had climbed the narrow staircase, he stood still in front of the door for a moment and listened. He faintly heard a soft, whirring sound. His surmise had been right.

He knocked and stepped inside. The small cages hanging from the eaves were outlined against the evening sky, and in the semi-darkness he vaguely saw the tea-basket on the table.

'It is I,' he said when she came round from behind the bamboo screen. He took her sleeve and guided her to the bench. They sat down there, side by side.

'I knew I would find you here,' he resumed. 'I am travelling back to the capital early tomorrow morning, and I didn't want to leave without saying good-bye. Fate has struck heavily, both at you and at me. You lost your brother and your sister, I my best friend.' He told her briefly about Chiao Tai's death. Then he asked anxiously, 'How are you going to get along all alone now?'

'It's very thoughtful of you to remember me, in your great sorrow,' she said quietly. 'But don't worry about me. Before leaving the mansion, I had my uncle draw up a document wherein I renounce all my claims to my late brother's possessions. I don't need anything. I have my crickets, and with them I shall get along all right. With them I shan't be lonely.'

Tao Gan listened for a long while to the whirring sound.

'I carefully kept those two crickets of yours, you know,' he said at last. 'The one you sent me and the one I found in your room in the Examination Hall. I too am beginning to appreciate their song. It is peaceful. And I am feeling old and weary, Lan-lee; peace is the only thing I am longing for.

He cast a quick glance at her still face. Lightly laying his hand on her arm, he resumed diffidently:

'I would be very grateful indeed if you would come to stay with me in the capital some day. With your crickets.'

She did not draw her arm away.

'If your First Lady does not object,' she said in her even voice. 'I shall be glad to think it over.'

'I am all alone. There is no First Lady.' Then he added softly, 'But there will be one. Any time you say so.'

She raised her blind face, listening intently. One sound was now drowning that of the other crickets, a sustained, clear note.

'That's the Golden Bell!' she said with a contented smile. 'If you listen well, you'll know that his song means more than peace alone. It means happiness.'

206

# POSTSCRIPT

In the seventh century A.D. the two leading world powers were the vast Chinese T'ang Empire in the east, and in the west the Islamic realm of the Arab Khalifs, who had conquered the entire Middle East, North Africa and Southern Europe. Curiously enough, though, these two cultural and military giants barely knew of each other's existence; the points of contact of their spheres of influence were limited to a few scattered trade-centres. In the latter hardy Chinese and Arab sea captains met, but in their respective home-countries their accounts of the marvels they had seen were dismissed as so many sailors' yarns. Since for this Judge Dee novel I wanted to place the judge in an entirely new milieu, I laid the scene of my story in Canton, the port-city which was one of the focal points of contact between the Chinese and Arab worlds.

The events related in this novel are entirely fictitious, but they loosely link up with historical fact in so far as the redoubtable Empress Wu was indeed scheming to seize the reins of government at that time. She actually succeeded in doing so a few years later, after she had become Empress Dowager. Then she clashed directly with Judge Dee, and his prevention of her from ousting the legal Heir was the crowning success of his career. For that phase of Judge Dee's life the reader is referred to Lin Yutang's historical novel, *Lady Wu, a True Story* (London: 1959; Judge Dee's name is there transcribed Di Jenjiay).

The faked proclamation mentioned in Chapter XIX of the present novel I borrowed from one of the oldest Chinese crime-stories.

The said ruse was employed by the Chinese Machiavelli, the semi-legendary statesman Su Chin, in the fourth century B.C., in order to avenge himself on his political enemies who had unsuccessfully tried to murder him. When he was on his deathbed, Su Chin told the King to have his dead body quartered in the market, announcing that he had been a traitor. Then Su Chin's enemies came forward to claim a reward for their previous assassination attempt, and were duly executed (see *T'ang-yin-pi-shih, Parallel Cases from under the Pear Tree*, a Thirteenth Century Manual of Jurisprudence and Detection, by R. van Gulik, Leyden, 1956).

The poison used by Zumurrud is described in the Chinese historical work *Nan-chao-yeh-shih*, in the chapter about the Ti-yang-kuei mountain tribe in south-west China (*Histoire Particulière du Nan-tchao*, French translation by Camille Sainson, Paris, 1904; see p. 172).

I may again draw attention to the fact that in Judge Dee's time the Chinese did not wear pigtails. That custom was imposed on them after 1644 A.D., when the Manchus had conquered China. The men did their hair up in a top-knot, and they wore caps both inside and outside the house. They did not smoke; tobacco and opium were introduced into China long after Judge Dee's time.

ROBERT VAN GULIK